THE BROCKEN

Other books by Pamela Hill:

THE BROCKEN

PAMELA HILL

ignaro mater substernens se impia nato
impia non verita est divos scelerare penates.
CATULLUS

St. Martin's Press
New York

Library of Congress Cataloging-in-Publication Data

Hill, Pamela.
    The brocken / Pamela Hill.
        p.   cm.
    ISBN 0-312-06310-5
    I. Title.
  PR6058.I446B74   1991
  823'.914—dc20   91-19818
                                                           CIP

First published in Great Britain by Robert Hale Limited.

First U.S. Edition: September 1991
10 9 8 7 6 5 4 3 2 1

AUTHOR'S NOTE

The Brocken is the highest peak in the Harz Mountains, until recently unattainable in East Germany. Witches still foregather there on the first of May, Walpurgis Night. If it is not immediately evident what connection all this can possibly have with a family of merchant bankers, the only thing to do is read on.

P.H.

1

'It is a peasant dance which originated in Germany. So many of our customs now are German.'

Nicholas Crowbetter turned his handsome head, its jet-black hair cut *en brosse*, a trifle to the left, although he knew quite well that the remark had been made by his elder niece, Athene. He did not look directly at Athene because there was no pleasure in it. She had lived in his house for a year, ever since her despised young stepmother had died; he could remember Athene herself as a large self-assertive girl, and she had turned into a large self-assertive woman. Her plump body, which had a permanently upholstered look, was encased in a gown of lilac-coloured satin, which did not become her, and had been put together badly by a country seamstress. Her nose had a strong-minded hook; her ice-blue eyes could stare one down beneath their heavy lids, and she had very little conversation. Altogether, the fact that she was wearing a lace cap over her frizzed reddish hair this evening was an admission to the world that, despite all her money, she was beyond the marriage market at twenty-eight. As the greater part of her considerable fortune, which came from her mother, consisted of shares in Crowbetter's Bank, Nicholas had no objection to this state of affairs; in any case his wife Jane had to see a great deal more of Athene than he did.

The waltz, which had just been vaguely derided, continued decorously, for this small dance, given at Crowbetter's house in Hyde Park Gardens, was for a select clientèle. It was also an opportunity to bring out Nicholas's younger niece Sarah, who was pretty and only sixteen. His late elder brother George – Nicholas could remember him through the lilt of the violins – had, after commendably marrying an heiress, made an error on the second occasion and had married the vicar's daughter.

This was not the way a Crowbetter behaved, and although nobody except, probably, Athene would say it was a judgment on him, George had died within two years at his country house in Hertfordshire of complications following a chill caught when out hunting in the rain. His widow had lived on quietly with Athene and the baby, and after she herself died Nicholas had taken the two girls in.

He smiled to himself; he had been able to make certain plans for Sarah. He thought of it, while watching the white-gloved hands of the young men scarcely touching the laced-in waists of the young ladies. His eyes, of a curious and unmistakable golden colour, sought out his son, young Nick, assumed now, at eighteen, to be fit for social duties. Nick was thin, blond like his mother, and had, also like her, no animation and very little talk. He transported his partner, a beefy-armed heiress, round the floor with a certain dutiful precision, but no ecstasy. On the other hand his handsome younger contemporary, Felix von Reichmansthal, was in demand by all the ladies present except three.

The golden eyes flickered for instants towards Nick's mother, Jane, a small blond thick-set woman who sat alone in a chair against the wall. It was not that the company had refused her the courtesy of a word, as their hostess; but Jane Crowbetter had nothing to say. She was worth a very great deal of money, which was why her husband had married her. The sole fruit of their union had been Nick, and to his father's distaste he lacked the brains and enterprise to seize the opportunity so evidently awaiting him in the steadily prospering Crowbetter's Bank. The only hope was for Nick to marry an heiress, as his father had done, and, on the first occasion, his uncle; but unless a young man cultivated manners and address, no heiress would have him, beefy arms or not. What was to be done with him remained to be seen.

Crowbetter's eyes scanned the young assembly until they came on a sight which displeased him further. A very young waltzing couple, a boy and girl, were holding one another too closely for decorum. Sarah Crowbetter was slender and beautiful, with tossing light-brown ringlets and, when they could be seen wide open, long-lashed eyes that were almost turquoise in colour. She had a queenly neck, joy in living, and, already, though she was so young, a shapely bosom older women envied. She danced with a light-footed abandon against the boy, who was handsome enough. What caused Nicholas Crowbetter to frown was that a clerk in his employment, however well connected – and the Loriots were related to Holland House – should presume to public liberties with his niece. Nicholas himself had recently arranged, with diplomacy and care, a resplendent marriage for Sarah. She had not yet been informed of it.

Athene, in her lilac gown, was sorry she had worn a lace cap tonight; it made her look old. Perhaps that was what prevented Major Laverton from asking her to waltz. An ice-blue eye rested on his small, somewhat red-nosed, mustachioed figure, resplendent in its regimentals; he was not dancing either. Athene surveyed him with a melting glance, or as near to one as she could attain; he caught her eye and bowed slightly, but made no advance. If only he would come to her! She had loved him secretly for over a year; it was due to her persuasion that Uncle Nicholas had invited him tonight. If there could be a word between them, only a word! But he had turned away.

Nicholas Crowbetter had never encouraged fortune-hunters.

Sarah Crowbetter and Hugo Loriot circled the floor, the talk between them minimal; they were long past the stage of polite conversation. They met each morning, as early as could be, before banks were open, to ride together in the Row, knees touching; and if the servants noticed Miss Sarah's disarranged veil, flushed cheeks, and air of well-being on return for breakfast, they put it down to healthful exercise.

They touched again now. She was aware of Hugo's hand on her waist, his gloved fingers entwined in hers. She no longer missed her mother, which she had done on first coming to London. Hugo's face and her own were close, their breaths mingling, his smiling eyes gazing into her eyes, their lips almost meeting. They had already kissed often. To become one flesh, soon, as soon as might be, was Sarah's ardent desire, and Hugo's. He murmured of it now; the sound of the fiddles and the pianoforte came faintly, though they still waltzed, and waltzed.

'I shall speak to your uncle tomorrow, after the board meeting has dispersed. He is always in a good humour then.'

'He has no reason to be in a bad one, Hugo. You are an excellent *parti*.'

They giggled, being very young, and twirled to a close as the music died. 'Tomorrow?' he said to her, thinking of their customary ride in this fine weather, with the sun on the horses' necks, and Sal in her tall hat and veil, and all the rest of it.

'Tomorrow, of course. But I shall not know what he has said to you by then.'

'I will send round a note, Sally.'

But there was to be no note, and no tomorrow.

Major Henry Laverton flicked his red-gold whiskers upwards with a quick, accustomed movement of one hand; they were his sole magnificence and he was inordinately proud of them. If only the old girl would stop eyeing him! He was perfectly aware of Athene's sentiments towards him, and it was tempting to think of the money, but otherwise a large, hook-nosed, pink-fleshed female about him daily and, to face facts, nightly, was more than he could endure. Nor did he relish the prospect of having to encounter Nicholas Crowbetter at some point in the business: that man had the reputation of ruining his enemies in subtle ways Laverton knew he could not match. He told himself that he was a direct chap who knew what he liked, had followed the fortunes of his regiment with some success, and could boast of bold encounters in Afghanistan and India. Nobody, in fact, impugned his courage. When at home, he liked to gamble for high stakes. That was almost his only form of social encounter, as he was by nature morose. For that reason, the invasion of his privacy by Athene's heavy-lidded gaze disturbed him; it was like being aware of a large parrot about to pounce on a small crumb, himself. He moved self-consciously away from the dancing, in which he had not joined – in fact, he regretted accepting the invitation – and went to sit beside his hostess, who as usual said nothing. Her pale-blue eyes were fixed straight ahead, watching her husband, whom she seldom saw.

Supper would be announced soon, but before then the musicians struck up a quadrille. It took a little time and laughter before everyone was placed, and Athene was sent down by her uncle to ensure that Sarah and young Loriot did not dance together again; it was becoming improper. Such a task appealed exactly to Athene's didactic nature. She took her young half-sister by the arm, led her towards a waiting gallant, there being no cards to fill up at an informal party; and, as a final stroke, provided poor Hugo with the beefy heiress who had earlier danced with young Nick. Duty done, she bustled away from the dancers as the music struck up its initial chord, then picked her way, like a large, determined hen, to where Henry Laverton sat by her aunt. Perforce, he rose to his feet, thanking his stars it was too late to have to ask the old girl to dance; lace cap or not, that was probably why she had come over. They were never too overripe to try.

Athene, however, merely smirked. 'It is pleasant, is it not, to watch the young people enjoying themselves?' she demanded. 'May I beg the favour of your escort in to supper, Major? It will be quite soon.'

Surprisingly, Jane Crowbetter spoke up. 'Major Laverton is escorting *me* in to supper,' she announced firmly, and Athene's face fell like a Greek mask, painted pink, that has slipped. They watched the quadrille to an end in bridling silence, then took themselves, Athene trailing behind on nobody's arm, to the supper-room.

Ices, conceits and jellies were consumed, and fruit cup, with a hock base, drunk. There was a chatter of talk round about, but the three, Jane, Athene, and Laverton, maintained a silence that nothing could break. Jane had asserted herself, as she sometimes, though rarely, did; having done so, there was, again, nothing left to say. Athene was in a state of furious and resentful disappointment; and as for Laverton, he ate his ice, being careful not to leave traces on his moustache. His nose, besides being red, was pointed. There was not the slightest reason why Athene should have fallen in love with him, but love is never reasonable.

Presently Nicholas came past, and enquired genially if they were enjoying themselves in this after all much younger assembly. 'I recall my own youth, and I used to like to dance; now I prefer to watch,' he said. 'It is like most things in life, and palls with time.'

Carriages were to be brought round at eleven, and after a schottische, and another waltz, the glow of the lamps showed yellow beyond the windows. The young ladies' shawls were fetched against the night air, and chaperones – these were not formidable, as this was a private party – betook themselves off

with their charges. Young Nick, emboldened by hock cup,
Felix and a few bloods went back to the supper-room to finish
the wine, but found that it had been prudently removed by
the servants. Everything in Nicholas Crowbetter's house was
accomplished smoothly, with economy, and in time.

He himself, when the last of the company had gone, had a
word with the housekeeper, both to thank her for the success
of the evening's entertainment – he was punctilious in such
matters – and to give her a message to be conveyed, without
fail, to Miss Sarah's maid tomorrow. Tonight would be too
soon; there would be scenes and pouting, perhaps tears, and a
lack of sleep. 'Tomorrow, when she asks for her habit to be
fetched, will be best. Is that understood?'

'It is understood, sir.' Like all his servants, Mrs Tobin – her
late husband had been Irish – held Nicholas in as much awe
as if he had been God. It was difficult to explain the power
that radiated from him, and none of them would have
attempted to do so. That his house was perfectly run, despite
the ineptitude of its mistress, was symptomatic of the regard
in which he was held. Any peccadillo meant dismissal; that
was understood also.

He went on and up. Jane's apartments were on the second
floor, and it was years since Nicholas had entered them. The
nieces, Felix and Nick occupied the third, and the servants
the attics. His own room, and that of Jane's official
companion, Mrs Milsom, faced one another across the first
landing, where the rich carpet gave way to drugget and
gilt-framed paintings hung. At one of these Nicholas stopped,
as he did every night.

It was the portrait of his grandmother, who had been a
Jewess. Her elopement with his grandfather had been the
scandal of the decade. Neither family would be reconciled, and
it was a Jew who was no relation, as Nathan Rothschild, who
had aided the young couple and helped to found the fortune
to which Nicholas's father, and Nicholas himself, had added in
their time, had stated. For Rothschild had taught his grandfather the craft of banking. Nicholas himself, with his trace of
Jewish blood, found that it came naturally to deal with money,
invest it, lend it favourably, predict its increase, prevent its
decline. Tomorrow, he would preside over a board of men less
able than he was himself, and would manipulate them as he

did his guineas. Meantime, he gazed at his grandmother's face. He could just remember her, as she had been in old age, hair still as jet-black as it showed in the portrait; nose short with flaring nostrils, neck long, face oval. She had been almost totally paralysed by then and had lain on a sofa, but had ordered her household till the day she died. He regretted never having had a daughter, who might have resembled her.

He turned away from the portrait and went to the companion's room, and opened the door. Harriet Milsom sat by a lamp with a book; she was fond of reading. She smiled, laid the book down with a marker at the place, came to him and kissed him on the cheek. She was a plump, comfortable creature of his own age, perhaps a little more, with fine eyes and dark hair smoothly combed on either side her face.

'Did you have a pleasant party?' she asked him. Crowbetter shrugged, and cast himself into a chair.

'I am always faintly thankful when these affairs are over,' he said. 'Nick did not distinguish himself. I begin to lose hope for him.'

'Eighteen is not old.'

He did not reply, and Harriet started to undress. She knew that was expected of her, and that it would take perhaps an hour; after that, she could sleep. It would not have done to be ready waiting in bed for him; he expected her always to wait up, fully dressed. She unfastened her bodice, let her petticoats fall silently, and put on her nightgown before removing her chemise; manners were always observed between them. They had been lovers for more than fifteen years, and there were few surprises. She even knew what Crowbetter was doing now, when her back was turned; he was gazing at the Danaë miniature.

He had it in his hands; it had been easy to reach out from where he sat and take it down from the wall. As he always did he took his eyeglass, which he kept on a ribbon and never otherwise used, and magnified the figure of a naked recumbent young woman visited by a shower of gold. He liked to think of himself as purveying the shower. The girl's name had been Maud Partridge and she had been his wife's first lady-companion.

Seeing her for the first time, he had been amused because she was so prim. Even her name was prim. She did not look up when he entered whatever room it was she sat in beside

Jane, netting purses; there had been a fashion then for that particular activity. Her mouth was set in a certain line of virtuous continence that reminded one of portraits of Queen Jane Seymour. Her hair was smooth and a medium brown, not curled, for that would have been frowned upon in her position. She wore a plain gown without braid, for the same reason. He had been immediately intrigued by her breasts; prudently concealed as they were, they resembled a child's. He could picture them beneath her dress, beneath her chemise, never having been touched by any man. No doubt they never would be. However, it was not long before he began to imagine himself handling them; and having begun, to continue in that occupation.

Maud was the perfect companion for Jane, who could be exacting to her inferiors. She fetched what was asked for, either from upstairs or down; disentangled silk, held wool, read aloud – but Jane did not enjoy reading or being read to – and, in general, knew her place. At first she did not eat with them, and a tray of food was sent up to her room; then, as it was infinitely dull alone with Jane, Nicholas ordered that Miss Partridge was to come down for meals, and might join them in the dining-room. Maud did so, without comment, or contributing to the talk, except to answer when spoken to. She avoided looking at Nicholas or raising her eyes.

He began to be in need of diversion. Jane was by then pregnant, which made it thankfully unnecessary to sleep with her any longer, at least meantime. Nicholas kept no regular mistress, for it would have caused gossip and harmed trade so soon after his advantageous marriage. Perhaps it was natural that the daily sight of Maud Partridge's lack of bosom made him anxious to remedy affairs; and, with Nicholas, to want something was to have it, on whatever terms.

As Jane thickened, it was considered inadvisable for her to take carriage exercise. Nicholas began to take Maud Partridge out for rides in his brougham instead, telling his wife it was time the companion took a little air. Once in the vehicle, with its upholstered comfort, he would talk to Maud; brilliant, winning, heady talk such as she could never have heard before in her life. Her stepfather, one understood, was a grocer. While Crowbetter did not give her much opportunity to reply, as her intellect was not what interested him, such answers as she was permitted to make were intelligent. He found her restful company. At last, now and then, her eyes would raise themselves timidly to his face. He was still uncertain of their colour; and one day asked her.

'What colour are your eyes, Maud?' He had used her Christian name without thinking, or perhaps deliberately. She flushed, dropped her gaze again, and he leaned forward, seized both her hands in one of his, and forced her chin up with the other. Maud was distressed; her flush deepened to crimson.

'Please, Mr Crowbetter – please –'

'Look at me,' he commanded. Still bashfully, she raised her eyes, and he saw that they were full of tears.

'They are green with brown flecks,' he said. 'Why are you crying?'

Suddenly he leaned further over and kissed her on the mouth. She gave a cry, which was lost in the kiss. She tried to wrench her hands away, but he would not let them go. He felt her mouth firm in the familiar prim line, with his own hard against it.

'Sir, you must not act in such a way,' she said when he had freed her. 'I cannot drive in the carriage alone with you any more. It has been most beneficial, but it is not proper in a married man to kiss a young female such as I am.'

'Then let us be improper.' He found the challenge amusing.

'No, Mr Crowbetter.' She had turned her head away, and this time was able to repulse him. She acquired a sudden dignity. 'Please have me driven back at once. I must never venture out with you again.'

It was evident that she would not yield to him, and as the weeks passed he found his resentment grow, accordingly; he was not accustomed to denying himself what he wanted, or letting others deny him. He began to want Maud increasingly, out of all proportion to the interest he had at first shown. His eyes followed her constantly, but with care lest Jane, dull unobservant Jane, noted it and perhaps gave the companion notice, though it was unlikely that she would dare take such a step without consulting him first. He kept in his hands everything to do with hiring and dismissal of the servants, among whom Maud could be counted as one. The thought in itself angered him; a servant to flout his wishes!

It came to him that he must find some way to force her to let him have the will that hardened in him, and without much difficulty he hit on a scheme. Jane had a favourite set of sapphires she often wore, a heavy necklace and earrings, also a bracelet to rest on her pallid arm. The deep stones gave her some animation. She kept them in a four-tiered jewel-case on her dressing-table, and herself carried the key. It was a simple matter to have another made, and to purloin the gems from their velvet-lined drawer. Nicholas did this, accordingly; and at a time when nobody was upstairs, stole with them into the companion's room and thrust them beneath Maud's mattress. Then he went out and closed the door, smiling to himself. It was only a matter of waiting now.

He had to wait longer than he expected; Jane did not require her sapphires for three days. During that time he watched the companion as usual; her eyes were lowered, as they had been when she first came; her mouth was prim, her little breasts beguiling. He pictured himself handling them till they swelled, kissing her mouth till it opened like a rose. He could hardly contain his impatience; it was only due to his discipline of himself during the day that his work at the bank did not suffer. To possess Maud Partridge would relieve his mind as well as his body. He began to think of her in her absence, even while talking with clients. She was becoming an obsession.

Then the plot succeeded. Some kinsfolk of Jane's were coming to dine, she looked for her sapphires, and they were gone. The outcry she raised was nevertheless muted; Jane would never make much noise, and sapphires meant little to her; she could after all buy others. This pleased Nicholas well enough; for several reasons he did not want the servants' hall to be apprised of the matter.

One reason was the turning of feather mattresses. He had known that, sooner or later, his housekeeper and one of the maids would go up to turn Maud's. His only worry was that they would go too soon, before the loss of the jewels had been noticed. But it was the end of the week, and his impatience was rife, before they plumped up and turned the feathers in their great linen bag; and out rattled the sapphires. Mrs Rae swooped on them, recognising them at once. The maid gaped.

'Don't you say one word about this to the other girls, or you're in trouble, Aminta Beaver,' she told the young servant.

Aminta, magically named, cast down her eyes like Maud Partridge.

'I won't say a word, 'm, I promise,' she replied.

'You'd better not. Leave all this to me. Now go down to your tasks; I'll finish here.'

She shook the mattress where it lay on the floor, determined to ensure that there were no more pieces entangled in it; then counted the rest, the earrings, the necklace, the bracelet; all present. That minx of a lady companion had taken the lot. She herself would tell the master.

Nicholas came home to find a housekeeper as pregnant with information as Jane was with his child. She asked for a word with him, very respectfully; and when the request was granted, produced from her reticule a package discreetly wrapped in linen.

'Sir, I didn't tell the mistress.' That was understood between them. She went on to explain where the sapphires had been found, without commenting further. Nicholas's golden eyes surveyed her with approval. She was a jewel of a housekeeper, worth every penny he paid her. Discretion was of more value to him than anything, even an ability to dust.

'Leave it to me,' he said. 'You have done very well. We will not call the police for the moment. Before dinner, send the young woman to me.'

When she had gone, he poured himself a glass of marsala from a decanter that stood ready. It slaked his thirst and confirmed him in his resolution. The prospect of Maud's standing before him, in his full power at last, pleased him greatly.

She came in. She had her guarded look, but that was habitual. She had no idea why he had sent for her. He set down his glass, and unrolled the bundle of sapphires. They gleamed in the light.

'You are aware what these are?' he asked her coldly. She raised her eyes in a look of complete innocence, and answered in her precise way.

'Sir, they are Mrs Crowbetter's sapphires. She wears them often. She lost them lately. I am glad that they are found.'

'She also will be glad, when she hears of it. You will be aware where, in fact, they were found.'

He regarded her pitilessly; she began to tremble, as though she sensed something that should not be; and when her reply came it was a whisper.

'No, Mr Crowbetter.'

'You are lying. They were found in your room, beneath your mattress. My housekeeper is a witness to it, and she had a maid with her. You cannot deny that you put them there, having stolen them first. By rights I should inform the police. You would have to endure a spell in prison which would hardly suit your ladylike ways.'

'Sir – I did not – I have not touched any jewels – I know nothing of it –'

'You are lying, I say. Do you want to stand up in court and let the lawyers do their worst with you?'

'I – I am innocent – a lawyer would know it –'

'Not in face of so many witnesses to the contrary. That you would be found guilty is a certainty; and after that, when you have come out of prison, who will employ you again? You would receive no reference from here.'

Her trembling increased; knees, mouth, her very innards grew weak. What was she to do? Mrs Crowbetter would not help her; she was completely under the dominion of her husband. And that man himself was merciless; the golden eyes stared her down.

'Please, sir – please – I have nowhere to go, my stepfather has married again, and he would not receive me –'

'He will certainly not receive you after this discovery, if it is reported in the newspapers.' Did a grocer read the papers? Nicholas was enjoying himself. She was weakening, he saw; soon now he would put his intention to her.

'What am I to do?' Maud cried. 'I have sworn that I am innocent, but you do not believe me.' The tears left her eyes and began to roll down her cheeks. He had kept her standing, and did not, even now, ask her to be seated.

'There is something you can do,' he said smoothly, 'one thing; I will advise you on it.'

'Oh, sir, anything – anything, I promise –'

'It is very simple, and must be done in silence. You will not come down to dinner tonight. A tray will be sent up to you, as formerly; then you will undress yourself and go to bed. You will not lock your door. At about eleven o'clock I shall visit you. I want no outcry then, no alarm to rouse the household.

I shall stay with you for a little while, then leave you. Tomorrow you will resume your duties as formerly, and nothing more will be said about sapphires. Have I your understanding in this matter? You are not, I have already found, a fool.'

She had given a long breath; her face was white, with the tears still on it. There was no doubt that she understood him. She was not, he was thankful to discover, one of those young women who had been kept in entire ignorance of what they might expect from a man in bed. That would hardly have interested him, even now. 'Well?' he said presently. 'Do you agree, or not? If not, I can assure you, it will mean prison for you, perhaps for a long time.'

She was standing very still, like marble. Then she inclined her head. 'I will do it,' she said quietly. 'May I go now?'

He could have taken her then, intrigued once more by her unexpected dignity. But he watched her go, and did not trouble to open the door for her.

Late that night he trod noiselessly upstairs in slippers, brocade dressing-gown and nightshirt. He had kept her waiting deliberately; it was some time past eleven o'clock. What he had to do would take very little time, he had assured himself; afterwards, he could be certain of a night's sleep to allow for certain important negotiations tomorrow; a client was coming from St. Petersburg, another from Vienna. Crowbetter had made himself go over some of the paperwork just now, before his valet undressed him. It was a discipline, and he had been obsessed with Maud Partridge too long.

He tried her door. It was unlocked, as he had requested. He opened it, entered, closing it again carefully, and prudently turned the key, though interruption was unlikely. Then he crossed to the bed, in which Maud lay. It was a narrow iron one, without curtains, the kind servants used; the feather mattress had been a concession to Maud's status. She lay silent, her eyes wide open, seen dark against the whiteness of her face by the reflection of lamps from the street below. He slid beneath the covers, pushed up her nightgown, and began to take her; carefully, for, as he had expected, she was a virgin, and Crowbetter prided himself, ever since certain expert instruction in his youth, on being able to remove a maidenhead without pain. He did this, and went on and up into her; she made no sign except for quickened breaths. Crowbetter began to handle her body, sliding his hands upwards beneath the heavy cambric nightgown which, he had noted with some amusement, Maud wore. He fondled her little breasts at last, covetously, feeling them swell and grow taut, all the time staying well up within her. Presently his overt thrustings, his determined caressing of her, brought her response, a harsh late cry, like an animal's; he crushed her mouth with his, to silence her. She began to urge her body helplessly, ignorantly, upwards in the rhythm of his own; and at the thought that he might be giving her pleasure sudden anger rose in Crowbetter, remembering the time she had made him wait, repeatedly denying him. He began to use her constantly, careful not to get her with child; between darkness and dawn he mated her several times. By the end she was sobbing with exhaustion, not loudly but hopelessly, like a lost creature. Crowbetter rose and left her presently, having slaked himself as fully as he might. Not a word had been spoken between them.

At breakfast – she had come down – he surveyed Maud pitilessly, knowing she could have had no sleep. There were blue shadows under her eyes and her mouth was bruised. Jane, placidly eating kedgeree, noticed nothing. She told Maud to fetch the pepper and Maud obeyed; her unsteady walk filled Crowbetter with triumph. He stared at her bodice; was it perhaps strained a little? It should be, certainly; he found that the matter did not now affect him. He himself felt no ill-effects from the lack of sleep; on the contrary, he had a sense of well-being that had eluded him for some time. He would not, he thought, go to her tonight; he had already given her – he smiled broadly as he climbed into the waiting brougham – something to remember that very few spinsters had: an education.

One thing had not occurred to Nicholas Crowbetter; the exercise in which he had indulged with Maud had increased his own need of a woman. Perhaps after all he would make more frequent use of the companion than he had foreseen. When all was said she was in the house, and it was convenient. He waited for a day or two; Maud must not think herself indispensable; he had one or two social occasions to attend,

and there was the Austrian matter, which concluded itself
suitably, though the Russian client had gone home for further
advice. Between times, at home, Crowbetter diverted himself
by watching Maud. Had she been disappointed, after all, that
he had not come back the next night, and the next? Perhaps by
now she would be aware that she had overrated herself.

But when he approached her after dinner that evening, in
Jane's presence, it was almost as it had been at the beginning.

'I will visit you tonight,' he said in a low voice. 'Leave off
your nightgown.'

The flecked eyes held panic. 'No, Mr Crowbetter, not again
– please, no –'

'But yes,' he said, his voice like silk. 'Remember the prison
sentence.' Jane was eating almonds, prior to going into the
drawing-room.

'You cannot do that now – the time has gone by since it
happened –'

'I can say that I have only just heard of it. Understand this:
I shall visit you as and when I choose, and not when I do not
choose. You should leave your door unlocked to be available
in either case.'

They were making up on Jane, who had by now gone first
out of the dining-room, her pale-blue skirts trailing. Nicholas
strode ahead and overtook her, giving her his arm, as should
have happened earlier when he did not remain behind for
port. She was growing heavy with the child, and he hoped it
would be a son. He addressed some commonplace remark to
her, and took no further heed of the companion.

That night he used Maud Partridge as he would have used
any woman, without either rancour or particular feeling. It
was the first of many such nights; when he had nothing better
to do, he would go to her. She began to recover her former
appearance during the day, and to walk evenly; no doubt she
was beginning to accept the situation. She ought, he
reminded himself, to be grateful for his attentions; their
remembrance must beguile the tedium of her days,
particularly as he put her in no danger of pregnancy. He had
in fact, begun, for his diversion, to teach her certain things a
mistress ought to know; and her breasts were growing full
with handling. It was a great deal better than nothing, and he

himself was no longer obsessed to the detriment of business.

Jane Crowbetter went into premature labour at seven months, and gave birth to a small fair-haired boy. The doctors said that she could have no more children. Nicholas was pleased that he had a son, but irritated concerning Jane; it was like her to have remained alive, but barren. Now she was of no use to him at all, being without social gifts, attraction or conversation. Yet he had married her, and some of her money had made the Austrian venture succeed. He often visited the puny baby, had found a good wet-nurse, and expressed the hope that one day young Nicholas would become a partner in Crowbetter's. The child's life was important; without it, the marriage was a mockery.

Although the birth had been early and the baby small, Jane did not recover for many weeks, and kept to her bed. During that time, Crowbetter generally dined at his club. The sole company, unless there were male guests, at home was Maud Partridge, and he had already decided that there was only one occupation they could share. Maud's education had been deficient; her mother's second marriage, made beneath that lady's station, had deprived Maud herself of the benefits of a finishing school, and thrown her into the company of tradespeople. She could play the pianoforte a little, but that did not interest Crowbetter; she was unhandy with cards, and although she was a good listener she had almost no talk of her own. It was evident why she was such an ideal companion for Jane, who had none either; the companionable silence, as Nicholas described it to himself, in which the two young women habitually sat bored him, with or without Jane. After dinner one night, when he and Maud had eaten it alone, he had laid her down on the sofa, opened her bodice, and taken her as they were; but the prudery she showed was almost like it had been at the beginning, and no longer excited him.

'The servants will come in – please –'

He had already eased down her drawers. 'They will not come in until I send for them,' he told her. 'In any case I pay them, not they me.' He forbore to add that he also paid Maud; it was perhaps unnecessary.

He exposed her breasts, which he again noted were filling out agreeably with his occasional fondling. 'Do you know that you have glorious breasts nowadays?' he asked her, kissing them. 'They used to be like a schoolgirl's; now, you may be proud of them.'

'Not here – oh, please, please, not here, Mr Crowbetter –'

But he had continued what he had begun, and finished at his leisure. He was growing a little tired of her constant gentility; he had taught her to begin to take pleasure in her body upstairs, so why not here? Tomorrow –

'You are a goose,' he said. 'Tomorrow we will drive in the Park.'

They drove in the Park. Once there – it was an unfashionable hour – he laid her along the rear seat, and took her again while the coachman's broad back ignored them, to his own diversion and Maud's confused shame. But such matters no longer occupied Crowbetter's full attention, and later he went to his club.

It was summer, and London was very hot. He had supper, and stayed late at Crockford's, playing against Count d'Orsay at hazard bank, and drinking champagne served on ice. Next day was Sunday, and he could be as late as he chose, and get as drunk as he chose, and lose as much money as he chose; but to his astonishment, between the golden haze and the heady bubbles and the sight of d'Orsay's glittering waistcoat, Crowbetter won. He did not win a small sum; he won a small fortune.

They drank together into the early hours, the Count talking with nonchalance about Italian painting; he would win another day. Nicholas, with more respect for money, declined to play again; through the deserted cobbled streets he rattled at last in his brougham, feeling the weight of golden guineas – it had not even been a note of hand, but coin of the realm – and thinking how he would go up and rape the life out of prim Miss Partridge to her undoing; even she must rejoice with him. He was let in, left his hat and cane, took the moneybags, and ran upstairs like a boy, borne on wings by victory and champagne.

He kicked open her door; and stood enchanted.

She had cast the covers off for the heat, and was lying naked; he had forbidden her to wear nightgowns nowadays. He had not troubled to look, as he was looking now, at her body in the abandon of sleep. Her breasts, grown beneath his hands at last like those of a goddess, swelled above her spread ivory limbs; her mouth, far from being primmed in a line, was open, moist and pink like the inside of a strawberry. He could at once see what he had made of her, and what she herself might become. His member thrust against his breeches; gold, champagne, and now this!

He remembered the gold; with that, he would awaken her suitably. He rummaged in the linen bags and brought out handfuls, enough to keep a starving family for a week; and cast it at her private parts. She was Danaë, he had decided, waiting for the shower of gold; and he was Mars, and a damned sight better than gold to any woman. He began to laugh; she had opened her eyes, her flecked and still timid eyes. 'Don't be afraid, m'dear,' he said tipsily, 'it's only I.'

He fell upon her then. The bed soon shook with his urgings and the gold coins rolled to the floor. Maud lay bewildered, not knowing what had happened; only what was happening now. At the beginning she hadn't liked it; she still wasn't sure it was quite proper; but there it was, only she hadn't been expecting it so early in the morning, when people would soon be getting ready for church.

'They must paint you,' he said thickly soon. 'They must paint you as Danaë, with the shower of gold. Y'know what happened to her? A god, think it was Mars – fine fellows, these gods – got at her, shut in her tower, forget why; and she had a baby. They said Mars had disguised himself as a shower of gold. Can't see, m'self, that it would apply, but there it is. Then the old father, who'd shut her in the tower, that was it, in case anybody got at her, put 'em in a trunk, her and the baby, and set 'em out to sea.'

'I must not have a baby – please, please –'

'Have no fear, m'dear, I'll see to it you don't. Always have seen to it. Trust Uncle Crowbetter. Now, this paintin'.' He leered, and fondled her thigh. 'I want you painted as you are, like that,' he said, 'on the bed, with your legs open, and the shower of gold.'

'I could not do that. I could never let a painter see me like this. I could never –'

'A little miniature, just a little one.' He thrust within her, bringing on her climax. 'I know a young feller paints miniatures on ivory,' he said through it. 'You wouldn't see him; he'd come and paint you, standin' at the door behind a screen. It has glass panels to look through.' He let his hands stray from her thighs up her stomach, at last caressing the ripe, perfect breasts. 'I'd stay here with you. You'll do it for me, eh? Let me show you some of the other things you'll do for me.'

He was using her hard now that the fumes of champagne had worn off. He was still elated; to have won all that money! And Maud, whatever she said, should be painted naked as Danaë, with that flush on her cheeks, and her moist pink strawberry mouth, and her – God, to think he had never looked at her before!

The miniaturist came in a few days, glad of his commission. It was made clear to him that he must be punctual, neither too early nor too late, and must work from behind a screen, because the lady was shy. About half an hour before his expected arrival, in the early summer evenings, Nicholas used to take a certain precaution. Lest Maud grow listless for the portrait, he made love to her vigorously until the painter came, thereby inducing something of the same glow and flush as she had had in natural sleep. Then he retired out of sight of the screen, ready to ensure that Maud stayed where she was and did not spoil the venture, and his own expense, by any untimely prudery. The whole proceeding entertained Nicholas Crowbetter; and it would be diverting, however long he lived, to have the miniature to scan, and remember the shower of gold coins he had flung at Maud Partridge to wake her up.

The portrait was finished before the summer nights changed, and the gold shower realistically inserted; it echoed the gilt frame Nicholas chose for the completed work, which at first was hung in his bedroom. He would look at it occasionally, recapturing such erotic stimulation as the episode had brought him. But, by then, there was another.

Towards autumn, when everyone returned to town, he was invited to an evening party at Princess Lieven's. He was still capable of feeling flattered at such an invitation; as a rule, he moved chiefly in banking circles, albeit international ones. This was, in fact, the reason why he figured on the particular guest-list; the Austrian representative with whom Crowbetter had dealt in London concerning the recent successful *coup*, was to be present, with his wife, having known the Lievens in Vienna.

Nicholas was greeted by his host, poor Bonsi, as his wife called him, who remained a dull and little-known stay to the life of a brilliant social and diplomatic butterfly. Bonsi murmured that they were mostly at cards, and did Crowbetter understand this very new game baccarat, from France? That land would never be defeated. 'They are always changing,' sighed the husband of Dorothea Lieven, and Nicholas reflected, on the way upstairs, that that might be the Prince's epitaph. His wife had had many lovers, notably Prince Metternich, for whom she had developed a passion, but who had deserted her shortly out of prudence; that diplomat knew when to stop.

They entered the salon, where the very new game was proceeding. Dorothea Lieven set down her cards and came rustling over to greet her guest, who was deliberately a little late. She was no longer beautiful, having grown thin and sallow over the years; but she had wit and address, and spoke in her challenging fashion to Crowbetter, while her worldly glance summed him up. He interested her; but meantime there were other matters. 'You must meet your Viennese partner again,' the Russian-born hostess told him, and he was aware that Dorothea was in some manner informed of the whole Austrian enterprise, perhaps had even had a hand in its success; she was in contact with everyone of note from here to St Petersburg. She preceded him, her oddly tied dark hair bobbing on either side her head, to a table where, as was the custom of the game, three people sat. 'This is Count Franz von Reichmansthal,' said the Princess, and a tall plump Austrian, not notable, rose to his feet and bowed. The client and his wife were there also; there was more bowing, kissing of hands, then Nicholas was placed at another table.

He had fortunately acquainted himself with the rules of the game before coming, otherwise he would have been lost in its complications. He had no time to think of anything but his cards for some time. When a halt was called he raised his eyes at last to the opposite pair of players. Who the third one was he never afterwards remembered. Encountering him was a clear green gaze, slanted like a cat's.

'My husband has no manners,' said Mélanie von

Reichmansthal. 'He should have made you known to me at once.'

Crowbetter had virtually no further memory of the game. He had never played as absently in his life. At one stage he recalled holding the bank, and at all points his hand turned up nines. He cared nothing; he was obsessed with the sight of the goddess, the enchantress, across the table. She had a skin like milk, without flaw; so, come to that, had poor Jane, but all comparison with Jane thereafter ceased. This creature was vibrant, alive, challenging, mocking him even now, so soon. Her hair was the colour of honey, piled in elaborate coils and ringlets about her head, held by a gold band such as Greek women wear on vases. Her ringed fingers were long and predatory, clawing in the money she won with evident enjoyment, but he knew very well she was shrewd enough to have made sure of its amount. Her mouth was naturally red, lacking paint, her teeth strong, white, and perfect. There was a foreign, almost a wild aspect about her, enhanced by high cheekbones which gave her more than ever the appearance of a cat. He had never before seen that particular shape of face on a human being. She wore earrings, fashioned of beaten gold to match the headband; they dangled as she moved. His glance roved down her long smooth neck to her body; she wore a gown of almost transparent sea-green silk, barely admissible to a virtuous house such as this pretended to be; the gown was cut so low that her breasts narrowly escaped their fullest revelation. And what breasts! Crowbetter forgot the others he had lately handled, had brought on from bud to fruition. There was nothing now in his mind, his eyes, his memory, but Mélanie von Reichmansthal. Without fail, if the heavens fell, they must meet again. He would follow her to the ends of the earth.

Lacking preamble, he seized the chance of a pause in the game, for refreshments, to go across. He was convinced that she was as keenly aware of him as he of her. The green eyes mocked him. He bent over her, speaking in a low voice.

'I am Nicholas Crowbetter,' he said, 'and I adore you.'

Mélanie laughed, with a flashing of her white teeth. He could see, now, that her thick eyelashes were darkened; it was the only artificial thing about her. She was the perfect animal,

but with a mind. He saw her look, assess him coolly, smile, and
sip her wine.

'Many men say they adore me,' she told him. 'It seems they
cannot help themselves. My husband adores me also. He
returns to Vienna next week, however, to see our son; he is
concerned about Wenzel's education.'

'You have a son?' Like Aphrodite, motherhood had not
stretched or sagged her; she had given birth, he had no doubt,
as easily as a lioness.

'Indeed. Wenzel is nine years old. He is a good child, but I
am not a good mother. I should stay with him, not come to
gaming parties in London. But I love society, and here I am.'

Her accent was very slightly unfamiliar; he could not place it:
it was not German. 'May I say that your English is excellent?' he
ventured. Mélanie smiled, and set down her glass.

'English? That is nothing. We Hungarians speak our own
Magyár, some Polish, a little Russian perhaps, and, naturally,
French and German. When one travels to many capitals it is
useful.'

'We are talking now to no purpose,' he said impatiently.
'When may I see you again?' His whole body was filled with
need; even to hear her voice again would assuage some of it.
She talked, he thought, directly of whatever was in her mind,
like a child; but there was nothing else childlike about her. This
was a woman of the world, such as he had never before met; on
a par with, though set apart from, the Lievens, the Dinos, the
Metternichs. She belonged to the set that travelled with
accustomed ease between London and Berlin, St Petersburg
and Vienna. Crowbetter felt himself provincial and underes-
timated; and the fact put him on his mettle. He could show her
what love was. His golden eyes gleamed; his mouth was set.
Mélanie surveyed him with her cat's glance, and her smile
grew.

'I ride in the Row most mornings, very early,' she told him. 'I
do not sleep late.'

'I will escort you.' It would make him late for the bank; that
could not be helped for once. After all, he was a director; if
clients had to wait till he arrived, *tant pis*.

Early on the following morning, as arranged, he rode across
into Hyde Park. The groom, who had had to get up early, was
also the coachman, and looked after the riding-horse and the

single carriage-horse Nicholas kept for the brougham. He was a taciturn individual with small mud-coloured eyes, not likeable, but that did not signify, as he kept the horses in good trim and drove expertly. His name, inappropriately, was Joseph Humble. Crowbetter rode out into the autumn sunlight, and forgot him.

He was conscious of his own appearance, and pleased therewith. He had had his valet shave him carefully at half-past five. His white stock was subtly tied, his coat and breeches fitted like a glove, showing his broad shoulders and reasonable waist; his boots had been polished to a degree of excellence concerning which he had, unusually, spoken a word of praise to the valet. As for his looks, he knew himself to be a personable man, a challenge to women, perhaps even the despair of husbands. He surveyed the facts coolly; one might as well admit to them at such a juncture as this. He rode on into the Park.

It was very early; a mist still lingered between the trees. Nicholas had imagined himself to be the first rider out, then saw that he was not. He should have known that she would be before him; he felt his heart pounding at the sight of her. She was cantering gracefully, light as the mist, her superb figure enhanced by a close-fitting habit, perhaps even more inviting than last night's revealing gown. The tall hat perched on her thick severely-dressed hair with nonchalance, its light veil flinging behind her as she rode. She saw him, and laughed, wheeling about on the sanded path. He urged his mount up to hers, and wished her a good morning. Mélanie did not reply; he was to discover that she had no time for conventional phrases. Instead, she smiled, again showing her magnificent teeth.

'It is dull here, as they will not permit one to gallop,' she said. 'I am used to the wide plains, ah! verst upon verst, where one may gallop one's soul away, and be at one with the little horse one rides. They are not large, the horses of my country, but tireless and light to handle, once they know the rider. This great animal is like a cow.' She looked down with dislike at the mount she rode; it was a dapple grey, and had cantered well enough, if without inspiration.

'Let us make what speed we may,' Crowbetter suggested, and they set themselves to canter again; riding from the first with knee touching knee, so that he was intimately aware of

her strong, shapely thigh beneath the skirt of the dark habit.
They rode round the paths, encountering no one. At the end,
he asked Mélanie to walk her horse, as he did his; he wanted
an assignation with her.

'I must see you again,' he said. He hungered to do so alone;
not in any public place, not in company with her husband;
only the two of them, herself and him, perhaps in an inn
room; he could think of nothing better. He pictured the bed,
and grew faint with desire.

The green eyes slanted round beneath the tall hat's alluring
brim. 'My husband is spending a few days, from tomorrow,
with the Duke at Stratfield Saye,' she told him, and his heart
leaped. Mélanie lifted her shoulders expressively; there was
no need to say which Duke. 'The Duchess is not a hostess, so
no ladies are invited,' she pointed out. Crowbetter thrust his
hand out and caressed her knee, possessively; he could not
help himself. Mélanie raised her thin arched eyebrows a little,
and moved away.

'You take a great deal for granted, Mr Crowbetter. I have
not yet said that I will be your mistress. Come to visit me
tomorrow. I shall be at home.'

He left her in raging uncertainty. To see her again, and not
possess her! They were made for one another, in body, in
mind; he was sure of it, had been so since he first set eyes on
her over the half-recalled game of baccarat. And now, must
he miss another morning at the bank, let opportunities go,
lose important commissions, only to wait politely at Mélanie's
beck and call over teacups, or glasses of marsala, perhaps with
other morning visitors present? And yet, she had taken the
trouble to tell him her husband would not be there. Surely
she would not have done that if she did not intend seeing him
alone?

In any case, he knew that he would go. She had enslaved
him: she had turned his bones to water, and would do so until
he possessed her.

He returned home, bade the carriage wait, went inside and
hurried upstairs. On the landing he surprised Maud
Partridge, coming down to breakfast. She shrank against the
wall to let him pass, her eyes wide open, staring at Nicholas in
his riding-gear. He wished her a good morning, and hurried
on; he would change into his customary suit of clothes,

swallow some coffee, and be gone to the bank. By the time he had washed and been dressed, had his stock re-tied and brushed his hair, and had gone down to the breakfast-room, Maud had left it. Her absence did not trouble Crowbetter any more than her brief presence had done; no doubt she had gone to Jane, who still kept her bed.

He forgot all women when he went in to his private office, which was a sizeable room with large windows, a bright Turkey carpet and a great mahogany desk. His chief clerk brought in the business of the day, and some from yesterday; Nicholas dealt with both, and also saw two interesting clients who wanted a loan to start mining for opals in Australia. The market was almost untapped, they said; and the stones finer than those of India.

'I have seen Australian opals,' said Nicholas drily. 'They vary, as Indian stones do. They are on the whole inferior.' Nevertheless he was intrigued by the proposition; they had said labour was plentiful and cheap; they had security to offer; in the end he made funds available, having an unfailing nose for the likelihood of success.

His next clients were my lords of the Admiralty, a concession which at first flattered Crowbetter. There had come to his office a Rear-Admiral, portly of body and with a face the colour of claret, and his subordinate, a Commander who had little to say in face of the blustering of his superior. The third man was the most important. He was plainly dressed, evidently a ship's architect and surveyor. He also said little, but when he spoke it was clear that he knew what he was talking about. The Rear-Admiral, as clearly, did not.

'Fact is, and we have to admit it, sir, ships have changed damned little since the French wars. Either we'd take an enemy vessel and use her as she was, or build our own to the French pattern.'

Nicholas sat in silence, listening; he was always willing to learn. He wondered why they had come to him in particular; his bank was small, and hardly prominent enough to attract a government department's interest. The Admiral's bloodshot eyes surveyed him.

'Dare say you're wonderin' what the devil brought us here. Speak up, Captain Symonds.'

Symonds began, expressively and using his long hands, to

speak. He explained his notion of a large sailing cruiser such as did not at present exist. He had brought paperwork: Crowbetter stared at the carefully measured drawings and plans. He was not expert enough to gauge their excellence; again, as always, he judged the man. This was someone he himself would trust. Only, my lords had come to a small and relatively little-known bank; why? No doubt they hoped for more favourable terms than they would obtain from the Bank of England.

'I will tell you in confidence, Mr Crowbetter, that we are givin' him a free hand,' blared the Admiral. 'If he's mistaken, we'll sink him along with his ship; eh, Symonds?'

'Exactly, sir. But you will not be disappointed.'

Symonds spoke with quiet assurance, and Nicholas decided to make himself heard. 'Why have you come here?' he asked them. 'An Admiralty contract is something at which the major banks would grasp. I take it you have not come merely to promote our fortunes at Crowbetter's.'

The Admiral cleared his throat, and flushed even more deeply than his natural complexion allowed. 'Fact is, it ain't a contract,' he said. 'I am bein' plain with you, sir. We are, as I said, givin' Symonds a free hand, but that means, of course, that all this is to be kept in the dark for the meantime, till it can be proved beyond doubt that he can give us what the country needs. If the country don't need it, there will be no more of 'em built. I myself believe that the venture will succeed; some of my fellows, who are reluctant to see any change in anythin' at all, don't; and there you have it. Will you finance Symonds privately, or not? Say the word.' The red eyes glared at him.

'If I finance this, and it is successful, can you promise me the Admiralty contract in due course? I realise that such an undertaking cannot be written down.'

'Can't say, can't say,' growled the Admiral. 'It depends on the Board. They're damned sticky, some of these fellers.'

'Then you had best go to the Bank of England, whence you can follow on in natural course, if the scheme succeeds. If it fails, I myself would in any case prefer not to bear the brunt of it. They can afford to do so.' He was in fact making himself out as less affluent than he was; there were plenty of funds to meet the request, but the fact that he had been approached in secret, and might not reap later benefits, angered him.

The Commander spoke up for the first time. 'We had hoped – I trust I may state it frankly, sir – that your rates would be more favourable than those of some others; it is, after all, not a large enterprise.'

'If I am not to be certain of a future contract, my rates will be the same as those of anyone else; and I may venture to suppose that you will find the same response elsewhere.'

'Then we will take ourselves off, damn you,' rumbled the Admiral, and rose to depart. Crowbetter saw Captain Symonds go with regret. He was certain that the man would be heard of again, and that his ship's design would be a success. Had he come alone, to ask for a loan to build and market it, Nicholas would have listened to him. But he was not going to be made use of by my lords, or anyone else. It did not surprise him, in a year or two, to learn that Symonds was made surveyor to the Navy, and that his large cruiser, built and copied many times, sailed the seven seas. Perhaps he himself could have made a fortune out of it; and again, perhaps not. By then, in any event, other things had happened.

The rest of that day's business was humdrum, and when the brougham drew up outside for him at closing time, Nicholas directed it to his club. He sent word back with Humble that he would not dine at home, and bade the man call back for him at half past ten o'clock. He would not make a late night of it, for the prospect of tomorrow's morning call was again filling him with anticipation. He had banished Mélanie from his mind all day; now she was back to torment him with half-promises. If tomorrow would come!

That evening he read the papers, in which there was nothing notable. He exchanged small talk with one or two members, and drank little. On return home, the house was quiet, with no sign of anyone except such servants as were still about. He looked in on his son, sleeping quietly in his cradle; Nick had not grown as fast as he should; he was still puny, perhaps backward. Crowbetter went to bed.

Next day he had himself driven to the address Mélanie had given him during their ride. It proved to be a narrow, elegant grey house near that of the Austrian Ambassador. He would have expected such elegance, although the house itself could only be rented in the circumstances. The door-knocker was that of a Greek head surrounded by worked and twisted metal. Had she worn the headband in echo of the knocker, or had she had it fitted to remind callers of the headband? Either was possible; she was deliberate, yet nonchalant. He felt his heart beat loudly again, waiting to be admitted.

The door was opened by a punctilious manservant. Madame was at home. Nicholas, his hat and cane taken, felt himself guided on and up, past a drawing-room which was empty of visitors and hostess alike; and up further carpeted stairs. At last he was shown to a white-and-gold door, which on being flung open revealed Mélanie, in bed.

'Come in, my friend. Did I not say that I would see you alone?'

She had said nothing of the kind; but he felt his senses fail him. She was lying on pillows of a delicacy one only found in France; their frills and embroidery enhanced her loose hair, which flowed about her. She had cast about her a filmy négligée in green and gold, revealing everything. She was smiling. He swallowed; strode across the carpet to her; and remembered nothing more.

He became aware of the fissure, the cleft, between lust and passion. His experience had been as wide as most men's; the debauching of Maud, which he did not for the present remember, was different; before that there had been the dullness of his marriage, and one or two other episodes in his youth, one of calf-love, but that had not been consummated. Here, now, was fulfilment; to plunge deep into her, to possess her, body and spirit, that laughing spirit that eluded him always, yet led him on. He emptied himself in her repeatedly; there was no more thought of prudence, none of anything except the glorious, ineffable present; his eyes feasted on her body, the pearly globes of her revealed breasts amid the tumbled green and gold stuff, transparent as lawn; all of her flesh had that same pearly sheen, that alluring smoothness, like the inside of a shell. At the same time he realised that she had hurt him; in their climax, she had bitten deep into his shoulder, laughing wildly, with a sound like a man's; it throbbed, and the blood stained her sheets. They lay in surcease at last, his hands still avidly gripping her.

'When does your husband return?' he asked. 'I must come

every day till then.'

'Perhaps I will not permit you.' She put out her long fingers and felt his cheek and jaw, savouring the roughness and the darkening, visible already, after his morning shave. He began to kiss her, and go into her again, and she laughed, with a different note from before, lighter, less dangerous. She let him do as he would, then answered him.

'Franz returns in a week's time. He is not a good lover. He is a German, and they cannot make love. You are different.'

He rode her hungrily. 'Why did you marry him?' he asked.

Mélanie shrugged beneath him. 'My family were poor; he was rich. It was arranged, as such things are.'

'You must come away with me. We will take a little house together.' He knew this was fantasy, or partly so; but they could not continue here as lovers with von Reichmansthal in residence.

'And your bank?' she said mockingly. 'And my place in society? Dorothea Lieven would not invite me to any more of her parties. She herself has had her affairs, but discreetly. We also must be discreet, my friend.'

'I will be anything you wish – anything –'

'Then make love to me a last time, and that will be enough. They will send us up a tray of luncheon.'

They were forced to vary the times of their lovemaking that first week. Nicholas could not indefinitely stay away from the bank in the mornings on the plea of urgent business, leaving everything to his chief clerk. As for Mélanie, she would not ban morning callers every day; she was proud of the social position she had built up in London. For that reason also, she was mindful of the outward proprieties as much as her lover had to be. No client would trust his money to a man who had filched another's wife, and Crowbetter knew it. A kept mistress of the ordinary sort would have been acceptable.

They would meet in the Row very early, as on that first morning, in order not to be remarked while there were few about; and would arrange a time to meet later in the day. The tea-hour was convenient; Nicholas would usually call then, sip tea impatiently, then go up to bed with Mélanie. It was still as it had been that first time between them; fierce, intense, harsh, all-consuming. He never felt the time pass. Mélanie had to instruct her maid to knock on the door each evening in

time for her to dress for dinner, or, as was frequently the
case, to go out at the invitation of some well-known hostess.
At times her devotion to going out angered him.

'You have only these few days with me, and you will not
give up one rout or ball so that I may stay longer with you.'

She flicked him on the cheek in a teasing way. 'You have
your men's dinners, do you not? And I wager you talk of
women.' She had sent for the maid – the girl was French, and
took the matter of lovers calmly – to dress her for a visit to
Baroness von Bülow, the wife of the man who was spoken of
as the future Prussian Minister: she was in England on a visit.
This was indeed brushing royal circles, for Gabrielle von
Bülow was a close friend of the Duchess of Clarence, who was
godmother to her children. Crowbetter knew that Mëlanie
had all this in her mind as she was dressed in a gown of
low-cut white satin, with diamonds in her ears and at her
throat. She was so lovely that he felt desire rise again, and
would gladly have detained her in order to fulfil it. But she
slapped him away absently; she would always go her own way,
and the fact spurred him on to desire her more than ever.

The days fled ever nearer to von Reichmansthal's return
from Stratfield Saye, and Nicholas thought of the German's
renewed possession of his wife with distaste. He himself had
already begun, in such spare time as he had, to scan the
newspapers for advertisements of small properties to rent,
inconspicuous yet convenient. It was not easy to find such a
place; everywhere in town there was the danger that they
would be remarked on coming and going, and he knew better
than to suppose that Mélanie would agree to being taken out
to Bloomsbury or Clerkenwell. Towards the end of the week
he was becoming desperate; nothing had been found, and
apart from the rides in the Row – her husband, she had said,
was not fond of riding – he had no means of seeing Mélanie
alone again.

He was wildly considering a few small rooms at the rear of
the bank, which had once been coachmen's quarters and
could be cleaned, decorated and furnished, when he became
aware that Maud Partridge was standing in front of him. He
laid down the paper with impatience; he must soon leave for
his office, and had not found what he wanted in the columns.
He forced himself to be courteous, however.

'Yes, Miss Partridge?' That he had been as familiar with her as he had was almost forgotten; it might have been years ago, or never. He had invested every one of the gold coins profitably, having picked them one by one off the floor; looking at her, he thought of that and nothing else.

She spoke pleadingly, her eyes wide open as they had seldom been when he first knew her. Once the sight would have intrigued him; now he hardly noticed it.

'Have I offended you?' she asked him.

Her hands were twisting together against her skirts; he had the sudden awareness that she was almost writhing with desire for him. The knowledge filled him with cold distaste. He raised his eyebrows.

'Assuredly not; in what way could you have offended me?' He smiled, and reached for the paper once more; he would take it with him. But Maud spoke again, not having moved from the place where she stood.

'You have not come to see me for a long time. When will you come?'

It was a humble request, like a child's; but Crowbetter was irritated. 'I told you,' he said, 'that I would come to you when I chose, and not when I did not choose. That is clear to you now, I hope.'

The tears had welled up in her eyes and were spilling down her cheeks. 'You are cruel.' she told him. 'You have ruined me, and now you abandon me. What is to become of me? What am I to do?'

He rose from the table. 'Why, go about your duties to my wife. You cannot say they are onerous.'

She gave a choking sob, and ran from the room. He strode into the hall, picked up his hat, and went out.

That evening at dinner Miss Partridge was not present. They had a guest, an old aunt of Jane's, who was deaf, so the talk was not diverting. Luckily the dowager went early to bed, and before doing so herself Jane approached her husband as he opened the port.

'Miss Partridge wants to leave,' she said timidly. 'Will you write her a reference? She will not obtain another situation without one.'

He looked at her; how dumpy she was, how overdressed, how lacking in all wit and charm! 'No, I will not write her a reference,' he said; the notion that Maud Partridge might take herself beyond his reach was in some way obnoxious to him; let her stay. 'Tell her that this is nonsense, that you are satisfied with her, and that she will remain.'

Over the port he forgot Maud. He had still not selected a house in which to meet Mélanie to make love, and von Reichmansthal returned tomorrow.

It was to have been their last ride together before the expected return at midday. She was aware of that, and would surely have made an effort to be early for him, to grant him the full hour of her company. But he waited, in the saddle, at the place among the trees where they met by custom in the Park, and there was no sign of her; he cantered aimlessly up and down the paths, and still she did not come; and after half an hour had passed he knew that she would not. He waited for a little longer, riding again up and down; then stabled his horse before the hour was up, and returned in an evil temper to the house. Had she done this to torment him? It would be like her; there was that devil in her, the devil that made her bite his flesh till it bled.

But when he reached home they handed him a note, directed to him in large sprawling writing. He realised that he had never seen her hand before. He dismissed the servant, and tore the letter open before going upstairs.

He returned yesterday evening, unexpectedly, it read. *He says I look pale, and will take me to Brighton for a few days for the sea air. It will be a great bore, because since the King left no one goes there. I hope at any rate to be at Almack's on the twenty-seventh; pray come to me there, and ask me to waltz. I waltz very well. M.*

The days till then were a torment to Crowbetter. He tried to fill the hours with work, cards, wine, company at the club; but there were the night hours, when he could not help but picture his mistress's possession by her plump, uninspiring husband. It was all he could do not to drive down to Brighton, but that would be foolish and would serve no purpose.

Lying in bed, with the lamp lit, he tried to read a French novel, but could not fix his mind on its contents. He closed the book, put his arms behind his head, and stared at the wall. Hanging there – he had not observed it lately, had forgotten its existence after briefly remembering it that time Maud

Partridge had come to him in the breakfast-room – was the Danaë miniature. The sight of it irritated Crowbetter; he got up, went over to it, and turned it with its plain back to him, hanging it that way round instead; but it was more obvious than ever, impossible to overlook. Tomorrow he would have it hung in the room opposite; then he recalled that that was his wife's room. Jane, then, must be moved upstairs; he thought of her as if she were a piece of unnecessary furniture. The portrait – it had its value, no doubt, which would increase with time – could be kept in there, afterwards, safely enough.

He lay back on the pillows and let misery overwhelm him again. How long till the evening at Almack's? And after that, how long again? He was not accustomed to being made to wait. He was as greatly driven by desire as he had been that first night at Princess Lieven's. She, also, would be at Almack's, keeping an eye on the proprieties; she was a patroness. It was amusing to reflect that the famous and select assembly rooms had been set on their course by a Scotsman named McCaul, who had turned his name the other way round. Few people knew this; it would be sacrilege to mention it openly.

Jane wept when told that she must leave her room and occupy the one upstairs. Crowbetter was adamant; he never visited her now; the luxurious first-floor room could be kept for guests. 'It will do you good to walk up an extra flight of stairs,' he told her heartlessly. 'You take no exercise of any kind, and you are putting on too much flesh. Upstairs, you will be opposite your companion; you may call her more conveniently if there is anything you should require.'

Jane's mouth set in a dreary downward curve. He didn't want her any more since they had said she could not have more children. That was it; he didn't care about the companion, or about guests, and in any case there was another room for them in the house if they came. Jane watched her familiar things being moved upstairs with a sense of hopelessness. She meant nothing to Crowbetter, nothing at all. If only she were clever enough to make him laugh and listen to her! Sometimes he would be like that with people who came, but never with herself, never when they were alone: they would dine together in silence, after he had been out all day.

She settled obediently into the upstairs room, however, and occupied it without further complaint. Maud Partridge heard the commotion, the coming and going, and knew that the visits from Mr Crowbetter to her own room were ended. She would toss and writhe on her bed at night, wanting him, as he had repeatedly taught her to do. Sometimes she thought she would go mad with longing, as if her whole body were on fire. But he was like a stranger now. She had tried to see him as he came and went, although since she had tried to speak to him that time he had given the servants orders that she was not to come down for meals in future, but to receive a tray in her room as she had done at the beginning. He did not want to see her, that was evident; why then did he make her stay?

The two unhappy women lived on the second floor, accordingly, and seldom spoke to one another; it was not often that Jane needed her companion except to fetch something or else put it away. There had never been talk between them from the beginning, and there was none now.

As for the baby, he was slow in learning to walk; but by this time it was fairly safe to assume that, unless Nick caught some fever or other, he would live. He occupied his nursery; nobody occupied the first-floor room; the miniature hung on the wall there unremarked, and Nicholas Crowbetter waited with impatience for the twenty-seventh of the month.

It dawned at last, and all that day he found it difficult to keep his eye on business. He contrived, however; and in the evening had himself attired in the silk knee-breeches and other appurtenances necessary to satisfy Almack's discerning patronesses; they had once turned away the Duke of Wellington himself because he appeared in trousers. Nicholas's stock was high, his hair again *en brosse*, his shave perfect, his coat a tailor's dream. He entered the famous King Street rooms with his heart pounding; and at once saw Mélanie.

She wore the same white satin dress she had put on for the von Bülows' rout. Her hair was dressed differently, left loose down her back, confined in front by the Greek band of gold. The earrings swung; he could see them from where he stood. She was waltzing already with Lord Brownlow, although she had promised him, Crowbetter, the waltz.

He made his way determinedly towards them, and when the second waltz struck up, made sure of it with her. To hold her in his arms, to sense the warmth of her flesh beneath the satin, made him as hungry as a wolf. He must have shown it in his face, because he saw Mélanie laughing at him.

'Softly, my friend, softly,' she murmured. 'You will have us refused admission in future; they are watching, remember.' The patronesses sat amiably enough, surveying the dancing. Dorothea Lieven wore yellow, and her diamonds. He had caught her glance and she inclined her dark head amiably, so all was well. He gave himself to the waltz; the lilting music filled him with satisfaction, yet sadness; when, when in all the world, was he to see Mélanie again?

He asked her. She smiled, murmuring.

'Do you know what you have done, you great brute? You have given me a child. I have allowed Franz the opportunity to believe that it may be his.'

'So soon?' His heart had missed a beat; if there was a scandal, his business would suffer. He saw her green eyes mocking him.

'So soon. I have missed what women have to expect, and I have felt sick daily. That last convinced me; I am never sick. It is your fault. It should not surprise you, *après tout*.'

'What are we to do?' he asked her. 'I still have nowhere for you to come to me.'

'Then we must do without.' The music had ceased; the couples were leaving the floor. 'May I procure you an ice?' he said. A country dance was being set up, and he could not bear the thought of its lack of intimacy.

'We must not be seen to be too much together,' she said. 'He will go to Wien soon, to Wenzel. I will send word to you. Until then, farewell.'

He saw her moving down the long line of couples as if she had no pregnancy to trouble her, her hair flying behind her in a long tress of soft honey-coloured ringlets. He waited all evening, but did not manage to speak with her again. Von Reichmansthal was not present.

Mélanie did not inform Crowbetter of the departure of her husband for Vienna; he saw it in the papers. It was not stated that von Reichmansthal's wife had failed to accompany him because of her delicate situation, but Crowbetter knew that that must be the excuse she had made. He was angry with her. She should have apprised him of the departure.

It would have suited his pride not to wait on her at once, but he could not help himself. It was Sunday, and he was free to suit his own book. He dressed carefully, in a dark coat, light breeches, and white hat; and betook himself to the von Reichmansthal house. He was admitted, and to his rage heard the sound of voices and laughter.

She had morning callers, mostly women, drinking negus. Their clustered bonnets drew together over the latest gossip; they were mostly well-known hostesses in their own right. Nicholas hardly separated them by name, though he knew them all; his disgust and impatience consumed him. Was he not to see her alone, after coming here especially to do so?

It did not appear that he was to be so favoured. After what seemed an interminable conversation with old Lady Mount Edgcumbe, who was growing deaf, and after unwillingly swallowing negus, which he disliked, he perceived the guests begin to leave. Mélanie came up to him.

'It has been a great pleasure to have your company, sir,' she said sweetly. 'Perhaps you will call another day? I bid you farewell for the time.' And Nicholas had no choice but to bow over her hand, and go out; yet when he did so, he found the maid Germaine ready for him in the hall. She said no word, but gestured him upstairs; nobody saw him go. He was thrust into Mélanie's bedroom, and left waiting, looking at the white-and-gold door, the dozen knick-knacks a woman had about her, the silver hairbrushes, the pots of rouge and pomatum, the hook for lacing bodices. He felt like a bear in a cage; and commenced pacing up and down, waiting for the last of the guests to go, when, surely, she would come.

She came. She entered the room like a whirlwind, laughing, twining her arms about his neck. They kissed repeatedly; he carried her to the bed, unable to wait. 'You thought, did you not, that you would not see me today? Here I am; and as anxious for you, you see, as you are for me. Crowbetter, Crowbetter –'

He was within her already. The notion had come to him that he must destroy the child, if it could be done; if it were born, and resembled him, his reputation was lost. He rode her hard and ruthlessly, therefore, hearing her laughter: force never made Mélanie afraid, but seemed to stimulate her. He thrust on, spurred both by the time that had elapsed since he had last taken her, and the need he felt to undo the results of his own imprudence. By the end, they both lay exhausted. Her hand strayed over his neck.

'You make love as my people do, strongly and without pity.
I like it. I have missed it all these weeks.'
'And Franz?' he said with jealousy.
'Franz does not matter.'
There was no sign that he had induced a miscarriage in
her. Perhaps, if he persevered, it would come.

Twice a year, once in summer and once in winter, Jane
Crowbetter was expected by her husband to give a somewhat
larger entertainment than was involved in the endurance of a
few guests for dinner. Endurance it was indeed for Jane. She
was aware that, like the Duchess of Wellington, she had none
of the qualities demanded of a hostess, and the occasion itself,
and its prospect, filled her with terror, thinking of
Crowbetter's all-seeing golden eyes regarding her, afterwards, with cold contempt. As for the list of guests, she left
that to him. Mrs Rae and the cook would see to the food, and
Crowbetter himself would undertake the wine.

On the list that her husband handed her on this occasion
Jane saw, with her short-sighted eyes, a new name, that of the
Countess von Reichmansthal. Thinking to please Nicholas,
she remarked on it. He told her that the Countess was
Hungarian and her husband Austrian, at present absent in
Vienna to arrange the education of their little son. 'I trust that
you will make her welcome,' he added. Jane, pleased – it was
not often that he made so long a speech to her – decided to do
so, smiled and nodded.

Crowbetter smiled also. Had his wife known, he and
Mélanie had been making love twice daily, morning and
evening, since the departure of her spouse two months ago to
visit their son. They had given up the Row rides, as unsuitable
to Mélanie's state; instead, Crowbetter would have himself
admitted, very early, to her house by a side door, go up to her
in bed, finding her with her hair already combed and
smelling delicious; they would couple together hard for an
hour, then he would dress again and leave for his office.
After the day's work, when it closed, he would return and,
unless there were visitors, in which case Nicholas would join
unwillingly in the talk, would take possession of Mélanie
again urgently, brutally, totally. It would happen wherever
they were, if they were alone; in the drawing-room, in the
bedroom, in a small private room she kept for herself in

which to write her letters. She seemed to care nothing; his ears continued full of the sound of her laughter. Nor had she taken harm from his thrustings; her pregnancy progressed inevitably. She had not yet thickened, but her bosom had grown full and tender; she had shown him her darkened nipples with pride, holding up her breasts in both her hands. Disquiet claimed Crowbetter every time he thought of the expected child, who might resemble himself. Also, he was cautious lest clients see or hear of him entering and leaving Mélanie's house too often: but if he was to continue in possession of her, there seemed no alternative.

The reception at Hyde Park Gardens took place on a clear dry evening, seldom troubled as they were here with the constant fog near the heart of London. The street became lined with carriages, some belonging to the socially élite, others to clients and their wives, or else directors of other merchant banks and theirs. One belonged to the Countess von Reichmansthal. Mélanie rustled into the house with her shoulders draped in a gold-embroidered pelisse of mulberry shade; when it was shrugged off it revealed her gown, low-cut as never before, of a raspberry pink no other woman present would have had the insolence to wear; a harlot's colour. Mélanie made her way through the staring assembly, caring nothing what the strait-laced thought or made evident: diamond earrings swinging, she was served with champagne, then duly met Jane Crowbetter, standing mute beside her husband to receive the guests. The two women regarded one another, Jane with complete lack of interest, Mélanie with ill-concealed mockery. So this was Crowbetter's wife! No wonder he needed a mistress.

Her host watched her back as she threaded her way beween the guests, noting that the men spoke to her while the women did not. He hoped that that did not signify the beginnings of a scandal which would involve himself. They had not made love this evening, because of the reception and his own necessity of seeing to the wine: but he had gone to her as usual this morning. He looked forward to tomorrow with renewed vigour. Tonight, though, he was careful not to pay any attention to Mélanie at all. He talked to other women; it was an occasion on which to ingratiate himself further with the families who had invested their money with his bank. He praised the diamonds of one, the Lyon silk of another. For so long Englishwomen had been without it during the wars with Napoleon that it was still considered a wonder to possess, although the wars themselves were long over.

The voices had risen to a pitch where one could hardly hear oneself speak, however, and the champagne flowed. The creams and jellies on the table were consumed; it was a successful occasion. Nicholas was congratulating himself, and was almost about to congratulate Jane; then a rustle of subsiding silk sounded nearby above the hubbub, and everyone fell silent. Mélanie von Reichmansthal had fainted. She lay crumpled on the carpet, her spilt champagne ruining her dress.

Crowbetter went to her, shouldering his way through; there was no scandal in the host's doing so, in fact it was expected of him. He called for the rest to stand back, to give her air; gathered her up in his arms, at the same time hoping that the miscarriage he had tried so assiduously to promote had taken place. 'Call the servants,' he said. 'The Countess must lie down upstairs.'

The servants came, the housekeeper, the footmen he had hired for the occasion, his butler, even his valet; but he himself carried Mélanie up the flight of carpeted stairs to the first-floor room. He laid her on the bed, while Mrs Rae unlaced her gown and arranged the pillows comfortably. Before returning to his guests Nicholas looked down at Mélanie. She lay like a broken flower, he thought: the bright skirts loose about her, her white limbs flaccid, the full bosom almost revealed above the unlaced bodice. He heard himself express the hope that she would soon be recovered: and saw the darkened eyelashes render him a wink.

'You were troubled about your reputation if you were seen to visit me, so I have visited you instead. You should be pleased, not scowling.'

'You should not be here,' he told her. Nevertheless he had given the servants orders that, of course, Madame von Reichmansthal was to stay the night, as she was not well enough to be moved. He had let it be discreetly known that she was in a delicate situation, and had sent her carriage home. When it was time, they would return with her daytime clothes and she would be driven back. That, at any rate, was what he had persuaded himself would happen; but already, knowing Mélanie, he suspected that she would make him a long visit. It was not, after all, unpleasant to have her across the landing from him, with the other women safely upstairs.

He had come to her after the guests had left, with the servants clearing up the chaos of used crockery, spilt food and drink, and wilting hothouse flowers ordered at some expense from a florist's. He had let himself in at her door and turned the key, then gone to her and peeled down the pink dress to her ankles, whence Mélanie kicked it away. Then they went about their customary business, anger spurring Crowbetter on to prick hard and dangerously, no doubt, in her condition, but he was determined by now to rid her of the child if it could be done. She accepted his attentions joyously, bending her body into an ivory arc to receive them; and began to make the sounds of a woman in ecstasy. He laid his hand over her mouth, to quiet her.

'Be careful,' he said. 'They will hear you.' He was well within her, and stayed as he was. Mélanie bit his hand, and he drew it away in anger with her; the mark would show tomorrow.

'Who will hear? What do they matter? I do as I please.'

'That is evident. That dress you wore tonight was improper; the wrong colour, and cut too low.'

'If you do not like the sight of me as I am, others do. I could be Lord Brownlow's mistress, if it suited me. Perhaps it does. He –'

Crowbetter crushed her mouth with his own in the way he had, to stop her talking. They made love again, insatiably. When it was done with, and she lay back sated, Mélanie asked languidly, 'Who is the young woman with the shower of coins in a particular place? I have diverted myself by looking at her, all evening until you came.'

'No one of importance,' he told her; Maud Partridge had not been present at the reception. He considered whether or not he ought to have the miniature removed while Mélanie was here; but she had seen it now, and its absence would be noticed by her.

He left her for the night, but returned in the early morning; finding her tumbled, sleepy, flushed and adorable. He plunged deep into her, finding himself unwilling to leave in

time for the office. Perhaps after all her bold stratagem
had been the right one; nobody would see or guess more than
that he himself entered and left his own house. He hoped
Franz von Reichmansthal would stay for a long time in
Vienna. So far there had been no word of his returning
home.

Mélanie, left alone, was brought coffee by one of the maids,
who was shocked at the nakedness she did not trouble to hide.
Later in the morning the door opened. It was the companion,
with a lace shawl from Jane Crowbetter, who hoped her
guest's condition was improved after a night's rest.

Maud made the speech carefully, having handed over the
shawl. Suddenly the beautiful woman in the bed pointed at
her with one long finger, and broke out into harsh laughter.
She laughed immoderately, cruelly, incessantly. Maud stood
almost reeling for moments, then looked round wildly; the
portrait of herself, the shameful and improper portrait, hung
on the wall here; she had not known where it was.

'Ha, ha, ha, ha,' jeered Mélanie. 'Did he give you a single
guinea for yourself, *aprés tout*? I wager not; he is too careful.'

Maud Partridge blundered out of the room. She felt the
sobs rising in her throat, and could not control them. There
was nowhere she could go to be private, nowhere in all the
house; Mrs Crowbetter was across the landing from her
room, and would call her for some matter any moment.
Maud's breast was heaving, the tears were running down her
face; blindly, she groped her way to the back regions,
avoiding the kitchens, and out to where the stables were.
There was a loose-box where there was no horse kept, unless
someone came on a visit; there was clean straw in it, and
Maud lay down and sobbed there, feeling her wretchedness
overcome her. The thick straw drowned other sounds than
her sobbing; she did not hear the foosteps that came, but
sensed a presence, and turned round, revealing a tear-
blotched face. A man, the groom and coachman Humble, was
standing looking down at her.

'You in a bit o' trouble?' The small mud-coloured eyes
surveyed her. Maud struggled up; it didn't do to tell the
groom what was the matter. 'I am in some distress, that is all,'
she said quietly. She would have gone out, but he barred the
way.

'Women's allus in trouble,' he said. He looked her up and

down in a way she resented, but perhaps he meant no harm. 'You can go up the ladder if you like,' he said. 'There's a bed there. Lie down till you're over it.'

Maud was not very anxious to lie on his bed; but without pushing past him she could not escape. In any case, for a little while, the attic would be private. She gathered her skirts in one hand and climbed the wooden ladder. Upstairs the sunlight flooded in from a roof window, showing a bed, none too clean, a chair, and a large straw hamper in which Humble kept his clothes. Maud stood uncertainly, then, feeling wretched, went after all and lay down. Her sobs were subsiding; she closed her eyes.

Some time passed. She wondered if Jane Crowbetter might be looking for her, and did not care. That woman, the beautiful mocking cruel woman, wouldn't stay long here. In a little while she herself would begin to feel better. Such things had to be endured.

Humble had meantime come up the ladder. He entered at the door, turning and fastening the hook on the inside. She hadn't expected him to follow her. She began to rise on one elbow, preparing to get off the bed.

'Lie down, and shut yer mouth,' said Humble. 'I know what women need. You was in the back o' the carriage with him, remember? In the Park.'

He passed his tongue over his lips. He was busy unfastening his breeches. Maud began to tremble. It wasn't ladylike to scream; they would ask why she had climbed up here at all. It wasn't – it wouldn't – oh, he was upon her, and had flung up her skirts, and – and –

The pallet bed began to creak rhythmically. Maud Partridge kept her eyes closed. The fire in her body quenched, she was solaced, it hadn't happened for a long time, and now – and now –

'I know how how to handle a woman, and a horse too,' said Humble, and spat on the floor.

The days passed. Mélanie showed no signs of leaving, and her lotions, essences, négligée and hairbrushes had been sent for, although not yet her maid. Germaine had, at this time of the month, it was explained, *ses règles*. She would come presently; in the meantime, might one of the servants appear after breakfast to brush out Mélanie's hair?

Crowbetter was fairly helpless in the matter; he would be gone by then, and Mélanie stayed in bed all day, making no effort to dress and get up. There were reasons why he did not care to ask Mrs Rae. That lady had come to him recently one evening, when he was on his way upstairs, attired as usual in her cap and blacks, with keys jangling; and had told him respectfully that he must look for another housekeeper. Crowbetter pretended to be bewildered, though he knew perfectly well what it was about; she had surprised him coming out of Mélanie's room early that morning, and had gone past with averted eyes.

'I have always served in respectable houses, sir. There are things going on here as don't please me. I'd be obliged if you would give me a character, to enable me to find another place, and I'll stay for a little, till Mrs Crowbetter has found someone else to see to things about the house. Then I'll go.'

'Mrs Rae, you cannot go. I rely on you absolutely, and so does my wife. We will never find anyone like you. Will you not think again?' He offered, in tactful terms, to raise her wages, but she shook her head.

'It isn't money, sir; I'm very well suited in that way, and every other, here, and I'll be sorry to leave. It's that foreign lady, sir, to put it plainly. You know better than I do what goes on.'

'The foreign lady, as you call her, is only staying for a little while, till her husband returns from abroad. Do not leave for that reason, I beg.' He had visions of all the maids leaving as well, of word spread abroad that his house was one with a bad name, and he himself an adulterer. He let his golden eyes plead with her.

The housekeeper sniffed. 'Well, sir, seeing as it is only for a short while; but it's time her husband was home.'

The servant sent to brush out Mélanie's hair was, cruelly, Maud. The order came, as usual, from Nicholas, and he put it in a straightforward manner, seeing nothing wrong with it; the companion had very little else to do, and so he told her. 'It will take you an hour each day, no more,' he said. 'Madame von Reichmansthal is accustomed to having her hair well brushed, and her maid is not yet here.'

Maud set her lips in a line and did as she was told, holding each lock of the long resilient hair as if it were the snakes of

Medusa. She had flushed when she was bidden to do it, and he observed that fact and thought how greatly her appearance was improved; in fact she looked almost attractive. If he had known the loathing with which she carried out the task, perhaps even he would have felt pity.

He had begun to spend all night with Mélanie, leaving her in the early morning after slaking as fully as he might the desire which rose and teased him again then; having slept entwined with her, his hands gripping her smooth warm limbs, naked beneath the covers. She submitted agreeably, her half-shut lids hiding amused eyes; no matter what the hour of day or night, she looked as another woman might when prepared for a ball. Nicholas would tangle his fingers in the long rich hair poor Maud would unravel tomorrow, would caress and fondle every part of Mélanie's body, the intimate clefts, the swelling tender breasts, the belly where his child still lay. He was by now so bewitched that the losing of the child was less urgent than the fulfilment of his constant need for her. He could have made love all day as well as all night, she told him, and laughed; always, there was her laughter. He would rise from her unwillingly in the grey dawn, and return to his bed to let his valet think he had slept in it.

Germaine the maid returned, and for a few days all was harmony; Mrs Rae said no more about leaving. The French girl was put to share the companion's room. 'Your Miss Partridge goes out a great deal,' said Mélanie to him one day, her eyes dancing with malice.

'Goes out? Where should she go to? She knows nobody.'

'Perhaps she has made an acquaintance,' said Mélanie softly. She was not unaware of the hatred Maud bore her; it amused her, and there was small other amusement here, except for the trays of meals and the regular visits of Crowbetter. She stretched her limbs and body luxuriously. What a lover he was, forceful, insatiable! It suited her, after the dullness of the plodding Franz.

In the following week, the Count wrote. He would travel back to London at the end of the month, and was bringing little Wenzel with him.

'A good evening to you, Crowbetter. It is long since we have seen you.'

Crowbetter had walked into his club out of the fog in the

winter street. His ill-temper was not abated by the sight of an egregious member, whom he disliked, standing before the roaring coal fire, while the porters hovered. He murmured some reply to the member's welcome, and made his way upstairs expecting to be greeted by his elder brother George, who was to dine with him and discuss affairs regarding his second marriage, which had taken place a year ago now: George seldom left the country. Their father had hoped to make him a director of the bank, but he was unsuited to it, and the task had fallen to Nicholas, providentially enough. They could dine together here more amicably than at Hyde Park Gardens, which had grown dreary since the departure of Mélanie.

George was late, no doubt due to the fog. Nicholas ordered himself whisky and sat and drank it, in too morose a mood either to chat with other members or to look at the newspapers by the fog-wreathed light of the smoking-room lamps. His mind harked back to the state of affairs at home, from which Mélanie had been removed on the return of her husband some months ago, and had thereafter vanished from Crowbetter's life. He had caught a glimpse of her once, swathed in furs and great with his child, driving beside the Count in their carriage, a small dark-haired boy accompanying them, his straight locks cut in a square fringe. As von Reichmansthal had evidently forbidden Mélanie to go into society because of her condition, Crowbetter had had no opportunity of meeting her since. There was little chance by now that the child would not be born: he had, therefore, accustomed himself to the prospect.

He still felt the need of Mélanie, however, and filled his days with work in order to banish her from his mind. In the evenings, though, the memory of her returned, as strongly as if she were present in the body. It was as though she would not let him go, while yet remaining absent from him. The birth was imminent. Crowbetter wondered how soon he would be able to glean details of the child's appearance. If he called at her house, as he might conventionally do, he would learn nothing in the ordinary way: it was hardly for a gentleman visitor to be taken up to a nursery, unless he wanted to appear openly besotted; and that was the last thing Crowbetter wanted. In fact he had avoided calling on Mélanie at all during these months, afraid that he might betray himself.

George was certainly very late. Undoubtedly the fog had

delayed him; perhaps, being of a somewhat timorous nature, he had not set out. Nicholas ordered more whisky, then still more, and got himself fuddled. He stayed there drinking steadily until ten o'clock, then decided George was certainly not coming. No doubt there would be a letter tomorrow, making fresh arrangements to meet and ensure an allowance for the young second wife, if anything should happen. One hoped that it had not done so; George was not yet old. He was a considerable shareholder in Crowbetter's by virtue of the rich bride he had married on the first occasion, who had enjoyed a fortune even larger than Jane's, made in whatever fashion by a grandfather in Jamaica. She had died four years ago, leaving a young daughter, Athene, who would inherit. Two years later George had made a fool of himself with the second marriage to a penniless young woman, and there was now an infant, another girl. Nicholas Crowbetter had not seen it.

He decided that it was too late to dine, and went out into the fog, walking less certainly than usual. The whisky on an empty stomach had dispelled his usual prudence, and he was aware, and had been so for some time, that he needed a woman. The thought of Mélanie was still with him strongly, but she was not here, might indeed never be here again; it was possible that, after the birth, von Reichmansthal would whisk her off to Vienna. The prospect filled Crowbetter with a dismal sense of loss. Only by satisfying his body might he forget her, for an hour: and with whom, and where? A prostitute brushed against him in the fog, murmuring her solicitation; but he would have no dealings with such creatures, there was too great a certainty of venereal disease.

He walked on, taking out his savage need in the exercise; he had told Humble to stay at home to avoid risk to the horse on such a night. It occurred to him, as he went, that he might make use of the companion, Partridge, again; after all he paid her for doing very little, and the least she could do would be to oblige him, on this occasion at any rate. He quickened his steps, for the fog had thinned by now and he could see his direction; and in less than an hour reached his house. Having been admitted, he asked for Miss Partridge to be sent to him, giving no reason.

The butler looked at him expressionlessly; damn servants, they knew everything. 'Sir, Miss Partridge went out about an hour ago.'

'Out? At this time of night? Where did she go?' The knowledge that Maud was not immediately available irritated Crowbetter. The butler cast down his eyes and said that he thought the young lady had gone round to the stables.

'The stables? What the devil for?'

'Sir, I do not know, but I saw her go in that direction some time ago, and she has not returned.' He knew, in fact, very well, but he wasn't going to get the blame from the master about what had been going on for quite a bit, and having said nothing about it.

Nicholas turned without further words and went out of the house again, and round to the stables, built as they were at an angle at the back. The two horses were in their stalls, quiet and pulling down clean hay from their racks by the light of a hung lantern; another shone in the upstairs quarters. Nicholas began to ascend the ladder steps, feeling himself steady enough despite the whisky in him, and halfway up heard a sudden long harsh babbling cry, the cry of a woman's ecstasy.

He did not remember gaining the door, which swung open; Humble no longer troubled to shut it. The man's bared jerking buttocks showed in the light of a cracked lamp; beneath them were spread the woman's exposed thighs. Crowbetter heard his own shriek of outrage; the couple pulled apart at once, the man bold-faced, the woman already shamed, struggling up and drawing together her bodice. Nicholas found himself thinking already that it was the last time he would see Maud's breasts. She had a soiled and handled look; her hair was tousled, and her mouth, like a harlot's, hung loose. She did not look at him.

Crowbetter spoke like ice into the silence. 'You will leave tonight, both of you.' he said. 'Here is your money until the end of the week.' He flung some coins on the floor. Maud Partridge suddenly began to wail: the man bade her be quiet. 'You can come with me,' he said curtly. The narrow gaze fastened itself on Nicholas.

'Can't let others do what you do yourself, can yer? You had your fill of her; turned her into a hot piece one way and another, I can tell you. I can use her myself. It's no loss to me to leave 'ere, except for the horses. I was fond of them. I won't get others, not without a character, but I don't need one from the likes of you. We can manage, her and me, well enough.'

'Go, then, and talk less. I expect to find you gone by morning.'

'We'll be going now,' said Humble. He strapped up his hamper, took it in one hand, grasped Maud by the wrist, pulled her after him down the ladder and out into the fog. Nicholas watched them go with a growing sense of unreality; his rage had faded. Maud, still held like a bitch on a chain, was lurching. He wondered idly what would become of her. Later, he heard that the fellow had married her, then put her out to work on the streets.

By that time, his attention was taken up with another matter. George had failed to keep the appointment for dinner because he would never eat dinner again. He had died of pneumonia following a hunt in the rain, after which he had failed to change his clothes. It revealed the kind of inefficiency which was like him, and had made him unsuitable to be a director of Crowbetter's. Nicholas went down to Hertfordshire for the funeral, saw the widow afterwards, admired the charming baby named Sarah, and took a dislike to the overstuffed girl of twelve, already full of her own consequence, who was Athene. He was not to foresee that she would inhabit his house, with Sarah, in another sixteen years. In fact, he offered the family a home with him at once, somewhat half-heartedly; but the young widow replied quietly that she would contrive alone. 'My husband was good to me,' she said. 'I will look after his daughters.'

Touched and relieved, Crowbetter travelled home, having made the necessary financial arrangements; he was, of course, trustee for Athene, and though George had not been able to sign the documents necessary to ensure a large jointure for his widow and support for his infant daughter, Nicholas would see that they received it. He had family feeling in such ways.

Jane Crowbetter was complacent. Since the departure of Partridge from the opposite room – perhaps her presence had prevented his visits hitherto – her husband had come upstairs and had slept with her every night. This was a euphemism, as Crowbetter departed within an hour; but Jane had been brought up by an aunt who believed in understating such things, and had also taught her that it was wicked to enjoy them. Jane admitted to the wickedness, to an insidious bliss that pervaded her stumpy body when it happened; but her resulting stiff embarrassment, her passive endurance, bored and alienated her husband; had there been any alternative, he would not have come to her at all. For the moment there was none; so he would appear in Jane's bedroom, say nothing, perform the marital act with a kind of absent-mindedness, and leave as silently as he had come. After her long neglect by him it consoled Jane, despite her upbringing, and gave her confidence. One night, she ventured to make a remark about young Nick.

'Lady Mount Edgcumbe says she knows of a tutrix who would suit him,' she said. 'She is a widow, who has been with good families, and is reliable.'

'What is her name?' muttered Nicholas, engaged in his own occupation. He was only mildly interested in his son's progress; the little boy was neither bright nor taking, and his father hardly saw him nowadays. He proceeded, hardly listening.

'I think that it is a Mrs Milsom.' Jane was a snob, and while she would remember Lady Mount Edgcumbe's title she tended to forget humbler names. She tried to recall, while Nicholas continued to disturb propriety, the virtues the old noblewoman had enumerated as pertaining to this Mrs Milsom. She had had an unfortunate marriage, evidently, but the husband was dead; there were no children, and the widow was said to be very good with other people's. 'It is not,' she said aloud, while the bed trembled, 'necessary for me to have another companion. This governess could have Partridge's room.' That was unwise; perhaps he would not come to her any more; but she had said it now.

Nicholas did not answer, relieved his need fully, and left. Although she was not very intelligent, Jane knew that silence meant he was considering the matter. She rearranged her nightgown and prepared to sleep; now Partridge had left, with her comings and goings, one slept particularly well. That there had been some matter involving Crowbetter Jane was almost certain; although perhaps it was only that the shocking portrait downstairs, with the shower of gold coins, resembled Maud Partridge closely. In any case, Crowbetter by now was paying her, his wife, full attention. Jane allowed herself to recall his recent embraces pleasurably, said her prayers in atonement, and slept.

2

It was so seldom that his wife made a suggestion of any kind that Nicholas accordingly sent for Mrs Milsom and interviewed her, with the possibility of appointing her to be in charge of his son. Nick by now was still undersized and thin, though later his height would improve; he had the pathetic air of a neglected puppy. His father did not go up with the new woman to see him, but sent one of the servants, and saw Mrs Milsom again when she came downstairs.

'Well?' His question was laconic; he did not altogether take to Harriet Milsom. She struck him as sly. She was dressed in black clothes, as became her widowed state; and although her fine dark eyes were an admirable feature, the expression with which they looked at him was not sufficiently subservient. Crowbetter reflected that he would see very little of her if she came, however; she would spend her time and take her meals upstairs with the child.

'How do you find him?' he asked her. The dark glance surveyed him unreadably.

'I think that when he has the constant company of someone who will love him and talk to him, he will progress. A lonely child is thrust in upon himself.' The reproach was unspoken, but it was there; Crowbetter had neglected his son.

He appointed Harriet Milsom, finding no reason not to do so, except that she made him uncomfortable. She was to come as soon as possible; and in a few days her modest baggage arrived in a hackney and was carried into the house. Thereafter Nicholas saw nothing of her except to receive her weekly report on the progress of the little boy, who improved somewhat under her tutelage. Perhaps one day, after all, he would be an asset to Crowbetter's Bank.

Work occupied Nicholas himself unceasingly; it kept his mind

from other things. He was filled with self-reproach for the
fate of Maud Partridge, turned as she was into a drab in the
alleys; if he had left her alone at first, as Jane's prim
companion, she would be the same still. Also, he was filled
with a crying need for Mélanie. It was about this time that
their child should be born. He had heard nothing of her,
having cut himself off from every kind of social exchange;
what was the use of those, with Franz von Reichmansthal
bending assiduously over her? Sooner or later he must
provide himself with another mistress, for Jane did not satisfy
him; but not yet. He kept his head down over the paperwork;
there had been several contracts of the kind he had formerly
refused from the Rear-Admiral, and he congratulated
himself in the supposition that his refusal had perhaps leaked
out and had given him status.

He was incessantly busy, therefore, and on a particular day
had given orders to his clerk that he was on no account to be
disturbed. The familiar surroundings, the bright carpet and
great light windows with their delicate astragals, soothed him;
this was home to him, far more, at present, than his own
house. He sat down to the papers that awaited him, and
worked his way partly through; then was disturbed by the
clerk, holding a letter. Nicholas frowned.

'I told you not to disturb me.'

'Sir, this is very urgent. The man who brought it told me
what it contained. He says a Count von Reichmansthal is
dead, sir. There has been a carriage accident. I did not think
you would wish to be left uninformed.' He hovered
uncertainly, grey and forever subordinate; he had been with
Nicholas's father, and would never rise higher than his
present place.

Crowbetter tore open the note, seeing the sprawling
handwriting. *Franz is dead*, it told him briefly. *Come to me when
you can.*

They had already put von Reichmansthal in his coffin and
closed it, the doctors having finished with him: he was too
badly disfigured to be other than a distressing sight. Candles
burned at the head and foot. The widow sat beside it, dressed
in black, her pregnant bulk made thereby less evident; her
honey-coloured hair was covered by a black lace veil. His first
thought, on seeing her so, was – and it shocked him – that

Mélanie was enjoying herself. He had seen the Austrian Ambassador come down the steps, and be driven away in his elegant equipage; no doubt there had been several such guests, come to condole. He himself knew better than to do so. They were alone in the room; he knew that she had timed her note to arrive so that he would come to find the others gone. He went to her; and could not keep his hands from fondling her upper arms in their incongruous black sleeves. To be near her again! To hold her, have her for himself!

She was smiling. 'Careful, my friend,' she murmured. 'We cannot make love beside poor Franz's coffin. And I am near my time, as they call it; the young devil is kicking in me.'

'What happened?' he heard himself ask. 'How did it occur?' von Reichmansthal had been a notable driver, one of his few distinctions; he had liked to drive at speed, and to handle the horses himself, without a coachman.

'He drove out to Marylebone,' she said. 'Fortunately Wenzel was not with him, and neither was I. I know nothing more except that they say the traces gave way; at that rate, the groom is to blame. One of the horses had to be shot; the other is merely grazed a little. They brought it home; it is in the stable now.' She appeared more concerned over her horses than her late husband. 'You cannot attend the funeral service in your state,' he told her. 'You must come to me, and bring your maid.' It meant that Mrs Rae would leave; that could not be helped, there were other housekeepers.

'For the child to be born in your house?' Her tone mocked him. Crowbetter felt himself flushing. 'Everyone knows that it is expected,' he reminded her. 'You will come to no one but me.'

On the journey, made next day before the funeral, she went into labour in the carriage, beginning to utter little sharp grunts and cries, with the tears streaming down her face. He carried her up the steps into his house, her black skirts trailing; Germaine followed with the bandboxes. Mrs Rae, in the hall, flung up her hands, her mouth prim. 'Fetch Mrs Milsom,' barked Crowbetter. The widow would have enough sense to help unlace a labouring woman and put her to bed. She came, calm and competent, and reassured him at once.

'I have delivered babies,' she said. 'Tell them to bring hot water.'

They carried Mélanie upstairs to her old room, and he saw her no more. For an hour, two hours, longer, the cries sounded, with intervals of unnerving silence, while Nicholas paced up and down his study. When Mrs Rae came, with her bonnet on, to tell him she was leaving at once, he told her to go, and to go to the devil. Shortly after that the sounds changed to a wild screaming, then ceased. Presently Mrs Milsom appeared, with a wrapped bundle in her arms.

'It is a son,' she said. Crowbetter was aware that she knew it was his. He stared down at it, relieved, that, at least, the world would not yet know. The baby's hair, drying out already to fluff, was honey-coloured.

Little Wenzel had been taken to his father's funeral, then returned upstairs to the rooms where he by custom lived. 'He will go back to my husband's people in Vienna,' Mélanie said lightly. She had made a good recovery from the birth, showed no interest in the baby, who was thriving with a wet-nurse; and none at all, any more than she ever had, in her elder son. However, as the rented house was being shut up and the servants dismissed, it was expedient to bring the boy meantime to Nicholas. Wenzel came, pale-faced and with correct manners; nobody knew if he had been fond of his father or what he felt about the death. He was led by the hand, the housekeeper, Madame Horthy, having come with him; and, as Mrs Rae had departed, Mélanie suggested to Nicholas that this Hungarian woman, who she said was also an excellent cook, should take her place. Nicholas agreed, as he would have agreed to anything then; he hungered for the time when he should again possess Mélanie's body, and could think of little else; but she was not yet ready after the birth. They had bound her breasts to stop the milk, and she ate voraciously. She looked more beautiful than ever, as if fecundity became her.

As to that, Crowbetter was determined that there should be no more children. It was by a dispensation of Providence that little Felix – it was his mother's choice of name – should fail to resemble himself, except that when his eyes opened they were golden. On another occasion matters might be less fortunate. He, Crowbetter, must discipline himself as a lover; already he had grown accustomed to the notion, thinking of Mélanie now as a kept mistress, safe in his house. He must treat her body as he had treated Maud Partridge's, painful as it still was to recall that episode. He prepared himself with eager anticipation for their first coupling since Felix's arrival. It had been hard on him to have Mélanie in the room opposite, and not to go in.

She was waiting for him on the arranged night, her hair loose about her. Germaine had rubbed her recovered body with essences, and she smelled of musk and flowers. Her flesh was taut and resilient, as if she had never given birth. They lay together, Crowbetter's desire struggling in him with his prudence; but he contrived the latter. Mélanie pouted a little, and fed him sweetmeats which Horthy had sent up on a plate, left ready beside the bed.

'You need not use me like porcelain,' she told him. 'I am recovered. Do you not suppose that a woman needs a man? Do as you used to.' But he would not; and by the time he left her she was still dissatisfied, tossing discontentedly on the bed. She must accustom herself to it, he told himself, as he had also had to do.

Wenzel's future had meantime been arranged. 'He will return to his father's people,' Mélanie had said. Nicholas hoped that the baby and his nurse would travel to Vienna likewise; he would be glad to have Felix out of his sight; the child's golden eyes perturbed him. But Mélanie would not part with the baby, which surprised Crowbetter somewhat; he had not thought of her as possessing maternal instincts. However she soon made her reasons clear.

'If he goes, foolish one, they will expect me to go also, to be with both my sons. I loathe Vienna; the etiquette there is ridiculous, and the Emperor is a fool.'

'Our King here is not a wise man either, they say.' George IV had died, in darkness and obscurity, at Windsor; and his sailor brother reigned. It was more than ever worth while knowing Gabrielle von Bülow; the new Queen was pleasant.

'That is different,' said Mélanie. She sat on the sofa in the drawing-room, it was Sunday, and shortly callers would arrive. Crowbetter had given strict orders to Jane that she must be present when anyone came; it was to be made clear that she was hostess in her own house, and Mélanie the guest, not the mistress. So the squat plain fair-haired figure would dispose itself near the tea-things, and dispense them in proper course; but the laughter, the wit, the talk, all centred round Mélanie. She was still in mourning, but wore her usual transparencies in black, with the pearly flesh showing through at arms and breast. Respectability, however, was doubly present in the form of Harriet Milsom, whom Jane had invited to come downstairs; the widow had a quiet, deft way of talking, different from Mélanie's diamond-hard repartee; poor Jane felt less solitary in her own drawing-room when the other woman was there, and the children were cared for upstairs meantime by their nurse.

It was on one such occasion that Baron von Reichmansthal, the dead man's cousin, who was a minor official at the Imperial Court of Vienna, came for his young kinsman. There would be a bright future for Wenzel; with the introduction to Court life, prospects of promotion would open up for him when he was a little older. The Baron, a plump personage who resembled his late cousin faintly, was pleased to see the boy make a correct entry, bow slightly with his heels together as he had been taught abroad, and wait to be addressed. He was told to thank Madame Crowbetter for her hospitality to him, and did so politely.

'Well, young sir,' said the Baron in German, 'are you prepared for the journey?'

Wenzel said that he was prepared. 'And the little brother, what of him?' the Baron asked with sudden perspicacity. He turned to face Mélanie. 'Would it not be best for all four to make the journey together?' he asked her. 'A mother should be with her children. The nurse can travel with us, and later return.'

'I am not yet recovered from Felix's birth,' said Mélanie languidly. 'As for the baby, he is too young yet to travel.'

'Then you will join us later, with him?' Their family ties were close, and had often irked her. She smiled, and said vaguely that she would come to Vienna at a more suitable time. 'Wenzel will occupy you fully, I don't doubt,' she added. 'Be a good boy, my son, and do as the Baron bids you.'

'His tutors have once more been engaged,' said the Baron solemnly. A smile lightened the little boy's pale face; he had liked his tutors, and Vienna was beautiful in the snow. He entered the coach with his relative, and they drove off; when they were gone, the room echoed to the sound of Mélanie's laughter.

'Thank God for that,' she said. 'I was afraid he was going to carry me off to the Hofburg. I will postpone my departure indefinitely, it goes without saying.'

Nobody answered, and the dark eyes of Harriet Milsom looked at her with their expression that was difficult to read.

Nicholas had regulated his lovemaking to a different pace from formerly. He no longer spent the nights with Mélanie; he would go to her after dinner, and leave at eleven. The time between was spent in a way that satisfied neither of them, but whereas Crowbetter was resigned to it, Mélanie was not. Once, when as frequently and of necessity happened, he withdrew from her early, before her climax, she formed her hands into claws and made for his eyes; he seized her by both wrists, and succeeded in calming her. But she was still angry; her eyes were filled with tiny flashes, like light on sea-water. She lay resentful and sullen under him after that, no longer meeting his ardour. In fact, he was keeping her both in clothes and money; von Reichmansthal had left everything in trust for the children and Nicholas felt that, in accepting the allowance for Felix, he was under an obligation to provide for Mélanie, and handsomely. She bought herself gowns, out of black by now and into grey and lavender; made of faille taffeta, crêpe and lace, satin and velvet and embroidered silk from India. She would use the carriage to shop, or ride her own horse, the one saved from the accident and brought round by her groom; not yet publicly in the Row, as she was still in mourning, but down the lesser streets, out to places that were almost in the country, where cows still grazed, like Neathouse and Paddington. Then she would bring back the horse to her own groom, to be rubbed down.

There was a story attached to the groom. He had come to Crowbetter again after von Reichmansthal's funeral, saying he could not obtain a situation, as he was blamed for setting the traces loose and causing the Austrian's death.

'An' I'll tell yer something, sir,' he said, looking at the tall man in well-cut clothes in whose house his former mistress was staying. 'Them traces weren't loose; I'd not have put 'em loose. Them was cut. They brought 'em to me afterwards. Been cut almost through, they had; just a little bit o' leather left to last out o' town. Then when there was a bit of a pull,

like, they'd break. That's what happened. I can swear it. The
master liked to drive fast, by himself. I'm telling you all this,
sir, hoping you can find me a job. When they hear that's
where I come from, nobody'll give me one, not other.'

Nicholas was frowning. 'Where are these traces now?'

'Don't know, sir. Wish I'd kept them. But it ain't no good
saying anything to anyone, not if you're the likes of me.'

Crowbetter thought earnestly as he stood there, his hand
over his mouth. He already had a coachman with whom he
was pleased enough, who had replaced Humble. This lad – he
seemed honest and von Reichmansthal must have been
satisfied with him – could give a hand in the stables, cleaning
them out, grooming Mélanie's horse, which would in any case
be accustomed to him. He made the offer carelessly, and was
unprepared for the sudden delight on the boy's thin face.

'Sir, I'll do the job proper, I will. You won't be sorry. I
promise.'

So he began to work, but Mélanie had not been pleased
when she learned after childbed of his employment.
Crowbetter could elicit no reason other than that she had
wanted to be rid of everything connected with von
Reichmansthal and her marriage. He was astonished by the
thought that had briefly crossed his mind.

'Show Papa four.'

Nicky moved the threaded beads with his thin uncertain
fingers. Since Mrs Milsom had made him the frame, he had
been fascinated with it; she told him little boys long, long ago
had used them and that they were called an abacus.

Nicholas watched his son's doubtful movements with relief.
There had been a time when he thought Nick was mentally
retarded, and still, for his age, he was slow; but with constant
attention and understanding he was making progress. The
four beads stood grouped together, red and green
alternately. 'They find the odd more diffcult. Now, Nicky, try
six. That is a big number. See if you can manage it.'

Nick struggled, but had to give up at seven. 'It will come,'
said Harriet. 'Presently he will begin to read, with pictures.'
She spoke to the pale little boy, who had his eyes cast down
for fear of his father, whom he seldom saw. 'By that time
Felix will join us, perhaps, do you not think so?'

Felix kicked in his cot, full of life and intelligence. Looking at the children, Nicholas felt the nagging headache between his eyes recede; it had troubled him intermittently for some days. It was possible that he was undertaking too much close paperwork at the bank and needed spectacles, 'which will make me into an old man,' he thought.

He watched the quiet movements of the governess – by now she could be called that – and tried to banish the memory of the very different woman with whom he had spent the last few nights. He had been unable to leave, as was his custom; she had greeted him charmingly wearing the pink dress in which she had once appeared and fainted in his house. It was incorrect, as Mélanie was still in mourning; but all of her conduct had been welcoming and charming, enough to beguile any man; on the first night she had served him – they had been alone for dinner, as Jane had a headache – a little supper in Hungarian fashion, prepared by Mrs Horthy. It had been full of rice and brightly coloured vegetables, and had had a flavour he could not name. The sweetmeats afterwards, which Mélanie kept always in her room, had it also, or perhaps it was only that he could not rid the taste of it from his mouth; even the wine, ice-cold, had a trace of it. He had behaved at first as he had used to do in the early days of their liaison; it was as though he could not have enough of her, could not penetrate her deeply enough, possess her arched expectant body urgently enough. Presently it was as though he himself had been allotted the drive of a bull, a he-goat; coupling with her repeatedly, hearing her wild laughter, her loud harsh cries of pleasure. She pulled him down against her, staring up at his black springing hair, his golden eyes; feeling the hardness of his muscular body, the shadowed groin, the matted chest: biting his flesh as she had used to do. She put her tongue in his mouth; when she withdrew it, she spoke like a sibyl, holding him fast against her.

'You are Satan,' she said. 'You have made love tonight as you should. You could stand on the Brocken and take all the women who came, and never tire.'

'The Brocken?' he asked her thickly, caressing her breasts. 'What is that?'

'It is time you knew. It is the peak in the Harz Mountains where, each year, witches keep Walpurgis Night. Satan is waiting for them there. They dance about him, then he takes them all, one by one.'

'You are enough for me,' he said, and himself took her again. They coupled unnumbered times: near morning, he stumbled back to his room, jaded at last and filled with self-disgust. In the few hours that remained he fell asleep, not restfully; he dreamt that he was on the Brocken, and that Maud Partridge, her mouth agape, came and danced naked with him and he lay with her; and Mélanie and Jane, and other women, naked likewise. The great peak soared black against the dawn sky; soon they must go back again whence they came.

He awoke sweating. His will was failing him; what he had sworn should never happen again had happened repeatedly. Yet the memory of Mélanie lying sated on the pillows, smiling like a cat after cream, beguiled him still: he could have gone to her again this morning. And he would go to her again tonight, and the next night and the next, now that she was rid of her sullens; after dinner: he knew it well enough. Yet now, watching quiet Harriet Milsom with the children, he knew for moments what Mélanie could never give him; rest.

'You are bringing my son on well,' he said, 'and my wife is glad of your company. I hope that you will stay with us.'

It was not like him, he himself realised, to consider poor Jane. Perhaps Harriet Milsom was teaching him to do so. He got up and went downstairs, knowing Nick would return contentedly to the abacus once he had gone.

Mélanie had never ceased carping and complaining about the presence of the young groom who had been in her husband's employment. She constantly pestered Crowbetter to get rid of him. 'Give him a reference and let him go,' she said, adding that when she rode out, the horse had never been properly groomed, so that his coat was dusty and made her habit filthy; Germaine had to scrub it in places when she returned. Also, the stable-boy forgot to give the bay horse enough water; mixed too high a proportion of oats in the fodder, so that the bay was skittish and often nearly threw her. Worst of all, he could not be relied on to secure the girths, so that she herself had to tighten them for her own safety. It was as though – but she was careful not to stress this – he wanted the former accident to be repeated.

Nicholas had developed a kind of obstinacy about the matter; he was not going to give way to Mélanie on every point. Besides, the new coachman, when questioned, gave his word that the lad was a good, reliable worker, and cared for the horses very well. Mélanie continued, accordingly, to ride out unscathed; until one day.

It had come on to rain, and in the ordinary way she would have returned at once, to avoid soaking her habit. Time passed, however, and she did not appear. 'Madame is late,' said Mrs Horthy to the maid Germaine, when they met on the stairs. The Hungarian woman tended nowadays to leave the housework to the maids, whom she supervised occasionally, unlike Mrs Rae who had had an eye to them every waking minute; and to spend her time in preparing tasty, spicy meals in the foreign fashion. Mélanie liked them so, Jane put up with them, and Nicholas had accustomed himself, although he would have preferred a good straightforward roast of beef. Now and again he would still go to his club, but preferred increasingly to dine at home; what came after dinner was worth waiting for, although his headaches still troubled him during the day. He was not in the house when Mélanie was delayed on her ride; he had taken the brougham and the coachman, and was in town.

Mélanie limped in at last with a limping horse, walking beside it, after the rain. 'That damned groom left the bay with a loose shoe,' she said. 'He must go; there is no question about it. We must send for the farrier.'

As it happened, Harriet Milsom was descending the stairs, saw Mélanie come, and went to assist if she could. 'You are wet through,' she said. 'Perhaps you would care to go upstairs and change your clothes, and I will lead the horse round to the stables.'

The green eyes mocked her. 'You? You are not accustomed to horses, surely.'

But the dark glance held hers. 'I was used to them in my childhood; he will be quite safe with me,' Harriet said, and took the hurt animal's reins. She led him gently round to his loose-box, removed his saddle, then bent to look at the right hind hoof. By that time the young groom had come.

'There weren't no loose shoe, madam,' he said when he heard. 'I wouldn't have let him out with one. His shoes were all right and tight, all four. I check 'em every time she takes him out. It's like the time when –' He flushed, and fell silent.

Harriet looked up from where she was examining the hoof.

'This does not need a farrier,' she said. 'It needs a horse-leech. The shoe has been prised off, perhaps with a knife, but, I think, something blunter. You should put a fomentation on the foot meantime. But I do not need to teach you your trade.' She smiled at him, her plump, rather melancholy face taking on the charm it had when she talked to children. The boy looked at her shyly.

'You're right, madam. I'll do as you say. And – madam – if you'd be so good as to put in a word with Mr Crowbetter for me, to say as I didn't leave no loose shoe, it'd help. Otherwise he won't believe me, this time, not after the last.'

'The last?' she said. But he would not speak of it, only shaking his head. She found out later on.

The result of that episode was a screaming scene from Mélanie and obstinacy from Nicholas, who had already heard the governess's version and believed it. He had dropped into the habit of visiting Harriet Milsom daily, on the face of it to watch the children's progress, but in fact because he enjoyed her quiet company and informed talk. The bay's wound healed; but Mélanie said she would not ride again, she could not trust the groom. 'You must please yourself,' said Crowbetter, and offered the use of the bay horse to Harriet. But the widow shook her head.

'It would not be suitable in my situation,' she told him. He applauded her prudence; and thought more of her than ever. Once he went to her with a blinding headache, and she sent word that he would not be down for dinner; instead, she cooked him an omelette on a little stove she had upstairs. He found it excellent, and felt better for the time.

All this did not make for improved relations between Mélanie and the governess. The former resented what she saw as an attempt on the part of widow Milsom to ingratiate herself with Crowbetter; and as for Harriet herself, she had a quiet, thorough certainty that all was not as it should be, even allowing for the situation which already existed. If Madame von Reichmansthal had in fact cut her husband's driving-traces and caused his death, she was capable of anything; and the severe headaches Nicholas Crowbetter was experiencing undoubtedly had their cause, although as yet the governess only suspected what it might be. It would take time to prove, and she must proceed carefully; she had gained a certain position, and a false step might lose her her situation. Prudence was advisable; and in the hazards of her forty years Harriet Milsom had indeed learned prudence.

The bay horse, its hoof recovered, was sent to Crowbetter's sister-in-law in the country, and ended its days grazing comfortably in a field. Meantime, Nicholas had belatedly asked George's widow and her stepdaughter Athene to stay, assuming that Sarah would remain with her nurse; but Sarah was brought too. Her arrival was a success, as she crawled about the nursery with Felix, and it was difficult to know which child was the handsomer and more amiable. Athene, on the other hand, was to be regretted.

It may have been at that stage that Crowbetter assured himself that nobody would ever marry Athene but a man who was after her money: and he would have to be a brave man at that. She was dressed pretentiously, albeit by the hands of a provincial dressmaker; her young stepmother could not control her, and Athene must have been given freedom to order what she chose for herself. Her hair, which might have been a feature, was frizzed to a degree that had long ago become unfashionable even out of town; and unless any bridegroom beat her into submission he would be ruled all his life. Young as she still was, she sat, assured as any matron, to listen to the arrangements it was time Nicholas made clear, as George himself had intended to clarify them at that ill-fated meeting in the club which had never taken place. Athene was much displeased when it became evident that Nicholas, as her guardian and trustee, would have control of her entire fortune till she was thirty. Evidently her father had judged her character, and her probable future, well. As for little Sarah, she was unprovided for; there had been no time. An advantageous marriage would be the best thing for her. If she went on as she had begun, this should be possible.

After the discussions were over Nicholas stood at the window looking out at the day. He glimpsed the governess, Mrs Milsom, going quietly out on her own concerns. He found himself wondering where she was going, and watched her black-clad figure vanish down the street with some interest. His head still nagged a little.

If he had known, Harriet Milsom was going to the chemist to

buy some soothing syrup for young Nick's cough. She made her placid way to the shop, which had a gilded mortar and pestle hanging outside, and a window full of coloured glass bottles shaped like globes. She paused for a moment, as the sight gave her pleasure; then went into the shop, and was taken aback. Mrs Horthy the Hungarian housekeeper was in there, and had just completed a purchase. It was being wrapped up in thick white paper and sealed with red wax. She turned with it, started a little at the sight of Harriet, and walked straight out of the shop. Harriet bought the syrup, and lingered for some time in order not to have the Hungarian woman's company back to the house: she did not like her, and knew that she herself was not liked either.

Nick was better for the syrup, which eased his cough. Later that day, after the children were in bed, Harriet went deliberately down to the kitchen. Mrs Horthy was preparing the spicy little meals Mélanie had persuaded Nicholas to accept at the dinner-hour; exotic smells rose from cooking pans, and the woman was stirring a sauce. She set it down to go to the stove, and in that process saw Harriet.

'What are you doing, watching me? You should not be down here; your place is upstairs.'

Harriet ignored the impertinence. 'I am interested in what you are cooking,' she said evenly. 'What is it called?'

'Ryba na černo, and svičkova pečene.'

'Are those Hungarian dishes?'

'They are Moravian. Now go. It disturbs me to be watched.'

Harriet Milsom went, having observed the chemist's package open beside the ingredients of the dishes. She had no means of proving what it contained, and she could not herself have enquired of the chemist; but she thought of a means of doing so.

Next day Nicholas Crowbetter had one of his blinding headaches. He was almost unable to go to work, but forced himself to climb into his carriage. After he had gone, Harriet sent for the stable-boy, who since the episode of the horse's injured hoof would do anything for her. She gave him money.

'Go to the chemist's, and say to him that Mrs Horthy did not order enough yesterday, and would like a small quantity more,' she told him. 'If he asks you what it was, say that you do not know, but that you were sent to collect it. All that is true. Do not give it to her; bring it to me.' She smiled her rare smile, and the lad nodded and went off. He returned in a quarter-hour, having been successful. When she was alone, Harriet opened the package. It contained a coarse-grained greenish-black powder, iridescent, which on closer inspection proved to be made up of tiny beetles. Harriet nodded gravely. She was satisfied.

She was waiting for Nicholas when he returned from the bank; she asked for a word with him alone.

He was impatient, which nowadays he seldom was with her. He felt ill, sick and, after last night with Mélanie, drained of all strength. It troubled him that his work at the bank was becoming humdrum and uninspired; he was losing his judgment, and losing business. He had been looking forward to a glass of brandy before dinner to relieve the nagging ache between his eyes. He stared at the black-clad woman standing before him and cursed all women. 'Well?' he said curtly. 'What is it?' It must be something to do with Nick, who was constantly ailing; and Nick bored him. He was like his mother, without inspiration.

'What I have to say will not take a moment, but it is very important that you hear it now,' Harriet said. 'You must not go in to dinner tonight. A substance is being put in your food about which you know nothing, and which does great harm. I can prove this; I have acquired some of it.' Quickly, she told him of the stable-boy's journey, following the errand by Horthy. 'I watched her prepare food yesterday,' she said. 'The chemist's package was lying nearby. I did not see her put it into the sauces: she was careful not to do so while I was there. But, knowing the state of your health lately – forgive me if I forget my place –'

'No, no, you are right in all you say. But be frank with me; what effect does this substance have?' He had whitened, but stood his ground; perhaps he had known for some time of the possibility of some such thing, and yet had found it inconvenient to believe.

She had flushed. 'You have asked me to be frank, and I will be so. It is made of certain insects, and it induces lust. I believe its effects are very strong.' She looked directly at him. 'While I am speaking with you, I may also say that the bay horse Madame von Reichmansthal rode, which returned home with what she called a loose shoe, had an inflamed hoof induced by prising off the shoe with a metal instrument. This was done to discredit the young groom, who told me – and there is no reason to doubt his word – that the traces of Count von Reichmansthal's carriage were cut, not loosened; cut through just enough to allow the Count to drive out at speed, then snap through, leading to the accident which killed him.'

Crowbetter had lurched to his knees at last; the tears were running down his face. He groped for her like a blind man, and buried his face in her skirts.

The polite world was astonished to learn that the Countess von Reichmansthal, who had lent so much sparkle to society, had returned to Vienna quite suddenly, taking only her maid and her clothes. Her younger son had been left behind, to the annoyance of the Baron, that close family man; but Nicholas Crowbetter firmly stated that Felix was to remain as a companion for Nick. In fact, he could not abandon the child to such a mother, and the little boy showed bright promise and might well, if anything happened to the elder in the meantime, become his heir. The possibility of gossip about Felix's golden eyes would have to be risked; he was, after all, the only one of his kind.

Mélanie had not left without a scene. She had taunted Nicholas with his poor performance in bed, which was why she had administered certain encouragement; what woman would endure a dull lover, except perhaps the governess? Her spite was fully directed at Harriet, whose part in the proceedings she had had from Horthy: but Horthy also had been sent packing. It was Harriet who now supervised the meals, Harriet who acted meantime as housekeeper, Harriet who was in charge of everything; and, although Mélanie would no longer be there to see it, Harriet who was moved to the downstairs room, while poor Jane, who had been unaware of anything that went on, stayed in her second-floor lodging. Harriet made a decorous mistress; few people were in fact aware that she was a mistress at all. She did not love Crowbetter, but knew which side her bread was buttered, and that she would never have a better situation than the one she possessed at present. Time passed, accordingly; Mélanie von Reichmansthal was almost forgotten, having left in a storm of protest which had almost disturbed the neighbours. Her going had been sped by Crowbetter's threat to tell the authorities about the cut traces and the injured hoof, and his own secret dosing with cantharides. He could prove nothing, she screamed at him, her face twisted like that of a devil or a witch. But he had ceased, in Harriet's arms, to dream of the Brocken.

During the years that followed, George Crowbetter's widow died, and the sixteen-year-old Sarah, and her half-sister Athene, came, as was natural, to reside at Hyde Park Gardens. After the brief mourning – the dead woman had not been known in town – Nicholas decided to give a small dance for his nieces. He had, by then, reasons for congratulation about Sarah.

3

Sarah Crowbetter and her half-sister Athene shared a maid whose name was Temple. She was a middle-aged bewhiskered dragon, and knew her place well enough to spend a long time dressing Athene and doing her hair, while Sarah waited. In her impatience, the girl had already put on her riding-habit, but could not lace up the back fastening. She fumed, accordingly, till Temple arrived, her long upper lip, with its moustache, drawn down. The small eyes regarded Sarah with disfavour and a kind of triumph.

'You're not to go out riding today, Miss Sarah. Mr Crowbetter has forbidden it.'

Sarah drew herself up. 'He can't have done,' she said roundly. 'He isn't up yet.' She herself, and Athene, slept on Jane's second floor in the room once used by Maud Partridge, and one smaller; there was a guest-room beyond, but it was large and cold, kept cleaned and dusted but seldom used. The comings and goings between Harriet Milsom's room and Crowbetter's downstairs were taken for granted by the girls and, by now, Jane. Sarah knew, accordingly, that her uncle was not yet up; there had been no movement below, no advent of the valet to shave Nicholas, nothing. Sarah stared at the maid in the certainty of victory; but it was Temple's in the end.

'He left instructions last night, miss, but said you wasn't to be disturbed, only I was to tell you this morning. Off with that habit, now, and we will lay out your blue stuff gown.'

Sarah clenched her fists, and tears of rage stood in her eyes. Not to see Hugo! But she *would* see him; nobody should prevent her, later, from slipping out into the street and walking to the bank, where he worked, at the time when he came out. Athene – and Temple – would say it wasn't the way a young lady should behave, but in that case they shouldn't stop her from doing as she wanted now. Uncle Nicholas must have some reason for stopping her ride, but she didn't care what it was, Hugo was all she cared about, 'and he feels the same about me, I know he does,' Sarah assured herself. She stared at Temple's disfiguring moustache; that woman had never had a lover.

Temple said nothing more, but laced her young mistress into the blue gown. It was not new, having been bought before Sarah's mother died, and that lady had assured her daughter at the time that it matched her eyes. Now there was nobody left to say things like that to Sarah, except Hugo.

Nicholas Crowbetter had had a word with his niece Athene at the end of the previous evening, with the empty floor scattered with débris from the dance, a lost ribbon, a shed flower. The golden eyes surveyed these rather than the big discontented young woman beside him, her frizzed hair coming uncurled, her dress limp, but not from dancing. Athene was filled with resentment at the way Jane had treated her at supper; she herself should have gone in on Major Laverton's arm, not Jane. Jane had a husband already. It had taken away all enjoyment from the evening for Athene, and she had looked forward to it only because he, the magical he, was coming, had been invited. She knew she herself was too old to join decorously in waltzes and quadrilles, but the two of them, he and she, could have conversed amiably in some corner; only, when it came to conversation, there had been nothing to say because Jane was there; stupid thick-bodied Jane, who gave herself sudden airs in a crisis. It might be a long time before the Major was met with again, and she loved him so!

She awoke to the fact that her uncle was saying something to her. As a rule Athene listened to his every word with care, because he had control of her fortune for a further two years and without his consent, she was nothing and nobody; not an agreeable reflection for a being who thought as highly of herself as did Athene Crowbetter. But now, what was he asking of her? She blinked her myopic, heavy-lidded eyes round to survey him, then dropped the lids; it was like looking at Zeus, and there was that story of the unfortunate nymph who burst into flames when she did so. Athene had enjoyed the brief benefit of a tutor with a classical education, employed by her father before George died and rapidly got rid of when discovered, afterwards, making love with one of the maids in the broom-cupboard. Her own name implied a classical bias on the part of somebody: she was well aware of it.

'– and so you must not let your sister out of your sight until all this is completed,' Nicholas was saying. Athene was aware of guilt in that she should have listened to what was being completed, and had not; had she done so, she would in fact have discovered that her uncle had given very little away, only saying that he had certain plans for Sarah and would make them known to the girl herself shortly; and that they were not to be marred by surreptitious meetings with young Loriot, now or later.

'You must possess yourself of any letters addressed to her, and hand them to me,' he said. He turned his gaze upon Athene, studied her complete lack of charm, and smiled. 'Believe me, you will not find me ungrateful,' he told her. 'I trust you to carry out my instructions to the letter.'

Of course she would do so. Dreams of Major Laverton floated through her mind again; his unappealing countenance shone in her imagination like Apollo's. Perhaps, if Uncle Nicholas meant what she hoped – perhaps in time, in a very little time, she would be able to obtain permission to, to – one hardly dared think of the bliss – to induce the Major to propose. He had not much money, only, as Athene repeatedly assured herself, his sword.

'I shall do everything you ask, uncle,' she said obediently. Crowbetter patted her arm, turned away, and presently went upstairs to Harriet. He had noticed Athene's infatuation for Laverton, as he noticed most things; but attached no importance to it except to ensure her doting obedience. Fortune-hunters came and went: and it suited the Crowbetter investments that his elder niece should remain unmarried.

The younger was a different matter. Nicholas sat next day, before the board meeting which was to take place at three o'clock, in the room where it would be; the fellow of his own office, but boasting a magnificent long oval rosewood table with an inlaid edge, removable in shining sections. Blotting paper and inkstands, with quills ready sharpened, sat at the places to be filled; a decanter of brandy and glasses were conveniently placed for directors to refresh themselves; and Crowbetter himself sat at one end, with the Earl of Atherton's financial adviser, a thin personage wearing an eyeglass.

'And so,' said the personage, 'I may tell his lordship that the arrangements are finalised and that he may proceed?'

'You may tell him so,' said Crowbetter, 'and that I shall be pleased to welcome his wife and son, as he himself is unable to travel, at my house when it suits their convenience.' Nothing could have exceeded Nicholas's charm. His very appearance was enough to hearten the delegate of an earl on a difficult mission; he wore a coat of mouse-coloured broadcloth, his stock was snowy, and his jet-black hair had of late years turned white at the temples, giving him added distinction. His teeth were not as good as they had been, and when he smiled it was with closed lips. He was smiling now.

'It would be best, I think, from what you have told me of Lord Witham's state, that the young pair do not meet till shortly before the ceremony.'

'I have not seen the young lady,' ventured the adviser. 'I was specifically instructed to do so.'

'As otherwise you were buying a pig in a poke? Never fear, she is a beautiful girl.' He described Sarah in brief terms. 'At present she has a cold, and keeps her bed; but you may take my word for it that she is everything that could be desired, both in looks and temper.'

'It is not an easy situation,' murmured the adviser, whose name was Mr Fox. 'Lord Witham has grown up under the influence of his mother, who belongs to a sect in the north which I need not name, but which has strict views on marriage and everything else. She keeps firm hold on her only son, and his father being an invalid makes the state of affairs even more difficult.' He fell silent, being afraid even now to say too much. No attractive young woman with a fortune would look, title or not, at Lord Witham as he was. This niece of Crowbetter's was penniless, and instead of bringing a dowry to swell the Atherton inheritance it had actually been necessary for the Earl to make over certain shares to Crowbetter's bank. It had all been due to the persuasion of the fellow now sitting next to him. Mr Fox subdued a sense of mild outrage, and sampled his brandy.

'I am certain that Sarah will smooth over any difficulty,' murmured Nicholas. 'A little more brandy? I must leave you briefly, though we will meet again when the rest come. I must have a brief word with the representative of a bank in Hamburg, who is waiting in the outer office at this moment.

Refresh yourself; I shall not be many minutes.'

He returned presently, with a large German whom he introduced as Herr von Eisenbaum. The good Herr knew very little English, and Crowbetter rang a bell which brought a clerk running.

'Send Mr Loriot in,' he commanded, and presently Hugo came, chalk-faced; he had been nerving himself to face Sarah's uncle after the directors' meeting, and now he was sent for before it. He wondered if there was trouble; she had not come to the Row this morning; but Mr Crowbetter was smiling amiably. He gestured Hugo forward to meet the banker from Hamburg.

'This is the young man of whom I told you, who has a great facility in languages,' he said. 'Is that not the case, Mr Loriot?'

Hugo's white face turned quickly to red, but he was pleased; it was true that he had picked up French and German easily, and had only to hear a word or phrase to remember it. His widowed mother, with whom he lived, was constantly reproaching him that he did not turn this talent to better account; but his work in the bank was hard, and he had little time to spare for any other. He gave a little bow, and answered the German's greeting correctly. Otto von Eisenbaum's shrewd eyes shone pleasurably in his large face. This boy would do, as Crowbetter had indicated in their brief talk outside, in bad English and worse German.

'I shall have a word to say to you later, Loriot,' said his employer. 'Come in here again when the rest have gone.'

Hugo's heart beat loudly beneath his blue cloth coat. This time, it must be about Sarah. It could not be about anything else. Well, he was ready for it; he had practised what to say. He bowed again, and went out as the directors began to arrive. He saw them take their places at the board, then shut the door after them and went back to his place.

Sarah had contrived to put on her bonnet and pelisse without the ever-watchful eye of Temple seeing her do so; and slipped downstairs and, almost, to the front door; but the drawing-room door was open. As she stole across the hall, Athene came out and barred her way.

'Where are you going?' There was not much love lost between the sisters; for one thing, there was the disparity in age, and for another their likes and dislikes were quite different. Also, while George Crowbetter lived, he had doted on the baby Sarah, a fact which Athene had never forgotten. She had despised Sarah's mother as a poor thing, in nature, birth, and finances; and maintained the contempt to include the dead woman's daughter.

Sarah drew herself up in the way she had. 'I am going for a walk,' she said, and again tried to make for the door; but Athene's solid presence prevented her.

'Then I will accompany you,' Athene said firmly.

'I do not want your company.' Sarah knew defeat already; it would not be possible to talk alone with Hugo now. She must think of something else; perhaps a letter.

'You cannot go out unaccompanied. It is not proper for a young girl to do so.'

'Then I will not go at all,' Sarah replied, and flounced back upstairs to her own room, took off the bonnet and pelisse, beat her clenched hands against one another, and went to her writing-table. It was not difficult to write to Hugo; they were so completely in one another's hearts and minds that it was as though she were speaking to him, waiting for his answer which would come at once, in whatever form. She folded the letter and hid it in her pocket. How was she to obtain a stamp? Temple was useless, Athene worse. Nicholas and Felix, who might have helped her, had driven off, to stay with friends straight after the dance. Could one perhaps ask Mrs Milsom? She was always kind, if remote, and might not refuse. Sarah went in search of her.

There was a little maid named Betty who was cleaning the passage windows. Madam was in her office, she said, doing the books; she'd just been in there, which was how she knew. 'I must hurry, miss,' she said to Sarah. 'It's my evening off, and if I don't finish them windows I'll be late, and my friend's waiting.'

She polished on, and Sarah made her way to the office, knocked, and went in timidly. It was interesting to reflect that the little maid had called Mrs Milsom Madam; by rights that title belonged to Aunt Jane, but she took nothing nowadays to do with the house, or with anything, come to that; she sat upstairs staring ahead of her, and nobody knew what she saw.

Harriet raised her head from the household books she kept in a neat copperplate hand. She was wearing spectacles with metal rims, which emphasised the fact that she was some years older than Nicholas Crowbetter, perhaps thereby being the more readily fitted to mother him. 'Come in, my dear,' she said to Sarah. She was always kind to young people. However when Sarah asked if she might borrow a stamp, Harriet shook her head.

'I have none, I fear,' she said. 'I write very few letters.' It was true; whatever her life had been before coming to Hyde Park Gate, she had left it all behind her; Sarah could not remember a single friend who had ever paid her a call.

'Your sister will give you one, no doubt,' Harriet suggested, 'or if you care to wait till your uncle comes home, he will certainly have them in his desk.'

Athene! Uncle Nicholas! One could not think which of them would be worse to ask. Sarah was suddenly assailed by a wild idea. She had no money, but presently she unpinned a small brooch from her dress. It had belonged to her mother, and was formed like a tiny bow set with seed pearls in gold. In calmer moments she would not have parted with it, but this moment was not calm.

Betty had finished the windows and was making her way towards the back stairs with her clothes and pail. Sarah picked up her skirts and ran. 'Betty,' she called out breathlessly. The maid turned. Sarah took her letter out of her skirt pocket. 'Will you deliver this for me? I know it is your day off. If you will do it, take this brooch. It is a very important letter. Will you do this for me?'

'Oh, miss, it's a lovely brooch. It's too good for the likes of me.' But Betty saw herself wearing it tonight on her second best dress, walking out with Joe, the butcher's boy; there had been an understanding of sorts between them for four months now, but Joe was flighty, a bit, being much sought after. If she wore a brooch like that it would – she almost giggled – it would fix him. 'I'll do it, miss,' she promised. 'Me and my friend, we'll walk that way together, and put it in.'

But Fate decreed otherwise; Athene, who had been told to keep an eye on her sister, came up the front stairs. The sight of a scrubbing-maid holding a letter was in itself suspicious; looking more closely, even with her short sight, she could see that it was in Sarah's writing. 'What have you there?' she said grimly, and striding forward twitched the letter from Betty's hand, fortunately leaving the brooch.

'That is my letter,' said Sarah angrily. 'You have no right to take it.'

'You may go,' said Athene to the maid, who crept away with her bucket. There followed the kind of sour exchange which was all too common between the sisters. Athene laid down the law; Sarah must neither walk out of the house nor communicate with anybody without permission. 'Whose permission?' asked Sarah pertly. 'Because you have more money than I do it doesn't make you my guardian. You're nothing but an interfering old maid.' Athene crimsoned. Sarah, overcome with fury and tears, ran back to her room; flung herself face down on the bed, and drummed her feet on the counterpane. For Athene to read what she had written to Hugo! And Athene would do so; she was exactly what one had just said she was. At least one had said it.

About that same hour of the day, Crowbetter sent for young Loriot again. This time, the boy came in looking white; he must without fail ask permission to pay his addresses to Sarah, and he found his courage fail him in face of the strong, cold personality confronting him. It had been easy to picture himself saying the words he had carefully prepared; it was less so in reality. He began as best he might. 'Sir, I –'

Crowbetter held up a hand, smiling. 'Presently. I have something to say to you, young man. I have been pleased with your careful and methodical work here; you seem reliable and courteous. I have, accordingly, arranged promotion for you, if you will accept it. It not only means greater responsibility and an increased salary, but will involve your working knowledge of languages. You have lately met Herr von Eisenbaum of the Hamburg branch. You are to go, if you agree, to work under him; having seen you briefly, he is willing to employ you, which is a compliment indeed.'

Hugo's face had brightened at first mention of the increase; not only would it please his mother, but he would be almost able to support Sarah, though not yet in the way to which she was used. But at mention of Hamburg his face fell. 'Sir, my mother –'

'Rooms will be made available for you, to which you may take your mother if you so wish. Hamburg is an agreeable city, perhaps more so than London.' Crowbetter had placed the tips of his fingers together and was regarding them. Hugo took the opportunity for the removal of that compelling gaze.

'Sir, if I do not accept? I have reasons for wanting to remain in London. I – desire to be married.' There, it was out; but not all of it. He felt his courage receding with every moment. Crowbetter was frowning.

'That raises awkwardness. This appointment would only be permitted you if you agree to remain single for at least two years. The work will take all your concentration, you may frequently be asked to spend time out of hours on the bank's business, interviewing clients, possibly some considerable distance away, in Saxony or Brandenburg. You must be dedicated, in short, to the bank; a wife would detain you. If you want the posting, you must agree to its conditions.'

In fact, he knew very well what Loriot wanted to say, and had swiftly invented the clause about single blessedness; by the time the young man found out more, if he ever did, Sarah would be safely married. 'Well?' he said now, a little impatiently. 'Von Eisenbaum leaves in a few days' time, and has expressed the hope that you will return with him. If you elect to stay here, it will be to a dull future; one does not refuse promotion from a merchant bank and expect it to happen twice.'

Hugo was wretched. He knew already that he could hardly support Sarah on his present salary, as well as his mother, who depended on him. If he went to Hamburg, surely Sarah would wait for him for the required two years? And he would write to her; oh, yes, he would certainly write. There was no time to think things over, he knew; with Mr Crowbetter, one seized an opportunity when it was offered. He raised his head.

'I will accept it, sir,' he said, 'and hope to give satisfaction.'

Crowbetter smiled; that was more like it. He watched the lad go out, then prepared himself to leave. Loriot had not even mentioned Sarah, though it had obviously been on the tip of his tongue when he came in. The vagaries of human nature, in particular those of the young, were especially diverting when oneself possessed youth no longer. And now he must arrange the journey, without either young man's return from the country house where both were staying, of Nick and Felix to Vienna, to visit Felix's mother who some years ago now had married the Baron. Thereafter the boys would travel on to Italy, to take the roughness off them; and return

by way of Paris. He did not want either of them in the house
at the time of Sarah's marriage; they were like brothers to her,
and when they saw the bridegroom might object. The whole
matter had required diplomacy, the exercise of which
Crowbetter had enjoyed. And now he must speak with Sarah
herself; and that promised to be less diplomatic.

It was as he had foreseen; Sarah, sent for, came in with red
eyes and a defiant air. Nicholas relished the challenge; after
the spiritless Jane and the recently slavish Athene, it was
refreshing to meet an adversary in his own household. But he
was certain of victory, in the end.

He cast a glance over his young niece. She was a queenly
girl: he had noted it often. The blue gown was old, but
became her; her hair was splendid, and needed no great
dressing to render it fashionable. She had fine eyes, good
teeth, and beautiful hands. Her foot was small and she moved
gracefully, even now when she was plainly out of sorts.
Crowbetter made no comment, knowing well enough what
was wrong. Instead, he put a commonplace query.

'Where is your brooch?' he said. Sarah put her hand to her
breast; how Uncle Nicholas observed every last detail! She
stammered some reply; she must have forgotten to put it on;
she did not remember. All the time her sense of outrage was
hammering at her; this was not what she had intended to say,
she had not meant to talk to him of brooches.

'So long as you have not lost it,' he said gently. 'It is after all
a matter of no great importance; shortly you will have all the
jewels to wear that you could wish.'

The blue-green eyes stared at him; what did he mean? He
was smiling his closed smile; Sarah suddenly felt that she was
in the power of a great cat.

'You are the future Countess of Atherton. They own, I
believe, a string of very fine pearls. At the moment the
present Countess wears them, but they will be yours in due
course. Pearls must be worn constantly if they are not to
wither. That is one of the things I have learned in the course
of my life; I pass it on to you for your edification. Will you not
be seated?'

He gestured her to a chair; but she remained standing. 'I
do not understand,' she said. She heard her own voice as if it
were a long way off. She, a future countess? But Hugo had

said nothing of any noble connection. He must have spoken successfully to Uncle Nicholas after all. Relief flooded her like a tide, then ebbed at the next words, which left her white in the face and trembling.

'You are to marry the Earl's heir, Viscount Witham. It is a most fortunate match for a girl with no dowry. He and his mother will visit us in a few days, and the marriage will take place here, in this room. A special licence has already been arranged. You will require a few days to buy such things as brides require. You will not find me ungenerous in this respect. Athene will accompany you, but the choice will be your own. I will instruct her accordingly.'

Sarah was standing very still: the trembling had ceased. 'You have overlooked one thing in your careful arrangements,' she heard herself saying. 'I will not marry this man. I will marry nobody but the man of my choice.'

'Who is young Loriot. He has been posted abroad. You will not see him, or communicate with him, again.'

Sarah flew at him then. Her hands would have taken him by the throat, but Crowbetter seized them; twisting her about, he flung her down on the sofa, standing over her masterfully. 'Try that again and I shall beat you with a riding-crop,' he said. 'You will do as I say. This house has sheltered you, penniless as you are. You will show your gratitude in the way I have described. Do not speak; what you say is of no importance.'

'You cannot make me – you cannot force me –'

'I can,' he said smoothly. 'You will go upstairs to your room now; no food will be sent to you until you are prepared to behave according to my wishes. I do not think that it will be necessary to postpone the Viscount's visit. Go now; do as you are bid.'

She did not; she ran out of the drawing-room, and tried to escape through the front door, but a footman was there, and prevented her. Crowbetter came out, and marched her by the shoulders through the hall and upstairs, while she struggled all the way, trying to bite his hands, trying desperately to free herself. Athene had come out of her room, and when she saw what was happening cried out 'Sarah, are you mad?' and hastened to help her uncle; against the pair of them, Sarah could do little. She was forced at last into her room, and the door locked on the outside; she heard their steps going away.

She looked frantically about the room, seeking a means of

escape; there was none. The window was small, being on an upper floor, and even if she could have got out of it there was a long, long drop to the ground; she could knot the sheets, certainly, but they would be too short. And if she did escape, where would she go? Hugo – she sobbed at thought of him – had been sent abroad, she did not know where. In her innocence she thought of him as already gone. The idea of going to his mother did not occur to her.

　She flung herself down on her bed. The hours passed; it was dinner-time, and the smell of roast pork came faintly up, but Sarah was not yet hungry. The indignity of what had been done to her since early morning filled her with a rage she could not contain; she tore at the counterpane with her teeth, and the useless sheets. Crowbetter linen! The house that had sheltered her! No doubt Uncle Nicholas had made a good bargain of this marriage; he never did anything for nothing. The grip of his hands on her shoulders still hurt her; the things he had said hurt her more. What was she to do? What in the world was she to do? She loathed Viscount Witham already, and his mother. She would never wear the pearls. She would rather die. Perhaps, if she stayed up here till she starved to death, she would defeat Uncle Nicholas that way. He would not perhaps have thought that she had so strong a will.

Sarah held out for three days. It might have been longer if Temple had refilled her ewer when she came as usual to empty the chamber-pot. Sarah had drunk all the water, and felt a little better; if she could keep alive on what they filled up with once daily, she might contrive for a long time. But Temple had gone to the door with her bucket, and had hardly turned her head when Sarah asked her to remember to fill up the jug.

　'The master says you're to have neither food nor water. You're to get nothing, miss, until you do as he says.' And she went out, locking the door. Sarah had been lying on her bed, and stayed there; terror and ruin faced her now. To die of thirst was more dreadful than anything, even perhaps than this marriage. She was already almost beyond thirst; her stomach felt as if it were cleaving to her spine with emptiness, and she was weak. It was time to face the truth; they could keep her here as long as they chose, and if she died they would bury her and say she had had a fever, or whatever else they chose to tell a doctor. Uncle Nicholas could make anyone say anything, do anything. She began to realise that she also would do as he said; and lay and contemplated the fact, staring at the ceiling. The hours went by; the thought of her humiliation, of the certainty that even the servants knew, was nothing to her continuing inward torment. She had writhed with it, and subdued the writhing; she had bitten her arm to drink her blood, but it was salt; the bite still showed on the clear flesh. It was all of it useless, as she should have known from the beginning; nobody could help her; in the end, she must submit.

A few hours before Sarah sent word that she would do as her uncle required of her, Athene had glimpsed a letter lying in the hall and had gone and picked it up. As in all households, the man of the family by custom read letters first, unless they were surreptitious; this one had come from foreign parts, and was addressed to Sarah. Athene downed her strong urge to know what was inside, and kept the letter to hand to Nicholas when he should come home in the late afternoon. She did so, and stood by while he opened it.

He smiled, and presently handed it to her, watching her face. The old maid would envy her sister her lover.

Hamburg. Thursday

My own darling Sal,

I trust that this will reach you safely, as I write in great haste. I was unable to say goodbye to you before leaving, as they wanted me at once. The work here is interesting and I am practising my German. Enough of that; what I want to ask you is, will you wait for me for two years, when I am allowed to marry? I have a pleasant set of rooms here, and we could find a little house. My mother is coming out to join me, although not pleased at leaving London; she may return. I will write again soon, but will make haste with this to catch the packet. I enclose my direction in Hamburg, to which I hope you will write.

I trust you are well. Believe me, ever your loving

Hugo Loriot

A street and house number were appended. Athene's face had reddened and her mouth grown prim. 'It is disgraceful, uncle,' she said, 'disgraceful.'

'But owing to your perspicacity, she will never receive it.'

He took the letter from her, tore it to shreds, and cast it into the fire.

Later that evening, Temple came down, triumphant. Miss Sarah had said she would do as she was bid.

'Then take her up some cold roast beef,' said Nicholas.

They watched, Athene, Nicholas and Jane, while a tray of meat, bread and butter and a glass of wine were carried up to Sarah by one of the maids. It was better for her not to eat too much at first; this would be her first meal for almost four days.

The maid who took up the tray was Betty, and having watched Sarah fall on the food like a young wolf, she spoke timidly.

'Miss Sarah, it's about that brooch. I've brought it back. I shouldn't have taken it, and I never did post that letter you gave me. But I'll tell you another thing; there was a letter for you today, in the hall. I can read a bit. I would have hidden it, but I didn't dare. Miss Athene took it, and I'll swear she gave it to the master; it's not there now.'

Sarah, the pupils of her eyes so wide that they looked dark, thrust away the tray.

'I don't want any more,' she said. 'Betty, you're the only friend I have in this place. When I go wherever they are sending me, when I'm married, will you come with me and be my maid? I'd sooner have you than anyone.'

'Lord, miss, I'm no hand at fancy dressing. But I'd learn, I dare say. I'd like to come.'

That left Sarah a little comforted. She let the brooch Betty had returned lie in her palm. It reminded her of her mother.

After all of that it was a different, colder person who came downstairs. They had taken Hugo away from her; her life had been arranged despite her wishes; the stranger she was to marry meant nothing to her and never would. Nothing could touch her or hurt her again; she might have been made of stone. She was certain of it; yet when she and Athene were riding at last in the carriage on the way to the shops for her bridal gear, Sarah enquired about Hugo's letter, as though it had been sent long ago.

'What became of it?' she asked. Athene sat in the opposite seat, attired in a puce velvet bonnet and pelisse which did not become her. She spent a good deal on her clothes, but would never look other than provincial. She gave a little self-satisfied smile, as of duty done.

'I took it to Uncle Nicholas, of course; he read it, then tore it up and put it in the fire.'

Sarah closed her eyes for an instant. With the lashes still lying on her cheeks, she said, 'Did you read it also? Do you know what was in it?' If possible, she must know, even now, now when it was too late.

'I had the opportunity to glance at it. What was contained in it was most improper.'

Sarah's eyes narrowed; she gave a little hard smile. 'Nobody, Athene, will ever write anything improper to you,' she said slowly. 'Nobody will ever love you; you are unlovable. Someone has loved me and I him, and however long I live I can remember it. But you will have nothing to remember. Rich as you are, no man will ever care for you. When you are old, you will be alone; ugly and rich and alone.'

'You are cruel – cruel –' They were approaching the shops, and presently must leave the carriage; Athene knew the tears which stood in her hooded eyes must not be allowed to run down her cheeks. She drew a long, sobbing breath. 'You think a great deal of yourself because you are marrying into the nobility, you penniless little bitch,' she heard herself say. Where had she learnt such words? No lady knew them.

Sarah gave a bitter laugh. 'Here we are at the store,' she said. 'Watch how I spend Uncle Nicholas's money, as I have none of my own. Only watch.'

She bought pelisses and bonnets and velvet slippers, silk stockings, filmy chemises, gowns for dinner and gowns for a ball, and a wedding-gown. She bought a fur tippet and matching muff, and a wine-coloured velvet outfit to wear with them. She bought drawers and petticoats trimmed with handmade lace by nuns in a convent in Paris, embroidered handkerchiefs, and nightcaps. The nightgown for her wedding-night could have passed muster in a drawing-room of the Regency. The rest were frivolous, but that was superb. Athene gasped. Sarah was spending far too much money. Where had she learned about such garments? That nightgown was barely decent; one could almost see through it.

'Uncle Nicholas said that I need not stint myself,' was all

Sarah said, when her sister remonstrated with her and begged her to stop. The bandboxes and packages would be delivered at Hyde Park Gardens that same day. Sarah climbed, smiling, into the carriage again, clutching a wrapped pair of morocco half-boots she had remembered to purchase at the last minute.

Athene followed, apprehensive, her late humiliation almost clouded over. Uncle Nicholas would be very angry with her for allowing all this. As for the things Sarah had said earlier, she would never forget them, never. *Rich as you are, no man will ever care for you.* Surely, surely Henry Laverton might care? She, Athene Crowbetter, had laid her heart at his feet.

Another self-important lady was about to enter Sarah's life. Honoria, Countess of Atherton, had been a Miss Studeley of Bourne, and neither let herself nor anyone else forget it. The family was so ancient that it was reputed to have sprung from a misdemeanour of Ethelred the Redeless. When she was married, by arrangement, to the then Viscount Witham, Honoria had been a handsome young woman with a well-developed athlete's body and muscular arms. By now, with lack of exercise – she seldom went further than the door to enter her carriage – the body had run to fat, the arms had thickened while retaining their strength, and Honoria's face had developed such a grievous triple chin that she looked like a toad, except that that maligned creature has beautiful eyes while Honoria's were dead. She had no joy in her; such as there might ever have been was quenched by the dreary sect to which she had attached herself and to whose meetings she would drive, dragging her son with her, on Sunday mornings and on several other prescribed occasions in the year. Sin was stressed constantly, its most pernicious form being the necessity of procreation; and Honoria showed such abhorrence for this that her husband, now Earl, had long ago turned his attentions to other women, mostly dairymaids. When his son was seventeen the Earl had a massive heart attack, and thereafter lived the life of an invalid, seldom stirring out of his room or, with careful and hesitant steps to gain it, his study. What he did, or thought, all day there nobody knew.

Lawrence Witham had been brought up entirely by his mother and had acquired his mother's views; he had none of his own. He was from the beginning a gloomy, frightened child, and turned into a gloomy and chastised youth, a prey to his physical urgings but oppressed by the thought of satisfying them. He was not too tall, stocky in build – he would in time run to fat like his mother – with dark curls, melancholy dark eyes which were seldom raised from the ground, and a great blubbering red mouth. His hands were clumsy, and sweated. Altogether the young ladies of the district – there were not too many, as other great houses were sparse and it had never been hunting country – avoided the thought of him as a possible suitor, despite the title; and their parents, having seen Witham also, did not force them. Had Atherton been a cheery squire who was known among them, it might have been different; but the Earl kept himself to himself except for the dairymaids, and the Countess was detested.

The state of the Earl's health made the Countess realise that despite the sinful implications, it would be necessary to provide an heir to the inheritance, as Witham was all that remained except for a cousin named Crowe who was a celibate clergyman in a charge near Sunderland, and who could scarcely be considered as a breeding proposition. Also, there had been a terrible discovery made among the cottages, where for some reason Honoria had betaken herself on foot; perhaps it was a premonition sent from above. She was just in time to find Witham unfastening his trousers as a prelude to adultery with the cattleman's wife. The door was not even shut. Honoria's bulk darkened the doorway; she trumpeted forth damnation and doom, seized her son, saying tersely 'Fasten yourself,' strode over to the woman on the box bed and administered a good slap to both her ears – later she sent the couple packing – and took Witham abjectly away. Never would he forget the homily his mother read him; by the time she had finished, the tears were streaming from his melancholy eyes and his mouth dribbled saliva. He was made to promise never, never to expose himself to sin again; had he been younger his mother would have whipped him, as Witham well remembered having happened on frequent occasions, the worst being the one when the Countess had caught him stimulating himself. Witham could never think of that occasion, even now, without a shudder of terror and remembered pain. By now, however, words alone sufficed.

From that time on, the Countess had hardly allowed her son
out of her sight; his bed was moved to the dressing-room next
to her own; she supervised Witham day and night, even while
he sat on the chamber-pot; and all this would have continued
unchanged except for the fact that her mind was by now
exercised, after a word or two from the Earl, by the urgent
need to find Witham a wife.

This was, as has been already stated, difficult. Tentative
enquiries among the few landed families about Atherton
brought a negative response. Honoria's peculiarities were well
known, and aristocratic parents were not going to expose their
daughters to them; nor, as stated, was Witham himself an
attractive prospect as a son-in-law. As for the young women
who attended the sectarian meetings, whose cast of mind
might have pleased Honoria, they were not, on the whole,
high-born enough to ally themselves with a problematical
descendant of Ethelred and a definite future earl. Another
mother would quietly have arranged that a humble, unde-
manding mistress should be made available until a suitable
marriage might be arranged for her son; but not the Countess.
For three years after the cottage episode Witham sweated and
endured his wet dreams and his morning erections in terror
lest they be discovered. He had been made so mercilessly aware
of sin in himself that he believed every word; to take pleasure
in anything at all was sinful; he was a creature of dust and to
dust would return, and so would the tenants. His lugubrious
life continued in this way, for he had been allowed to make no
friends and had never been to school, having endured a tutor
closely supervised by Honoria. There was very little hope for
Lawrence, Viscount Witham, until the advent of Mr Fox.

Mr Fox had for some time been making advantageous
investments for the Earl, and of late had shrewdly decided that
the best concern to handle these was Crowbetter's Bank. He
had, accordingly, had several meetings with Nicholas Crowbetter over the past years, both on Atherton's behalf and his own.
It was at one of these, over the brandy, that he happened to
broach the subject of the Viscount's marriage, or rather the
difficulty of arranging one. He did, in fact, unburden himself a
thought too readily for total discretion, but the excellence of
the vintage could be blamed. Crowbetter smiled understand-
ingly, and refilled Fox's glass.

'It is unusual for a title to go a-begging,' he remarked. Fox stared into the golden depths, then up into the golden eyes; it occurred to him that their colour was the same; also, perhaps, their effect.

'A relatively ancient title,' he agreed. 'To find a young lady of suitable birth who is willing –' He did not finish the sentence; he had already explained.

'I know a young woman of suitable birth, but she has no money, although her half-sister, who remains single, is very rich.'

Fox pricked up his ears; would there be a possibility of the half-sister being available? 'No,' said Crowbetter. 'Athene is unable to bear children, and in any case is too old for your bridegroom.' This was to slander his niece, who could no doubt have produced an heir; but Nicholas had had Sarah in mind from the beginning. He had mentioned Athene's fortune deliberately, with the implication that it might one day accrue to Sarah; that nothing was less likely need trouble nobody at present. In any case, as Nicholas knew well enough, the Athertons were in possession of a fortune from coalfields and a happy income from his own investments on their behalf.

He went on to describe Sarah; invited Fox, who was in London for a few days, to Sunday luncheon at Hyde Park Gardens to inspect her by daylight; and discreetly, but unmistakably, made it clear that should she marry the Viscount under all the circumstances, a substantial investment would have to be made in Crowbetter's securities. Fox was somewhat scandalised. 'If she brings no dowry – and if her birth is after all not notable –'

'Her birth is respectable enough; my family fought in the Civil Wars, and until last century owned land in Warwickshire. As for the dowry, I have already made it clear that there can be none. My brother married a rich heiress on the first occasion, but all of that money went to their daughter when she died; and his second marriage was, alas, a love-match, and the bride was penniless, though beautiful. When you set eyes on Sarah, you will see for yourself that she has inherited her mother's beauty, with a certain addition of her own. She would grace a coronet of strawberry leaves with dignity, and she should prove fertile.'

The mention of so agricultural a word made Mr Fox drop his eyeglass and start to polish it carefully; at the same time he was thinking hard. It would do no harm to accept the invitation to luncheon, see the young woman, and take back a report to his master; as for the Countess, one could leave her husband to deal with her. The main difficulty would be the demanded investment, not that it could not be afforded.

He came to luncheon, as guests frequently did, and his presence was unremarked among the rest. He saw Athene first, and commiserated silently. When Sarah entered, late, wearing her ordinary blue gown, her light-brown curls bobbing, her queenly neck and bosom, and her delicious walk, a matter for admiration, Fox knew at once that his own mind was made up. He would take a report of Miss Sarah Crowbetter back to the Earl. The rest was a matter for the Athertons to decide. Crowbetter himself had implied that as soon as the conditions were met, the wedding could take place. The young woman's agreement was assumed.

'That damned fool of a man has forgotten to pack my best buckskins. I'm going to ride home for 'em.'

Felix von Reichmansthal, aged sixteen, his honey curls tumbled, got up from the hair trunk he had just been reducing to inward chaos and surveyed Nick, with whom he shared a room at the house near Chichester where they were staying at the invitation of one of the young men who had raided the wine-bottles without success in their company after the Crowbetter dance. Unfortunately, on reaching Cheyneys, their host's father proved to have a habit of shooting his foxes, which meant that he was ostracised by the county. There were, therefore, few diversions to be had in the way of visiting company, hunting, or the paying of calls; all that sufficed to pass the time, during which it rained a great deal, were paper and pencil games played downstairs with the two plain and giggling little daughters who made up the remainder of the family. Felix was bored to distraction already, and looked forward to the end of the visit, when he would repair by arrangement to his beautiful mother and her second husband in Vienna. There was only one redeeming feature here; in the stables he had early discovered a horse that was worthy to be a hunter, and he intended to ride it back to London, fetch his buckskins, and return.

Nick watched Felix dully; he could not keep up with the lightning decisions and customary brilliance of his junior. He

minded the pencil and paper games less than Felix did; in fact
they suited his manner of thinking very well. He reflected
dismally that he would be left to explain to his hosts where
Felix had gone; it was always the way of things.

'You can't ride all that distance,' he ventured. 'It may rain
again. Take the post.'

'I can ride anywhere, rain or shine. It will pass the time till
we can go. Tell them for me, there's a good fellow.' And he
turned about and went off; he was already dressed in his
riding-clothes. Once the slim upright figure had gone, Nick
transferred his stare to the disordered trunk. He knew a
slight urge to tidy it, but no doubt the servants would do so. It
was a mistake to let them think that there was nothing to
occupy their time.

Felix had let the horse show its paces on the first part of the
journey north, and as he was an experienced handler he was
able to give his mind to other things as they went, taking
pleasure at the same time in the speed of their going, the
lovely curve of the hunter's neck beneath his occasional hand,
its flying mane, the ease of the saddle, his own delicate
possession of the stirrups. 'There, now, my beauty,' he
murmured, and it seemed as if they went faster for the caress;
and he remembered how, with his usual insouciance, he had
told the groom at Cheyneys that he would be borrowing the
animal for a day and a half, and to tell his master so. Then he
thought of the coming visit to Vienna, to his mother; she was
a legend to him, for it had been agreed that Crowbetter
should bring him up in England and send him to an English
public school. This had been done, in company with Nick;
they had both left early, for Felix had done no work, not
because he could not but because he would not; and as for
Nick, he could not. They were to go together on the Grand
Tour, as it had used to be called in the time before the French
wars; after that, he supposed his stepfather would find him
some post, though the diplomatic service would be difficult as
his German was shaky. He did not want to work in
Crowbetter's bank.

They reached Dorking, amid a light patter of rain; and by
then Felix was hungry. He found a likely inn, handed the
horse to a groom with instructions to water it and put it in
shelter till he returned; and went in to a welcoming fire, his

cheeks bright with the ride. He settled down to a juicy steak and a bottle of good red wine, and would have stretched his legs before the fire later, but he must make for London before it grew dark. To his dismay, two things went wrong; the bill was larger than he had expected, leaving him somewhat short of money, and when he got out of doors the rain was teeming down. He debated whether to stay the night at the inn, but decided he could not afford it; it was better to press on, and when he reached Hyde Park Gardens the groom there would give his horse a good rub down, feed it, and put it in the empty loose-box; and he himself would have a bed for the night and a handsome breakfast before leaving again for Chichester.

The rain, luckily, was at his back, so that his eyes were clear to see the way; but it was a bedraggled and soaked young rider who cantered into the outskirts of the city. The streets were quiet by now, except for a few carriages making for the theatres or for evening parties and balls. Felix guided his tired horse to Hyde Park Gate, cosseting it through the traffic. He saw the great solid houses, and the green familiar Park, at last thankfully; almost, he was tempted to stay for a day or two, to shorten the dull visit at Cheyneys; but that would be ill-mannered, and he had no doubt tried their patience enough by going off with the hunter at all.

He walked it round to the stables, slid from the saddle, and shouted for the groom. The lad came hastening down the ladder which Maud Partridge had often mounted long ago. He exclaimed at Felix's state.

'Lord, Master Felix, you're wet through. The wedding'll be over.'

'So is this beauty wet; give him a rub and a hot bran mash.' What wedding? He made no sense of that, and did not ask; he was anxious to get himself into the house, to a hot hip-bath, and a change of clothes. He strode round to the main door from the mews, and hammered on it. The rain was still trickling down his neck; he was beginning to be cold.

The door opened, cautiously. Felix was amazed to see all the domestics assembled formally in the hall; the butler, the two footmen, all the maids ranged in a circle behind the house-keeper; only the groom had stayed away, no doubt being judged too malodorous for great occasions. The awed present-ation of caps and aprons intrigued him; what the devil was going on?

'You're just in time, sir,' the butler said, handing him into the circle; he was too well trained to remark on Felix's appearance, his flattened hair and dripping clothes, his face wet with rain. 'They will be coming out at any minute, sir, to go into supper.'

The wedding. There must be a wedding in the house; the drawing-room doors were closed. Not old Athene, surely? The thought made Felix double up with laughter inside himself, despite his discomfort. He turned and asked the butler that very question; Felix von Reichmansthal had little regard for the proprieties.

'Is Miss Athene being married?' He tried to keep his face straight; but the golden eyes danced. The man answered gravely.

'No, it is Miss Sarah. Miss Sarah's marryin' a lord.'

At that moment the doors were flung open. The wedding party emerged; the bride herself, white-faced and with eyes dark with shock, on the arm of a lumpish young man. Felix loathed Witham at sight, then hardly looked at him again. His eyes were all for Sal; dear Sal, who had been a sister to him, who had romped with him long ago in the nursery, for they were the same age, on her visits from the country with her mother, and then had come to stay. Sal had been married to this lout, and he had heard nothing of it beforehand, nothing. They had got him out of the way so that he –

He flung himself towards her, embracing her and crushing the bridal gown. 'Sal, what the devil – you cannot do this, you – I will not let you, I –'

But he was only sixteen. She had not moved or responded; she was like a statue carved in marble, or some more fragile stuff. The bridegroom raised his dull eyes and stared for a moment, then dropped his lids again as Crowbetter, leaving Honoria who had come out on his arm, strode forward.

'Take yourself off, you young hound, change your clothes and be gone to some hotel. You cannot stay here tonight; the house is full. Go quickly; there are occupants in your room, and it will be required after supper.'

There was no invitation to him to go in to supper. He was left staring after the retreating party, the bride and groom, Mr Fox who had been groomsman as there was no other; the Countess once again, gross as a toad, on Crowbetter's arm; an attenuated clergyman who, as Felix did not know, was the cousin who might inherit, and walked with his eyes down, modestly as was his way; and, last of all, Athene, Jane Crowbetter, vague as ever, and Mrs Milsom, unobtrusive in her blacks. There were no guests. The door of the dining-room closed after them. The domestics dispersed about their business, and still Felix stood there, a prey to the deepest anger he had ever felt. To do that to Sal! She hadn't wanted it; you could tell from the look of her. They had forced her to it, as like as not, by whatever means, while he himself was away. It had happened damned quickly. It was Uncle Nicholas's doing; everything here was. Uncle be damned; everyone knew the old man was his own father, they had the same eyes, though it was never spoken of.

There was a hand on his sleeve; the linen-maid, who was a kind soul and older than the rest. He stared at her good red face with an unreal feeling. These people lived in the house, led their lives, and one never thought of them, hardly saw them except by accident.

'You get away upstairs and get them damp things off, Master Felix, and I'll see them dry. There's a clean shirt of yours ironed ready, and the rest where you know, and I'll get you a bite from the kitchen, if you'll eat it quick. They won't be long in there.'

She cast a glance at the closed door which showed what she thought of the whole proceeding, but said no more. Felix went thankfully up to his room, longed to lie down on the bed which had been made up for somebody else, perhaps the clergyman; stripped, and thankfully rubbed himself down with a towel the woman brought, put on his dry clothes and ate the bite of food. Looking out of the window the rain had ceased to a patter; he could not go to a hotel, as Uncle Crowbetter had decreed, because he had not enough money, and he was damned if he would ask the old devil for any; he would bed down in the stable, among the clean straw. It was cleaner than sleeping with the groom.

He handed the linen-maid what was almost his last guinea. 'You have saved my life, I daresay,' he told her. 'I would have taken a pleurisy otherwise.'

'Get along with you, Master Felix.' But she was pleased; her wages were not excessive, and she was not to know that he was short-changed. 'Hurry, now; they'll soon be up here.'

She carried his wet clothes away to dry them, but he did not think he would return to the house tomorrow after what would have taken place. There would be more money, enough of it, later; Crowbetter, damn him, had arranged credit for them both all over Europe; one could always buy another riding-kit. He hastened out of the house, back to the mews, and found an empty loose-box to lie down in; his horse, next door, moved gently, pulling down its hay and, once, drinking the clean water filled into the trough. Felix slept after a time, loathing the thought of what was happening to Sal at the house; his mind shied away from it, but being young, he did not stay awake all night. In the morning, he awoke ravenous, went out and found a passing cow, which came by daily for her owner to sell fresh milk for children and households. He grinned, gave the woman his last coin, and downed a draught of still warm milk which sustained him on the way back to Chichester.

Sarah fared less well. The wedding night was to be spent in the guest-room, which had a dressing-room attached. She had hardly been in either since, as a child, she had played in them; hide-and-seek with Felix and Nick, who had always been too slow to find anybody, and when it was his turn had as a rule been found wandering about trying to think of a hiding-place. The bed itself had made a good one, if too familiar: between its four twisted pillars of dark wood there hung thick curtains, which left the rest in shadow. Sarah found herself put in there now, having been undressed by Temple, whose primmed lips conveyed evident disapproval of the flimsy nightgown. Athene, who had not been a bridal attendant, would accordingly not have her maiden eyes sullied by the sight of a bridal bed; so she was not present.

Sarah flexed her spine against the mattress and pillows, which were unused, hard and cold. She began to regret the thin nightgown. In any case she had begun to shiver; the wedding ceremony itself had been like a bad dream, the sight of her bridegroom worse; his mother was fat and evil, like nobody Sarah had ever met before; and she herself was uninstructed in the duties of marriage though she had several times heard Felix make knowing jokes she did not understand. But Felix had not joked tonight; and now he was gone. As for Hugo, he was far away; she must not even think of him.

The door opened. She had been expecting her
bridegroom, whatever part he was to play; but she had not
been expecting his mother as well. She knew immediate
resentment that the Countess should see her in bed. The vast
woman led forward her son, who did not look at his bride,
though at supper Sarah had seen his glance slide furtively
now and again towards her. He had said nothing all through
the meal, and except that she had heard him make the
marriage vows he might have been unable to talk. He was
silent now; it was Honoria who spoke.

'Do your duty, Witham, but remember, stop as I told you. I
shall be next door.'

The dead eyes swept Sarah, lying half seen in the shadows.
'I will not bid you good night, daughter-in-law,' she said. 'I
shall return presently.'

What did she want? Why would she return? Why, in fact,
was she here at all? Sarah turned in bewilderment to the man
who was her husband; and saw him advance upon her, with a
red glint in his eyes like a bull. He wasted no time; he climbed
into bed, rolled upon her immediately, and began what he
had not been allowed to begin with the cattleman's wife.
Sarah bit her lip in pain, terror and discomfort. If that old
woman hadn't been next door, she would have cried out to
him to stop. As it was, nothing would make her utter a sound.
She endured what he was doing; she heard his grunting
breaths, felt his heavy weight squeeze the breath out of her;
he was inept and clumsy, and too large in his parts to take a
narrow virgin kindly. He panted on, and she thought the
thrusting and jerking would never cease; when she heard his
mother's voice it was almost a relief, though anger flared high
in her.

'Now, Witham, that will do. You must come away.' She
pulled down the covers. The powerful arms were about her
son, pulling at him; he disengaged himself, left the bed
sullenly, and allowed himself to be led away. Sarah remained,
dishevelled and a prey to absolute fury; how dared this
happen? Within herself, having learned of it from no one, she
knew that had he been allowed, even he, to continue, there
might have been some pleasure, in the end; but that had been
wrenched away from her, and her privacy with it. It was
intolerable; and she could tell no one here. Aunt Jane was
useless, Athene would bridle, and feign ignorance, Uncle

Nicholas – not that she would go to him – would say some caustic, worldly thing. Mrs Milsom? That was possible; she had been married, after all. Before they left for Atherton tomorrow, she, Sarah, would go to her. This state of affairs could not possibly be the lot of all brides. She pulled up the disordered covers again, and tried to sleep.

Harriet Milsom was engaged again after breakfast with the accounts, an activity which was much resented by the new housekeeper; but Harriet had found that it was essential to keep her mind occupied, and the meticulous duty filled the hours till she could find others. As she could no longer be described as the governess of Felix and Nick, and as Jane Crowbetter was beyond the need of an official companion, these took the form of reading or taking brief walks, till Crowbetter himself came home. She did not think of him until it was necessary; her attention was fixed on the columns of figures in black ink on a long white page. Earlier, the ink in the book had turned brown. It was a model of particularity over the years if anyone had wished to study it, which was unlikely.

There was a scratching at the door; Sarah entered timidly, dressed for travelling. Harriet did not rise, as she would once have done; she was a respected figure in the household, and one of its members had come to her. Nevertheless she was disturbed at the girl's pale looks and shadowed eyes.

'Be seated, my dear.' They had already said good morning at breakfast. Sarah shook her head, and leant against the door.

'The carriage is ready to go, and they will be looking for me. I wanted a word with you, if you will spare the time.' Suddenly, in an outpouring of words, she described the wedding night. Harriet listened expressionlessly.

'It is quite wrong for his mother to have come in,' said Sarah. 'The rest I could endure, although it was unpleasant. Will it always be like that?' She was suddenly, helplessly a child. The older woman's dark eyes studied her. 'No,' said Harriet Milsom gently, 'it will not be so bad after the first night. You will grow accustomed to it.'

'If only *she* keeps away, perhaps I can.'

'I understand,' said Harriet slowly, 'that the Countess is a very strange woman. She has strong religious principles of a kind which I myself would not share or, indeed, condone. One may not judge her as other mortals. Perhaps, in time, if you are your charming self to her – and you can be charming, Sarah, if a little wilful at times – she will grow fond of you, and will allow you more freedom in such ways.'

'I don't think I want her to grow fond of me. She never leaves *him* alone, or takes her eyes off him. She has dreadful eyes. She has made him as strange as she is herself.' The blurted words were resentful.

'Then it will be your duty to make him a little less strange. It can surely be done; the Viscount is only twenty.'

Sarah shuddered. 'I want to be left alone, that is all. You were married once. Were you happy with your husband?' It was a question she hardly dared ask; Mrs Milsom was a mystery, and nobody enquired about her.

'No,' said Harriet quietly, 'I was not. He used to beat me. He was often drunk. He died of drink when he was forty, leaving me with the necessity of earning my living. That will not happen to you. You have much for which to be thankful; a great name, a high place, no doubt respected in society; you could become a leader of it, if you so wish.' She changed her course of talk before Sarah could speak of the past. 'Did you, my dear, sleep at all, afterwards?' she asked gently.

'No,' said Sarah miserably. 'It hurt. It kept me awake.' The daring nightgown had been stained with blood in the morning: it would never be worn again. She could still feel pain in her inner parts. It had been horrible, all of it; and now she was being sent away with these strange, revolting people.

'Perhaps you will sleep tonight, with this.' Harriet had risen from her place and had gone to a pearwood corner cupboard in which she kept medicines for the household. 'These tablets are made of herbs, and are harmless, but induce sleep; I sometimes use them myself,' she said, handing Sarah a small package. The turquoise eyes looked at her gratefully.

'You have given them all to me,' said the new Viscountess Witham. 'How will you contrive without them?'

'I do not always use them, and in any case can obtain others.'

The door opened without warning and Crowbetter stood there, displeasure on his face. 'They told me you were here,' he said to Sarah. 'The carriage is waiting, and so is your husband, and the servants are lined up to see you go. Make your way downstairs at once.'

Sarah suddenly went forward and kissed Harriet Milsom on the cheek, a familiarity in any other circumstances, but the only thanks she could give. Then she turned without a word, and left. Crowbetter jerked his head at Harriet. 'Come,' he said. 'We may as well see them depart.'

She followed him, not being given his arm – he never acknowledged her in public – and reflected, not for the first time, on his growing arrogance, the incessant nature of his nightly demands, his complete lack of consideration for her as a person, although at times he employed her mental capacities when he needed reassurance. They went downstairs, and saw the carriage go; the bride, her husband, his mother, the clergyman Mr Crowe, and last of all Betty the maid, who at Sarah's request had been allowed to come; one more servant more or less was unimportant. The Countess had brought no maid of her own. Mr Fox remained in London, at his club. The carriage bowled off with its occupants, no slippers being thrown by anyone. It was not that kind of occasion.

The carriage swayed on, going ever north; soon town was left behind. Sarah had stared out of the window at the grubby houses and the dogs in the streets, the markets, the people, without interest; later she stared at the scenery. It was unexciting, and as they progressed grew flat. She was aware of Betty beside her, smelling of harsh soap. Her presence was a comfort, also the possession of the little package of sleeping tablets Sarah had put in her own reticule. The horrors of a night without sleep were new to her, and another would, she was convinced, drive her mad. She did not turn her head to converse with her husband, who sat opposite in his customary silence, from time to time passing his tongue over his thick red lips and looking mostly at the carriage floor. Further off, the Reverend Mr Crow could be heard making desultory talk with the Countess, who disapproved of his High Church views. He was saying that he hoped shortly for promotion as Rector. 'That is worldly,' replied Honoria. 'There should be no differences in rank for anyone occupying a position of influence in religious matters. No one can say that bishops are necessary.'

This remark quelled all talk for some time, and Sarah watched the countryside change from green to brown; brown moors, stretching for more miles than it was possible to see. They stopped at an inn, and ate in silence after John Crowe had said grace.

A second inn was necessary for the night. Sarah was shown up into a wide bed, with a pallet provided for Betty. She was nervous lest her maid as well as her mother-in-law might witness what would surely come; but Witham did not appear. In fact his mother was teaching him to discipline himself. By midnight Sarah went to take one of Harriet's pills, returned past the sleeping Betty to her own bed, and thankfully passed the rest of the night in slumber. Next day she felt better, and they resumed the journey, the future Rector having returned, by public chaise, to Sunderland.

Atherton Castle was reached at last by a long fenced drive lacking trees. Fencing was, she was to find, a feature of the estate and had been ordered by Honoria some years ago to keep out sheep. These grazed on the moor, and were of a thin breed Sarah did not remember from her own country childhood. If she had known, most of them had foot-rot; the marshes were close. Neither Atherton nor his wife took much interest in the fate of the tenant farmers, except to see that they paid their rents. This aspect was supervised by Honoria herself, as she declined to employ a bailiff.

Sarah was made known to the Earl soon after arrival, when she had been greeted by a tense circle of servants in much the same formation as the party who had seen them off at Hyde Park Gardens. There was no attempt by Witham to carry her over the threshold, which was a relief; and the servants themselves seemed to glance in permanent trepidation at the Countess rather than the bride, as if concerned that they might somehow be doing the wrong thing, and be reprimanded. From there, Sarah was led to her room to refresh herself; when she had done so, Honoria appeared at the door.

'I will take you to my husband,' she said, using the terse way of speaking, and seldom at that, which she had decided on as suitable for the little bourgeoise her son had married. They went downstairs and along corridors where framed portraits hung; glancing at these, Sarah saw that her husband's thick lips, body and limbs were not inherited, as several of the Atherton ancestors could be described as personable, tall, and slim, with broad shoulders. It must be from his mother that

Witham had inherited his total lack of physical charm; yet a portrait of Honoria herself at the time of her marriage showed a reasonably fine girl. A later one, painted with her son as a child of six, was pointed out by her briefly. Witham, even at that age, looked cautious and sullen. His education must have commenced. The Countess's chin had begun to be double. Sarah made no comment on the portrait, and they made their way to the Earl's study.

He was seated in a leather armchair and made no effort to rise. She could see that he had been a handsome man in youth. Dissipation and illness had ruined him; his nose was marred by purple veins, and the eyes which surveyed her with worldly knowledge had heavy bags of flesh beneath. Sarah was sorry for him. Perhaps he would become a friend.

'So you're the gal, eh? Do your duty; that's all we ask. There are no Athertons left except that damned parson. Give Witham a son within the year, if you can; look as if you could; send word as soon as it starts. I don't see many persons nowadays. Good day.'

She was taken out of the room, her head in a whirl. Of course what Witham had done two nights ago must be to make children; at least, she supposed so. Would once be enough, or must it happen again?

It happened again that night. As before, he was vigorous but wordless; before too long a time had elapsed, his mother came in once more and took him away.

The ensuing days did little to relieve Sarah's misery. On Sunday she, Witham and the Countess entered their carriage and were driven to the building where the sect held its weekly meetings. The servants, Betty among them, walked the two miles. The building itself was of drystone, having been built fifty years before when the lay preacher who started the whole business had come to Atherton on his travels. Beside the place was an ash tree, and Sarah remembered hearing that that was often used to discourage witches. She hesitated to comment; in fact she had acquired the habit of saying nothing, whatever happened; perhaps she was growing like Witham. During the journey Honoria made one speech from the shelter of her grey bonnet.

'You are too elaborately dressed for this occasion; in future, wear something sober, as others do.'

Sarah took this blow with others. She had taken some trouble to instruct Betty how to dress her, and do her hair, thinking that there might be ladies present who would want to meet the new Lady Witham. She had selected her wine-coloured outfit, with the fur tippet and muff, because it was colder here than in London. Now she was made to feel overdressed and conspicuous; her cheeks flushed in mortification.

Nor did the service console her, after they had reached it by crossing a ford which splashed the carriage-wheels. In the days when Sarah's mother was alive they had often gone to church in the country: the old parson had been gentle and friendly, had known all his parishioners, and had come out afterwards to chat with them at the lych-gate. Certainly the church they had all attended sometimes from Hyde Park Gardens had been more impersonal; but it was nothing to this. On entering the grey building, a chill struck Sarah to the bone. Men and women in dull clothes were seated in rows, keeping their eyes down. They showed no evidence of prayer, curiosity, or friendship. Sarah found herself seated between Witham and the Countess, her husband furtively pressing against her in a manner she already disliked. A lay preacher got up and led the proceedings, ranting on for more than an hour in a way Sarah had never heard or imagined before; after a time she stopped listening. There was no singing. Presently, one after another, the members, mostly men, rose to their feet and held forth in extempore fashion about damnation and sin. It all went on for what seemed a very long time. If only Hugo or Felix had been here, to steal a glance at one and laugh! But there was no laughter in this place; never would be. The pew was hard beneath her, Witham's sweaty presence close. Sarah decided that whatever was done to her as a consequence, she would not come here again.

She had remembered, during the exalted ravings, an altercation some days since with her mother-in-law. Sarah had gone out of doors, had found a neglected garden which did not greatly interest her, then the stables, which did. She had been used to ride as a child, though Mélanie's abandoned bay had been considered too large for her; and here was a gelding ready in his stall. Sarah went in and talked to him; he was friendly, and she let her hand caress his soft nose and stroke his neck, which needed grooming. There was in fact no sign of any groom, though there must be one; and suddenly, relishing the notion of a ride, Sarah went and found a saddle in the tack-room, then strapped it on to the gelding's back. The leather was dry and hard with age, but somebody must be used to ride him, as he made no stir. She had settled the girths, and was about to tighten her own stirrups, when a voice interrupted her. It was that of her mother-in-law.

'You are not to ride,' said Honoria. The dead eyes held a cold distaste.

'Why not? I can handle a horse. It is bad for him to be always in the stable.'

'That is not your concern. He belongs to my son.'

'Then he neglects him. His coat is dry.'

'You are insolent,' said Honoria, as though she spoke to a servant. 'Return to the house. I will have the groom remove the tack when he comes in.' The groom proved to be an old man who drank. Sarah turned on her mother-in-law furiously.

'How do you expect me to pass my days? If I may not ride what is there left for me to do here? It is the dullest place on earth.'

'You may come to meals, read, walk, and do your duty to your husband. You may also instruct your maid; she is not yet experienced. Most young women would find all this enough to occupy their time. You may also pray. Go back to the house, and fulfil your obligations.'

'Why may I not ride as well?' Sarah made herself say lightly. She patted the horse; she had made a friend of him, and would certainly visit him again. To be owned by Witham was a misfortune she could well understand.

Honoria's many-chinned face had flushed. 'We need not discuss the reason why you may not ride,' she said. 'Walk if you wish; that is healthful, only take care not to go beyond the fences. There is dangerous bog land not far off.'

Sarah had gone for walks daily, as a result, and had even walked off some of her anger. Now, after the dismal service, she spoke up in the carriage on their return journey.

'I will not come to that appalling place again,' she said. 'I think they are mad. If it is not raining on Sundays, I shall go for a walk instead.' The turquoise eyes stared into Honoria's dead ones. Witham said nothing. The Countess suddenly gave way. It was, after all, inadvisable to stop this

strong-headed young woman from doing certain things
which did not impede pregnancy.

'Your maid will accompany you in that case,' she said, 'but
there must be no riding.'

Sarah walked, accordingly, on weekdays and Sundays, in
rain and shine, with Betty tagging behind her. It was better
than going with the rest, but dreary not to be able to
penetrate beyond the estate, with its everlasting fences.

Some time after the above events, a ruined man was making
his way down Regent Street, keeping for choice within the
shadow of the arcades. It was not that anyone would yet
recognise Major Henry Laverton as ruined, as he maintained
his usual jaunty walk; but unless a miracle saved him – and
miracles did not happen as a rule in Laverton's dispassionate
if eventful life – it would soon come out, and be all round
town. The whole thing, to make it even worse, was his own
fault. He had sworn not to gamble in the officers' mess again,
at least not for high stakes; but the intermittent fever which
crazed his otherwise cool brain had set him on fire again with
its unpredictable heat. He had launched into a foolproof
method which had never yet failed him, against Foxe-Scrope,
of all men, a challenge if anyone liked; and had hedged a bet
that the nine would come up, and it had not, for the good
reason that it had been in Foxe-Scrope's hand from the
beginning. The bidding had gone sky-high by then, and at
the end, while putting a good face on it, Laverton knew that
he must find seven hundred guineas within the next day or
two, or else send in his papers and blow out his brains. At
least, that was the honourable course.

There was not a chance of finding the money. He had
never had that kind of luck since the day when, with a bullet
crippling his bridle-arm, he had gripped his horse with his
puny thighs outside Jellalabad in 'forty-two, and laid about
him, one-handed, with his sword. General Pollock had
congratulated him afterwards and would have appointed him
to staff, almost certainly, but other interests as usual
prevailed. In the shadow of the arcades Laverton scowled
behind his flamboyant moustache, remembering that and
other wrongs real and imagined.

The fact was that he was not popular. The other officers in
the regiment disliked him, while admitting his physical

bravery. After twenty-five years of having seen all service Henry Laverton had not attained the rank of Colonel, despite his exploits in Afghanistan and India. Other men younger than he had been promoted; he watched the gazettings with bitter jealousy, while his morose nature drove him ever further in upon himself. He had few vices, however, other than the occasional bout of irresistible gambling. He had never married, was uninterested in women and preferred little brown Indian boys; but that sort of thing did not do here; one risked being cashiered if it got out. Come to that, his plight was as bad now as if that had happened. He had thirty-five guineas in the bank, and no prospects.

He had just told himself again that miracles do not happen, when he saw one approaching in the near distance. He had not seen Miss Athene Crowbetter for some time; not, if his memory served him correctly, since the informal dance at Hyde Park Gardens, the invitation to which he had regretted accepting. The spinster was looking particularly unattractive today; overdressed as usual, in fringed ivy-green velvet of that especial shade which does not flatter a high-coloured complexion. Her hook-nose jutted. She wore half-boots and, perched on her frizzled hair, the inevitable pork-pie hat. Temple the maid trailed behind her. They were shopping.

Athene saw him, and the instant's enchantment on her face told Laverton that the spell he exercised over her, God knew why, had by no means lost its potency in the time they had been apart. Possibly absence had strengthened it. She advanced upon him – he was a small man – holding her parasol like a weapon, and flourishing her reticule in her large free hand. Her countenance was wreathed in smiles.

'Major Laverton! How truly delightful! How do you do? I trust you are well? We have not met for long – too long.'

She looked archly at him. Laverton gave a slight inward shudder, but responded politely, not however overdoing his greeting. The quick brain that had saved him at Jellalabad, that had worked out the foolproof method which after all only failed once, acted now like lightning that would scorch this poor fool and her affected pretensions into cinders. He gave Athene his arm, gallantly taking the reticule from her.

'Allow me to escort you,' he said. An observer might have noted that the two pairs of eyes which gazed into one another were identical; both being pale-blue, cold, intent, and heavy-lidded. Temple, following behind, wrinkled her nostrils in an inaudible sniff. Her feet were killing her, she wished Miss Athene would have done with it and go home, but there wasn't a chance of that now this hanger-on had arrived, not that he was any catch, nobody would see anything in him, not even her; too small, little thin legs, and the tip of his nose turning red; if it wasn't for the whiskers, there would be nothing worth mentioning. Temple, who kept herself to herself, did not even trouble to listen to what the pair were saying, which was perhaps as well.

Athene had not much imagination, and when she had thought of a remark she considered apt, she would employ it more than once. She repeated, accordingly, the statement that it was a long time since she and Laverton had met, which gave him the opening he wanted. He looked at her gravely.

'My dear –' he pressed her hand against his side very slightly, without being overly familiar, and that and the caressing name – he had never used it before – so delighted Athene that she became receptive to anything. 'My dear, that is due to your uncle's ban. He forbade me the house some time ago, after I had approached him with the request that I might pay my addresses to you.' It was all lies: he had of course done nothing of the kind.

'That you might – that you might – I did not know you felt as I did – my uncle had no right –' She was flattered, confused, transported, no longer by any means her everyday self; filled with exaltation and, at the same time, resentment at the behaviour of Uncle Nicholas. He had gone too far this time! There had, it was true, been fortune-hunters in her youth, and he had rightly sent them about their business; but Henry was different.

She turned a beaming face to him. 'I do not dissemble,' she said. 'I will gladly receive your addresses. We need consult no one. I am of age.' She tittered unbecomingly, and he almost withdrew from what was rapidly becoming a commitment. On the whole, though, it was convenient that she should have fallen without hesitation into his rapidly prepared net. His mind worked swiftly; a special licence; he could just pay for it. Afterwards – he knew wry amusement within his narrow

heart – funds would be more than available. A wife's property
was after all her husband's.

Having been brought up in the country till she was thirteen
years of age, and having – although of course one looked
away immediately – glimpsed the occasional mating of
animals, Athene was not as ignorant of life's facts as many
unmarried townswomen of her day. Unknown and unad-
mitted to herself or anyone else, she had the strong sexual
appetites of the Crowbetters, which Henry would, deliberately, never fully satisfy. For the moment she lived in bliss so
intense that it could not be real; and yet, when their
arrangements were made – Temple had had to wait a long
time while they walked along together – she knew that it
would certainly happen; she was to be married to Henry
Laverton, at St Clement Danes Church, the day after
tomorrow at four o'clock in the afternoon; as Henry said, they
had wasted enough time. The notion that he had nourished
the passion for her, in secrecy, that she felt for him almost in
public left Athene with no nagging doubts as to why a small
red-nosed man should so inspire her to devotion. Love knows
no logic, and poor bridling, outwardly self-assured Athene
had waited a long time. It was not that at first sight of
Laverton she had particularly singled him out; she could not
even recall where it was she had first seen him; but tales of his
military exploits had reached her somehow, and his reported
bravery had made him a god in her eyes very quickly. Lonely
women have to have an object to adore, whether it is a poodle
or, like Madame von Schwellenburg, two pet toads in a dish.
Athene had adored Henry Laverton in presence and absence
now for almost four years. He had filled her mind and her
waking dreams. She was not troubled by sleeping ones; she
slept excellently, snoring a little. This of course she did not
know, for there had never been anybody there to tell her.

   She had been instructed, with subtlety and outward
deference, about every last detail of the plan. She was to tell
Temple that she would be away for the night to visit a sick
friend. The night itself they would spend – oh, bliss – at
Brown's Hotel in Albemarle Street, which Athene had at
times visited to tea in female company and about whose
antique respectability no one could feel other than assured.

Thereafter – this aspect of Henry's bravery left Athene almost breathless – they would take a cab to visit Uncle Nicholas at his bank. Henry would then confront him, in her company of course, tell him they were married, that that, and the night they had spent together, had been witnessed, and that there was, in short, nothing Uncle Nicholas could do about it. As for money, it had not been mentioned. This fact gave Athene a reckless feeling of contentment; all her life it had been considered of such importance that, as she now told herself, she had hardly been allowed to live.

She confronted Temple, who had been able to steep her feet meantime in a hot footbath below stairs. The woman cast her eyes down as a good servant should, and said yes miss and no miss, as indicated. In fact she was well aware of what was happening, and in a quiet way was enjoying it; if she lost this situation as a result, she could get another; an experienced lady's maid was always in demand. The picture of that little man in bed with great bouncing Miss Athene, with her hook nose, gave one to laugh, in private, of course; and she, Ann Temple, would tell nobody. 'I shall not require you, Temple,' her mistress said, a trifle coyly; she could perhaps be forgiven for feeling coy and being unable quite to disguise the fact. 'No, miss,' said Temple, and went to pack the things required for a one-night stay with a sick friend, including a clean nightgown and a comb. She had also been instructed to tell members of the household that Miss Athene had a bad cold and was keeping her bed. 'You may dispose of the food which is sent up,' said Athene. Temple knew better; when the laden tray came, she would help herself to plenty of the choicest morsels before consigning the rest to the slop-bucket. The dining-room food at Hyde Park Gardens was a different matter from that served in the kitchen.

Henry Laverton and Athene Crowbetter were married at the time and place arranged, two chaps from the officers' mess, sworn to secrecy meantime, standing in as witnesses and, vaguely, as groomsmen. Afterwards they wanted to escort the bride and groom to their hotel for a few drinks, but Laverton, with less than five guineas in his pocket, discouraged this; and they melted away, leaving Athene, blushing with happiness, and her silent bridegroom in a cab. They reached Brown's, were shown their room, went down for dinner a little early as

Henry was already in uniform and there had been nothing packed into which Athene might change; and imbibed soup and munched tournedos in silence as there was, quite suddenly, nothing to say. From time to time Athene glanced at the man who was her husband. She saw nothing about him that she had not seen before; he was dear Henry, no different, a little silent perhaps, but she herself was so, most unusually; it was not often that she was at such a loss for words, but – deliberately, she directed the course of her mind back to Hyde Park Gardens to wonder if they had discovered her disappearance yet; she did not think so. Temple was discreet, and nobody would want to visit her with a bad cold. She gave her maidenly titter, and spoke aloud. There were few other guests yet in the dining-room.

'I do not suppose that they have discovered my absence. If they have, they will not know where to look.'

Laverton himself hardly knew where to look, for directly opposite him, at a small intimate table, was this large-bosomed woman with whom he must presently sleep. He hoped that he would contrive, at least to a sufficiency that would prove the marriage to have been consummated. He had never felt less like proceeding; and it must be done. He thought of the money, and consoled himself.

'Tomorrow,' he said, 'we'll show 'em.'

She put out her hand, with his ring on it. Laverton had got it at a pawnbroker's, and it had reduced his available change. There would be just enough to buy himself a brandy or two before going up to her. Fortunately he did not care for cigars.

Athene was faced with a difficulty even Laverton had not foreseen; when she started to undress, she could not unfasten her corsets. They were laced up from the back, and Temple always did it. She knew panic; if Henry should come in and find her still not ready, still at the most unbecoming stage of female attire! But she was practical enough to send for the chambermaid, who proved adept; and Athene rewarded her suitably. She had brought enough money with her for an emergency, of whatever kind: Uncle Nicholas had never grudged her a handsome allowance. She began to think of him almost with affection as she eased her large plump body into the clean nightgown. Then she looked towards the bed. Should she get into it, or would it look more suitable to wait for Henry in a chair? What did one do in the circumstances? If only she had someone to advise her! She had no thought or memory of her half-sister Sarah, so much younger and quite alone, who had had no one to advise her either.

The dilemma was solved by the entry of Laverton, who had enjoyed his brandy, in fact more than a couple, as he had hit on the practical notion of putting them on the bill. He now felt capable of the task before him; after all Jellalabad had been worse; once the thing was done, that would be that.

Athene was standing uncertainly in the middle of the room, the nightgown failing to cover her feet, which he noted had corns. 'Get into bed, m'dear.' he said in military fashion. 'I shall undress.'

He undressed; she had never before seen a man's body; like the times with the animals, she looked away. Perhaps it was best to close one's eyes altogether. Athene kept them shut, presently felt him climb into bed, felt him grope for her; excitement rose in her which she did not understand as his moustache brushed against her chin. What followed was not unpleasant, after the first, but not nearly long enough; she admitted it afterwards freely to herself; perhaps in future one would grow accustomed, or he – but he had not said a word; after the episode, he turned over and slept. So did Athene, before long; having first reflected that it would be in order to confront Uncle Nicholas on the morrow. Despite the slight disappointment, for it was certainly that, she could say, after all, that she, Athene Crowbetter, or rather Laverton, was properly married.

Next morning, Henry obligingly laced her corsets himself; not only was he relieved that the business had been accomplished, but he had a slight favour to ask. He wasted no time, and put it tersely.

'I am a trifle embarrassed for money at the moment,' he told her. 'After all, the licence, and an officer's pay –' She looked at him blankly; she was seated at the dressing-table struggling to get the comb through her thick hair, which was tangled with the night's activities, and pulled from the roots painfully. 'In short,' she heard him say, 'I fear I shall have to ask you, m'dear, to pay the shot.'

'The shot?' She thought innocently of some military matter, perhaps something to do with a gun; but that illusion was brief. He told her the truth, standing aggressively by; she had not noticed before – yet how could she have failed to notice? – how sharp and, really, red at the tip his nose was. Dear Henry. It was a part of him, like – well, one must listen to what he was saying. Athene listened in a docile fashion quite foreign to her; and, realising at last that he meant the bill, said somewhat hesitantly that she would be pleased to pay it. In fact, she hoped that she had brought enough money with her after all; she knew very little about the cost of hotels.

They went downstairs, had breakfast, and paid; Laverton took her purse from her, emptying out the guineas. Athene watched with mild shock; nobody had ever done that before, but, after all, a husband had certain rights.

'There were the brandies as well, sir,' said the clerk. Laverton counted out the money carefully. He had hardly tipped the waiter. Apart from his gambling, he was, by habit and nature, mean. Also, they must keep enough for the cab to Crowbetter's.

Crowbetter's was seldom crowded, as most transactions took place by correspondence or else involved lengthy talks with clients from abroad who had called by appointment in person. They were fortunate, therefore, in being admitted to Nicholas at once, as Athene was known in the bank; she was one of the few female relatives who had ever been there, her signature having been required on certain occasions.

They were admitted to the inner office arm-in-arm, as a good husband and wife should be. Crowbetter looked up from his desk in surprise; he had understood Athene to be in bed at Hyde Park Gardens with a bad cold. He said so, rising to his feet to greet her and the fellow who, for whatever reason, escorted her here. He knew Laverton slightly, having been induced in the first place to invite him to the house at the suggestion of a certain General, a client. He could not resist a twitch of inward humour at the spectacle of large Athene on the arm of this stunted military officer.

Athene spoke first, having forgotten to kiss her uncle on the cheek as was the polite habit. 'No, Uncle, I was not in bed with a cold. I was – tell him, Henry.' She turned a face flushed with pleasure and trepidation – Uncle Nicholas had such a penetrating glance! – to her husband.

Laverton wished she had come out with all of it, instead of

leaving it to him; but spoke in his turn, stating that he and
Athene were married, that it had happened yesterday before
witnesses, and that they had spent the night together and
were man and wife. Athene's flush deepened almost to
crimson; men were sometimes so explicit; dear Papa had been
the same, in a way. Now –

There was silence.

They waited. Athene waited, expecting an outpouring of
cold wrath. Laverton waited, a mouse playing with a cat.
There was nothing Crowbetter could do but accept with a
good grace, he was convinced. He was not in the least afraid
of the notorious man; fear was not one of Henry's
weaknesses.

'I think,' said Nicholas after a long pause, 'that I had best
see you alone.'

He rang the bell on his desk for a clerk, who came. 'Pray
escort Mrs Laverton to the outer office,' Nicholas said.
Athene, radiant with triumph that her status had been
recognised, went out. The clerk congratulated her discreetly;
he had been here a long time.

Crowbetter wasted no time of his own. He sat down, faced
Laverton, and did not ask him to be seated. The little officer
however cast himself into a chair uninvited, his thin legs in
their braided trousers flung out insolently.

'Well, you scoundrel, how much do you want?'

Laverton stiffened; he was touchy, and had come of good
family. 'Sir, I believe I have the right to my wife's property;
you insult me.'

'How much is it?' Crowbetter made as if to take up a quill
from the penholder. Emboldened, Laverton told him,
expecting a draft to be written out at once; it had been, after
all, extraordinarily easy.

Crowbetter laid down the pen. The golden eyes surveyed
Laverton with cold dislike, also a quiet inward triumph.

'A gambling debt, perhaps?' he ventured. Laverton
brushed his moustache upwards with a finger.

'You have no right to ask that, I believe. I have outlined the
position.'

'But I have not yet outlined mine. You may not be aware – I
do not think that this marriage would have taken place if you
had – that I am in full charge of Athene's inheritance until
she is thirty. That will not be for two years; ample time for

you, my friend, to be arrested and thrown into a debtor's prison.'

Laverton's jaw had dropped, leaving a gap between moustache and chin. 'Damn you, I'll have the law on you,' he said. 'A wife's property is her husband's; no question of it.'

'Have the law by all means, if you can pay a lawyer. I will not advance you a penny with which to do so. A legal action takes a long time; in the meantime, if you send in your papers as I imagine you will be compelled to do, the bailiffs will come, and carry out their duty. I shall do nothing to save you; you have had no pity on Athene; I shall have none on you.'

Laverton's face was transformed into a snarling mask. 'It's Athene's fortune that interests you, you damned Jew and moneylender. It's –' He sagged suddenly. 'To resign my commission will mean the end for me,' he said. 'The army has been my life.'

'If your life were to end, that would be a good thing for everyone; but I do not think you will take it. You have called me a Jew, and with some reason; my grandmother was Jewish, and I am proud of it. Money is to me what the army no doubt was to you; a consuming interest, a way of life.'

'Then for God's sake lend it to me. I will repay it somehow. A turn of the cards – I am often lucky –'

'Athene shall keep her money, at least while I have control of it. Afterwards – if you are still on the face of the earth – when you are let out of prison, no one, unfortunately, can prevent you from spending it as you will. I do not anticipate that even that great inheritance will last long in your hands.'

He rose. 'I think that we have talked enough,' he said. 'I will speak with Athene; I would prefer that you were not present.'

Laverton bristled. 'Naturally, as her husband, I shall be present.'

'Then you must be prepared to endure what I am about to say.'

'Damn you to hell for a blackguard,' muttered Laverton sullenly.

Athene was brought in. Henry Laverton had the manners to pull out a chair for her to be seated, and she turned her pallid blue gaze on her uncle. She said nothing; since marriage, she had grown somewhat silent. Nicholas began to speak at once.

'I will tell you the truth, Athene, although it will be hard on

you. This man married you because he had lost seven
hundred guineas at play and cannot pay his debt. In the
army, when that happens, an officer must resign his
commission. Many take their own lives.'

'Oh no, no,' cried Athene weakly. '*Henry –*'

She turned her face, a mask of tragedy, towards her
husband where he stood behind her chair. But Henry was the
silent one now; he neither spoke nor moved to comfort her.
When she thought of it, he had never offered her comfort.
He had never offered her love. It was she, fool that she was,
who had loved him; so dearly, for so long!

'Have no fear,' said Nicholas drily. 'He will live.'

The tears began to course down Athene's cheeks; presently
great gusty hiccupping sobs came from her. She could hardly
have heard all the rest of what Nicholas was saying, which
concerned the debtors' prison, the bailiffs, and other
unpleasantness. All she knew was that Henry had tricked her;
then she realised that Henry was after all in distress; and as
women in love will, she replaced the reality with the dream
and loved him once again, and forgave him, and knew she
must help him whatever befell.

'Pray, advance the money, uncle,' she begged, still
hiccupping slightly and putting a hand to her mouth. 'It is
after all nothing to us; there must be –' She named a sum,
with the interest accrued to Crowbetter's. Athene was not
entirely ignorant of finance. Henry Laverton blinked; there
was more there than he had thought. All hope was, perhaps,
not lost; but there was Crowbetter, damn him. That could not
be got over, nor could the next two years. He made himself
move slightly nearer to Athene. He must think of something;
perhaps only of one thing. It was a battle, after all; much like
life.

'I have already told your husband that I will not agree to
advance him a single penny.'

'But he will go to prison! He will go to prison!'

So she had heard that. The disgrace, the discomfort and
squalor, seemed to rouse more emotion in her than the
resigning of one's commission, Laverton noted sourly. If he
could have been saved that! But there was no way out now.
Foxe-Scrope would grow suspicious after a few days; he
himself had promised that he would raise the money, had
signed a docket to that effect. Foxe-Scrope, damn his eyes,

was vengeful; he would take it to the finish. There had been bad blood between them on certain occasions. In any case, it was not a situation that could be permitted socially; he, Laverton, would be an outcast; he knew it well enough.

Athene suddenly collapsed sideways in her chair and her hat fell off. There were no women in the bank, and it was left to Crowbetter himself to loosen her fitted neckband and try to revive her with brandy; he looked up presently at Henry Laverton, who had not touched her.

'I think that you should go,' Nicholas said. 'She will return to my house, but you will not enter it.'

Laverton looked once at the pricked bubble of a woman in the chair, then without further words turned and marched, his back erect, out of the office and out of Crowbetter's. He had three and a half guineas in his pocket, and his arrears of pay to come.

When he had gone, Crowbetter quietly sent for the clerk, who arranged for a cab to take Miss Athene home.

To say that Athene lay between life and death for the next four days would be to exaggerate. Certainly she was much exhausted and distressed after her ordeal at the bank, and on arrival home Temple unlaced her, put her to bed and brought her a cup of tea. As she was supposed to be in bed anyway, nobody asked any questions or, thankfully, made any visits; Athene only wanted to be left alone. She had a great deal to think about; after the first misery had departed, her mind, which was not without its shrewdness, began to assess her situation. As time went by, it began to seem perhaps not quite so bad as it had once done.

Had Henry, in fact, deceived her? According to his own relation – and how she would always cherish the memory of that walk together up Regent Street, when he carried her reticule! – according to that, he had asked Uncle Nicholas for her hand long before the sordid business of the gaming debt. That was unfortunate, but she could have paid it, and saved poor Henry from disgrace and ruin. The thought of the form that that would take made Athene break out crying again; and Temple, who had been congratulating herself that Mr Crowbetter had not, after all, held her personally to blame for anything, hurried in on her unreliable feet and asked if there was anything wanted. It was evident that something had gone wrong, she didn't know what, but could guess. In fact, she herself was mistaken. Athene had come to realise, over the dreary hours, that a large part of her own concern was not for Henry, shortly to be hauled off to prison – how truly terrible! – but for that part of herself which, had she had any sense of humour, Athene could have described as the gateway to bliss. It was true that bliss had not quite been achieved, but it was surely possible that at some future date, given all the circumstances, it might be. At any rate, she had had a foretaste; and would not let the possibility go without a fight.

The first thing was to see Uncle Nicholas. She got up, had herself dressed, and having had the cook informed in time, went down to dinner. Nicholas was at home, and greeted her amiably, as if nothing had happened. Jane asked how her cold was. Mrs Milsom had remained upstairs. There was no company.

After dinner, Athene deserted Jane and went back into the dining-room, where Nicholas was sitting alone over his port. He raised his thin black eyebrows.

'I thought that we had finished with that subject,' he said gently.

'No, uncle. There is one thing. That is why I had to see you in private.' She was twisting her hands in the blue draped apron that had been fashionable some years ago, but Athene was always behind the times in her dress. Her left hand still bore Henry's ring. She began to speak nervously, telling her uncle how Henry had assured her some days ago that he had been forbidden to call at Hyde Park Gate because he had asked to be allowed to pay his addresses to her. As the story stumbled out it sounded increasingly unlikely; Nicholas was regarding her with pity.

'That is all nonsense,' he said. 'He made no such request, and I gave no such order. He has deceived you sadly, Athene. Try to be happy with us; you are much better rid of Laverton. He would have spent all your money, then left you.' He did not tell her of the power Laverton might wield in two years: a lot could happen by then.

He had said what he had of set purpose; he knew that Athene had a healthy respect for her own bank statements and, when he discussed them with her as sometimes happened, a measure of the creative delight he himself felt in selecting shares to swell them. But now she felt no delight at all, poor creature, and turned woefully away. Henry had been lying to her, after all.

Later, in bed, she wondered if perhaps it was Uncle Nicholas who was lying; he was perfectly capable of it, the object being, no doubt, in this case, to keep her fortune under his own control. She did not know which version to believe, and spent hours cogitating to and fro in anguish; then certainty came to her like a glow of light. She had sworn to love and honour Henry Laverton, forsaking all other, for better, for worse, for richer, for poorer – if only she could send him that money! – and she would abide by her vow. They were husband and wife. Nothing except death could alter that. And, at this moment, she did not even know where he was. Sending in his papers would be kept private, surely; but then where would he go?

It was a whole month before she heard; an agonising, lonely month when the days dragged uselessly, with her mind a well of misery and unending worry about Laverton. Had he perhaps fled abroad? For him, it would no doubt be the best thing that could happen; but for herself, to think of the lonely years, if she could not join him! And there was always the question of money; he had none, his occupation was gone, like Othello's – the analogy did not occur to Athene – and her own allowance from Uncle Nicholas, though handsome, would not keep the two of them even if it was continued in the event, which was unlikely. In the end she consoled herself by realising that Laverton, unless he had been gaming again, could not possibly have found the money for the fare.

She spent many hours on her bed, and lost flesh. Temple was silent and helpful, if not openly sympathetic, which was as well; Athene still had enough spirit to have snubbed her. Her mind was fixed on one person, one star in her dark firmament, which grew ever brighter and more desirable with absence. She forgot the meannesses, the probable lies, the overt unkindness, remembering only the loved one, her own man. If only he would write! Had he indeed written, and had Uncle Nicholas purloined the letter? The possibility racked her for days and nights; she remembered that it had happened to Sarah, typically not blaming herself for that episode. If she asked Crowbetter he would probably deny it; in the meantime, her darling might be short of food, of a roof over his head, and certainly of safety if the bailiffs were looking for him quite yet. Athene was ignorant of the niceties of High Court actions, nor did she know that *in absentia* Laverton's case would be heard, and judged. The time passed, and with it Athene resolved to be ready, if he should send for her; she got up, dressed, and went for a shaky walk, with Temple behind her. She found, against all expectation, that she enjoyed it. She would go for others, daily. She had lain too long in bed.

Salvation was at hand in the form of a grubby urchin of ten years old. He had been hanging about the street for a long time between the mews and the front door, and he was not the kind of person habitually to be seen in Hyde Park Gardens. Athene, who had at last stepped out, wearing her half-boots and a winter coat, glanced at him with open disapproval: but instead of vanishing as he ought to have done, he sidled towards her, with a gait like a crab; he was used to darting suddenly up alleys before trouble came to roost. He brought out a letter from his dirty and ragged jacket, and handed it to her. Athene's heart leaped; she had only once seen Laverton's handwriting, on the marriage register. It was small and careful, written with one of his own beautiful hands. (In fact, for a man, Henry's hands really were one of his assets; she remembered them well, small, white, and delicate, with shapely fingers.) She felt her heart stop its leaping and begin to beat again strongly, pleasurably. Henry must be well, or he could not write.

"E said to give it to you,' remarked the urchin briefly. He had been given a full description of the lady and there was certainly no mistaking her; but he was left in uncertainty whether to call her miss or 'm. He glanced at her gloved hand for the bulge of a wedding ring, but was still not sure. There was one matter, however, in no doubt.

"E said you would pay me,' he put it unequivocally. 'I walked all the way.'

'All the way from where?' She fumbled in her reticule; the same reticule Laverton had carried for her on that hallowed, never-to-be-forgotten occasion in Regent Street, and produced a shilling. The boy snatched it, bit it from force of habit, said 'Poplar' over his thin shoulder, and vanished, disappointed.

Poplar? What was Henry doing there? It was not, surely, a respectable place; she had heard of it, but had never, of course, been in that direction. She retraced her steps to the house, unwilling to be seen opening a letter in the street; its very exterior was grubby from being carried somewhere on the urchin's unsavoury person. That did not matter. The letter was from Henry. 'I have forgotten something,' she cast back at Temple, and said it again to the butler when he opened the door. She hurried up to her room, almost – the notion occurred to her – on winged feet. Once there, she opened her letter. It gave, indeed, an address in Poplar.

4th February, 1862

My dearest Athene,

 Forgive me for troubling you once again. I had hoped that you could put me out of your life, as matters stand. The thing is that I expected to live on my last pay for some time, but my creditor agreed to take it as interest on the whole debt, and I have nothing. At the time I write I have hardly had a meal. I have even sold my hairbrushes; they were ivory, as you will remember. If you can help me, I will be grateful. I have no one else to whom to turn.

Your ever loving husband,
Henry Laverton

He was hungry! He was entirely forsaken! She would help him, of course; and she must go to him, and at once. She glanced at the window; it was still cold winter daylight. She would take a cab to Poplar. It did not matter what she told them here; she was going to visit the sick friend again, anything. She did not even remember what she said. Without Temple – after all, she was a married woman now – Athene left the house again, found a cab waiting near the Park, got in, and impatiently watched the horse's buttocks rising and falling for some miles in the rhythmic exercise of its accustomed duties. Gentility was long left behind when the cab reached its lamentable destination. A crowd of urchins, inevitably resembling the one who had brought the letter, crowded immediately round it as Athene got out.

'Go away! Go away!' She waved her umbrella defensively at them; she was no more tolerant of social differences than she had been in Sarah's day. She turned and told the cabman to wait; it might be difficult to find another in this deplorable region. 'Suits me,' he said, not very respectfully, fanning away the urchins with his whip. They dropped off, as there were no pickings. 'Mind your purse,' the man added, considering not his customer but himself; if her purse was slit, or pinched, she wouldn't be able to pay the fare. He watched her pick her way across the rubble-piled street, wondering who in the world and all glory she was; probably a charity worker, one of them rich ones. She had already asked him for the particular direction she required, and he had driven as near to it as he could. He could do no more, and settled down to snooze till her return.

Henry's lodging proved to be up a flight of rickety stairs, smelling of cabbage-water. Athene climbed them carefully, her heavy skirts held in one hand, her heart suitably beating, but her mind still cautiously aware of the risk of a sprained ankle; the heels of the half-boots were moderately high and, had she known, gave her the effect of a picking hen.

At length – it had been up several flights – she knocked on a door whose paint was peeling. The door itself was cheaply made, warped and hung badly. For Henry to be in such a place!

The door opened. A small clean-shaven man stood there, in civilian clothes. Despite everything, he looked in moderate health and was dressed like a gentleman; but Athene gave a wail.

'Henry! Your moustache! It has gone!'

She would have flung her arms about him despite the vanished glory, but he told her unemotionally to come in. 'Better not let 'em hear,' he muttered. 'Shaved it off; thought perhaps I wouldn't be known without it.'

'It was *beautiful*. You must grow it again as soon as you can.' The difference between the small, relatively magnificent officer and this little ordinary being was almost too much; this was not Henry, but a different person, certainly of less standing. But, without thinking about it, he moved his hands to close the door; and his hands were still beautiful. They were, Athene told herself fondly, like those of a duke in a seventeenth-century portrait, the nails well cared for. Of course Henry was a gentleman; an officer and a gentleman. He had smiled at her last remark, which he seldom did; the sight gave her sudden pleasure.

'Henry, you have *beautiful* teeth.' It was true; the moustache had understated them. They were a further asset; even, present, shining, and real. Henry was full of delightful surprises. If –

'It was good of you to come,' he told her civilly. One must be civil; she had undoubtedly brought the money. Being a true Crowbetter, she did not give it to him yet, but held on to her well-remembered reticule. He must cozen her, he knew. He had relished his solitude and privacy, and the thought, as well as the sight, of Athene made him sour.

'I could not help coming, as soon as I had your letter. I would have come long before, had I known where to find you. Why, why, did you keep me waiting so long? Did you not know how anxious I would be?' She recalled the miserable days, the dark hours of each night.

'You wouldn't have done any good,' he said practically. 'Whatever had to happen is over.' He turned away; not to anyone, not to a soul on earth, would he relate the humiliation of, at last, sending in his papers, enduring the avoided glances of his former brother officers as he went out for the last time; and all the rest. A hand-to-mouth existence was not beyond him in some foreign fort, a challenge, in fact; to be uncertain of one's very life was one thing; but now his life was no longer in danger, only – and Henry used an almost forgotten word – his honour, lost by the very fact that he still lived.

His long silence, and his turned back, chilled Athene: he had not even kissed her. She burst into tears, snuffling and hiccupping as she always did; she would never learn to make a social grace of crying.

'Oh, Henry, can't you be kind to me? I love you so much, and you don't even trust me enough to tell me anything at all. I'm hardly a part of your life.'

The last vowel came out on a wailing crescendo, and Laverton knew that he must placate her. In his language, when a woman asked a man to be kind to her it meant only one thing. 'Come on, then,' he said tersely, and took her by the elbow. 'I didn't mean it; I've been worried, you know.' He guided her to the sofa, which had been upholstered many years ago in grey velvet and was now much rubbed.

'Oh, Henry – yes, dear, of course – but I have a cab waiting –'

'Let it wait,' he said grimly. He laid her down; contrived the

heavy skirts, the complication of the drawers, and set to work.
It was a matter of earning one's living, after all; as well one
way as another, but it was hard going and he lacked
enthusiasm. He was aware, none better, that he had not
satisfied Athene on the wedding night. Now, he must do so,
perhaps, a thought more thoroughly; she wouldn't keep
bringing money otherwise, or not for long. At last he
achieved a certain position convenient to them both, and
managed to hold it for some time. He heard her speak,
breathy with achieved satisfaction.

'Henry, you must be got out of this dreadful place.
Somewhere more suitable –'

The sofa had begun to sway remotely: he remembered that
its legs were not too strong, one having been recently mended
with glue at his own request by the landlady. He allowed his
thoughts to dwell on it, not daring to picture the collapse of
both of them to the floor. 'No good,' he replied to Athene's
last remark eventually. 'Have to keep out of sight. If I'm seen
by anyone, it's all up with me, you know.'

'Oh ... Henry ...' Athene was beginning to sense a certain
well-being fill her; at the same time, she could not forbear
thinking with her customary prudence of the cabman waiting
outside. 'I could write to my sister, Lady Witham, in the
north,' she murmured presently, proud in a vicarious fashion
of Sarah's title, which would impress Henry. 'There is surely
some small room in Atherton Castle where you could be
hidden. They would never look for you there, and I – I could
visit you.'

He grunted, and she became alarmed lest the strange
wheezing noises that had lately been coming from Henry
might mean that the darling, after all his privations, would
shortly succumb to an infection of the chest in this unheated
room. Without one's drawers – that was, in all the
circumstances – it was very cold indeed. If Henry were ill, of
course, she would nurse him, even here, but meantime – oh,
oh, oh –

Henry knew when he had achieved enough. Just as the
insidious delight was spreading fully in Athene, he withdrew;
leaving her deprived and, partly, ashamed. It had been
almost sordid, as well as chilly, in here; and yet had almost
been, almost, like heaven.

She endured the fading of the dream once again, as she

would always have to endure it; got up off the doubtful sofa, saw to the tapes of her drawers, and the proper rearrangement of her skirts. For some reason she wanted to cry again, but Henry must not think of her as always crying. Men were, as she had found even in Papa's time, impatient of tears. It was a mercy that the landlady, assuming there was one, had not come in.

Henry, unemotionally fastening his own clothes, was congratulating himself. Athene's heavy transports would have daunted him, and in any case he had seen her age on the marriage certificate. Twenty-eight wasn't too old to get in calf. Athene looked more, especially when her large face was blubbered and swollen with crying, to his own cold embarrassment. He must try to stay civil, however.

'The money, my dear,' he reminded her hopefully; she had been about to depart with her reticule unopened. She gasped, gave it to him, and he counted out the guineas, allowing her to retain the cab fare and a tip. Athene watched in worship; this was the action of a masterful husband. Laverton let her go alone down the stairs; he had not, for safety's sake, escorted her to the waiting cab.

> *14 Hyde Park Gate, the 6th of February, 1862*
> *To Viscountess Witham, at Atherton Castle.*
> *My dearest Sarah*
> *I trust that you are well. It is some time since we met, I believe not since the day after you were married. I hope that your new position is agreeable to you and that you are happy.*
> *I have a great favour to ask, but you are after all my sister.* (At this point Athene had vacillated between the correctness of 'half-sister' and a slightly warmer overtone, and had decided on the latter, despite her adverse opinion of Papa's remarriage and its results.) *You have a large place, no doubt with many rooms. A very dear friend of mine, Major Henry Laverton, whom you may have met here, is in great trouble and must conceal himself; I will not harrow you with details of which I myself know very little. Would you – or rather would Lord Witham and his parents, above all – agree to house Major Laverton quietly for a little while, hopefully until the storm blows over? He is a gentleman, of good family. I beg this favour of you; I know that you will not refuse me, and I hope that your relatives by marriage will not do so. I have no doubt that you can persuade them to agree, if you will try.*

There is very little news from here; we go on in the same way.

Your affectionate sister,
Athene

From Atherton, 10th February, 1862
Dear Athene,
Your letter surprised me; I had not expected to hear from you again, as we were never friends. You acted most cruelly in the matter of a private letter of mine, and I am unlikely to do you any favours at all. I remember Major Laverton chiefly for his ugliness; I believe he is a most unpleasant little man and has been in disgrace which will shortly bankrupt him. (As you see I have grown a trifle more worldly in such matters.) I would not have him here for the world, and I shall not mention the matter to anyone here at all.
You ask if I am happy. I do not suppose that the answer concerns you greatly. I walk a great deal. There is no news otherwise.

Your ever dutiful half-sister,
Sarah Atherton

So that was that.

Athene was not defeated. She was fighting for her man, and a certain battleship aspect she had always possessed became more than ever visible in her appearance. As regarded that, she soon thought of a stratagem. Henry must on no account be allowed to remain in that dreadful place in Poplar: one answer might be for him to go to Scotland, where one understood the law was different, although she herself was not at all well acquainted with the details of his particular case. After reflection she decided that Scotland was unsafe, if available to herself somehow, perhaps, occasionally; she could say that she was visiting Sarah. The prospect made Athene actually titter for the first time in very long indeed. But she soon sobered, for she saw, within herself, and clearly, that there was only one thing left for Henry to do to escape prison; he must escape abroad instead. Her own deprivation was a minor matter.

The ability of Henry to maintain himself was of course important. In earlier times men had enlisted in foreign armies, but Athene was not certain that this could still be done, and she hesitated in any case to suggest it to Henry, whose feelings on the whole subject might be, understandably, raw. She thought instead of a better plan, which after all involved very little sacrifice on her part: she never wore her mother's emeralds. They were of great value, and had been kept in the bank until Athene came of age; but they were still set in the lighter fashion prevalent in Regency times, and made large Athene look somewhat top-heavy and, if possible, wan. She had never troubled to have the setting changed, accordingly; such stones were meant for a green-eyed woman, which admittedly dearest Mama had not been. That strange foreign woman, the Countess von Reichmansthal, whose position in Hyde Park Gardens had been so ambiguous, could have worn them; but she had naturally not been given the chance. Now, the emeralds could be put to real use for Henry. One trusted that he would not gamble their value away.

She had no idea of how to sell jewellery, and asked Temple. That discreet personage did not openly enquire as to why one of the richest women in London should suddenly want to sell anything at all; she mentioned pawnbrokers, but said she believed they never gave the value.

'But that is dreadful,' said Athene. Suddenly she crumbled her defences and took the maid into at least a part of her confidence. 'They are for a very, very dear friend, who is in need of money,' she said. 'I can think of no other way of providing enough.'

'Best give them to him, miss, and he can sell them himself,' replied Temple, who had never stopped using the title by which she had been used to address her mistress from the beginning. Miss Athene somehow never would seem like a Mrs, whatever had happened. The pale-blue eyes surveyed her gratefully; Athene blushed. So Temple had guessed! For a servant, she was remarkably shrewd.

'I am most grateful for that suggestion,' she said, and when she was alone sat down and wrote Henry a letter to the Poplar address.

> *14 Hyde Park Gardens, 14th February, 1862*
>
> *My dearest Henry,*
>   *This is St Valentine's Day, and as you will see, I am sending you a Valentine! I do hope that you will be pleased with the suggestion I am about to make; it is, I think, the best thing for you, after all.*
>   *I have certain jewels. They belonged to my mother. In the ordinary way – but of course you are not ordinary – I would never, never part with them. However I trust that they would fetch enough (I believe*

that that is the vulgar phrase) to keep you in comfort where you must soon go, which is, I fear, abroad. I have thought about this matter very carefully, and, sad as I am to lose you, even for almost two years (the time, after all, has already passed a little), I believe that in your own best interests, and indeed for your safety, it must happen.

I suggest that you do not go to France. The Emperor of the French is not, they say, a respectable person, and anything may happen there. I suggest instead that you travel to Holland. (Here Athene reflected that the Dutch, who were reputed to be a sober and God-fearing people, would be less likely to gamble and probably fleece Henry of the money he would soon possess than their Gallic counterparts.) *The packet, I understand, leaves in that event from Harwich. I have never been there, but I could travel to meet you at some inn, to be chosen by yourself – gentlemen know so much more about these matters than us poor females – if you let me know where, and I will bring you money for your fare and the emeralds, which you can sell for yourself abroad. It would of course be impossible for you to do so in England at the moment, and I myself am quite ignorant of the procedure in such cases.*

Now, Henry dearest, do not gamble this money away. It is all that you will have to keep yourself in comfort and security until I can, hopefully, join you with wide-open arms when, at last, we are free of Uncle Nicholas.

My best love to my Valentine. Inform me about the time of sailings, and the inn.

Your most loving wife, for ever and ever, my own darling,
Athene Laverton.

The Major received this missive from his landlady, a thin grey creature of few words who brought it up with his unappetising midday meal. He ate the food, then opened the letter with mixed feelings. The money Athene had lately brought had lasted, he had paid for his board and lodging, some seventeen guineas were left over, there was little on which to spend them, and he did not want to have to encounter Athene again too soon. However, when he read the contents his wide, thin, attractive mouth – it was another asset – curved upwards.

Money. He would risk going abroad for that, knowing what flight might entail for a wanted debtor. Provided the thing was done quickly and quietly it might serve: Harwich was less carefully watched than Dover. On the whole, the old girl's suggestion of Holland was not a bad idea; but he would use it as a base, not a centre. He would of course take the occasional trip to Paris, not for the reasons most men went there, but then Henry Laverton was not altogether as most men. Better still, there was a mountain resort named Baden-Baden, known to the informed few since Prinny's day, which would entail a somewhat longer journey, but was worth it; he might recoup his losses there. Altogether – and he looked at the grimy window, then the dreary room, remembering meals of tough neck of mutton and cabbage, no company, not that he always needed it: nowhere to go lest they spot him outside – altogether, he almost looked forward to the inn at Harwich. He was even grateful about the emeralds; that stone was notorious for deceptive imitations, but Athene Crowbetter's would be real. Good old Athene; good old girl. He would try to give her something not too solid to remember him by, before they parted meantime on the flat eastward shore.

Athene was happy. Henry had written her a most affectionate letter, almost loving; he was, of course, more reserved than she in such ways. He had named the inn, and the time that he would be there, about four hours before the Dutch packet sailed; they would meet for a little meal, and perhaps – but one must not anticipate.

She told her story about going to stay with Sarah, and nobody appeared to disbelieve her; there was after all no reason why they should. She had Temple pack her things, but Temple must not accompany her; this journey was to be conducted in order to smuggle Henry out of the country, a proceeding which must take place before the minimum of informed witnesses. Also, she would go by train. How Henry would travel to Harwich Athene had not enquired. It was safer to leave him to his own experienced devices.

Trains were dirty, and Athene was concerned about the fate of the special gown she had put on to greet Henry on arrival. She also disliked, in a first-class carriage, the presence of a man with a cigar. He was otherwise inoffensive, but she wished that there had been a Ladies Only compartment on the train; but a search had revealed none. Athene disliked the smell of tobacco, and the brown colour it left on everything, including one's clothes; thankfully, Henry did not smoke. She addressed the spread newspaper behind which the man sheltered and said, politely,

'Do you very much mind putting out your cigar? I find the air a trifle oppressive.'

A pair of pale-blue eyes, much the colour of her own, looked out above the lowered newspaper behind the perniciously ascending column of noxious vapour. The man said nothing, but wound down the window and threw his cigar out. 'Thank you so much,' said Athene. 'That was most civil of you.'

He still said nothing. He seemed a silent person. At first, when she had seen the eyes, she had had a moment's wild hope that it might be Henry in disguise, travelling to Harwich. But if so why should he hide himself from her? A cigar, though, would be one way of eluding his pursuers. He would never be suspected of smoking one.

She found the inn at once, for it abutted above the sea on to the jetty, its sign swinging cheerfully in the early spring wind. Athene walked in almost jauntily; she had achieved the journey, and nobody had stolen the emeralds! That man in the carriage had caused her some alarm when he had first come in, leaving the two of them alone, locked together, as it were; anything could have happened. But he had been perfectly polite, in particular about the cigar, and in any case the emeralds were in as impregnable a place as possible, stuffed well down Athene's front, inside her corsets. They had pricked a little on the journey, so that she could make sure, when she moved, that they were still there. She pictured them with affection if not love; the twin bracelets, the drop earrings edged with diamonds – those were truly beautiful – the necklace, rich with gleaming stones, and a brooch. It was perhaps a mercy there was no tiara.

Henry was waiting in the tap-room, and rose to greet her. He looked a trifle shabby, poor darling; but she had brought money as well.

Henry had, though Athene would not yet know it, downed several brandies to fortify himself, but brandy took some time to affect Major Laverton. He bowed over his wife's hand most politely, repressing his distaste at her clothes. She was wearing, in his honour, a new black-and-white plaid dress of the kind the Princess Royal had made fashionable on her honeymoon a couple of years or so ago, with a narrow

crinoline skirt – thank heaven, he was thinking, the wide ones
went out when they presented difficulties in doorways and
other places – and the unaltering pork-pie hat. It was a
conspicuous outfit, Athene was a conspicuous woman, and he
himself had wanted to remain inconspicuous. As it was,
everybody in the tap-room was staring.

'We'll have a little drink, and then go upstairs,' he said. 'I've
ordered a tray sent up. Brandy, eh?'

'Oh, Henry, I have never drunk any. I do not think – a
small glass of madeira, perhaps, after the train.' She lowered
her voice. 'How did you come?'

He smiled. 'On a horse, m'dear. I was in a cavalry regiment,
after all.' He raised two fingers to the landlord, who appeared
presently with a pair of identical glasses filled with liquid of a
dark gold colour. When Athene sipped hers, it was not
madeira after all. Dear Henry had absent-mindedly ordered
brandy for them both; so like a man!

But she did not like it much, and reverted to low-voiced
talk. 'Do you think it is altogether safe, dear, to mention the
past quite so openly? But I am glad you got here safely – on
the horse.' She smiled, and sipped a little more brandy. There
was no doubt that it warmed one.

'Not difficult, not at all. After trekkin' ponies in the Hindu
Kush a man can ride anything.'

He stared at her, not altogether with approval, and Athene
refrained from assigning, in her mind, anything coarse to the
allusion. They finished their brandy. 'Another?' said Henry.

'No, no, I have had more than enough. I really feel quite –'

The landlord had come over. 'Supper's ready, sir. It'll be
sent up the minute you say. It's chicken, sir; a good spring
chicken, and they've given you the room with the Maryland
quilt.'

Athene was intrigued. 'The Maryland quilt?' That must be
from the United States of America. After all, a port, with
ships sailing in, would have a great many sailors coming here
with custom.

That proved to have been the case. 'A ship's captain
couldn't pay his shot, and left the quilt – his missus had made
it, evidently – in exchange,' said the man, who appeared most
willing to talk. Athene nodded wisely; she knew by now what a
shot meant. 'But we're not –' she began. Henry dug her in the
side with his elbow, and she fell silent.

They went up. There was a large bed, with the quilt spread on top; it was worn by now, but had many interesting colourful patches all sewn together. Athene would have liked to examine it more closely, but she found that she could not see quite so clearly as usual. Also, the supper tray was immediately brought up, and she found it necessary moreover to go behind the screen. When she emerged, having rinsed her hands afterwards at the ewer, she was able to eat a few mouthfuls of the spring chicken and to drink a glass of wine.

Laverton set aside the tray presently. 'It's hot in here,' he said, 'and the packet doesn't leave till four.' There was a fire burning in the grate, properly for the season; all told, it was a very good inn. Laverton went to the casement windows, and flung them open. The March wind whistled in, bellying the curtains and bringing its North Sea cold in a gust.

'I think, dear –' Athene began. She had appreciated the warmth; but dear Henry, after all, was used by now to that chilly place at Poplar, not to mention the Hindu Kush. She remembered, in her childhood, hearing of the wartime campaigns there, in the snow.

Henry said nothing. He came over and began to undress her. The gown came off; her petticoat slipped to the polished boards; then his fingers, his white and beautiful fingers, delicately unlaced her corsets. As he did so, the emeralds rattled incontinent to the floor. Henry gave a laugh – he laughed very rarely – went down on his knees, and scooped up the gleaming treasure with his hands.

'Good old Athene,' he said. 'Good ol' girl.'

She somewhat resented being called an old girl; after all, Henry was older than she. Should she perhaps call him old boy, as a joke? But that was a term used by gentlemen among themselves, in a certain mood; best not risk it.

She began to giggle. Henry finished stripping her, laid her meantime on the Maryland quilt, and set the emeralds down carefully by themselves in a pile on the table, thereafter bundling up Athene's clothes. He then went to the window and threw them out. He turned round and leered.

'Tide's comin' in,' he said. 'Better without 'em.' He eyed her consideringly, still without enthusiasm.

Athene was aghast. 'Henry! All my clothes! What shall I do?' For a moment the fumes of unaccustomed brandy cleared, and she saw her predicament unvarnished and plain;

then the fumes closed in again. Henry said nothing. He was undressing, with efficiency and speed. He laid his own clothes neatly over a chair, military fashion.

A small naked satyr then leaped upon Athene. She had never seen, much less imagined, Henry like this. As on the wedding night, she closed her eyes; but what was happening now was not in the least like the wedding night. It was heady, furious, glorious. She had never known anything like it in the whole of her life. Presently he would – oh, oh, oh, oh, *oh* –

Henry continued. Chaucer would certainly have eulogised him. Brandy was splendid stuff, although in the regiment he had never – but Athene, rapt and transported, had finally raised her mature body in ecstasy's arc. The ultimate in bliss was almost hers; almost. At that same moment, there came a thundering on the door.

'Damn them,' said Henry aloud. He did not stop; for the moment, he could not. The door was not locked and a policeman walked in. In all of his life the officer had never seen such a sight; he would remember it to his dying day, which luckily was fairly far off. A large pink naked woman lay on the bed, with a small naked man bouncing up and down on top of her, like a pea on a drum. This was the man he had come to arrest, and delay was not, in his profession, called for.

'You are Major Henry Laverton?' Henry turned his head; he had almost let everything go with shock; damn the fellow. 'I am. Who are you?' he said thickly. He withdrew from Athene.

'It don't matter who I am, sir, but it matters who *you* are. I have to arrest you as a debtor in the act of absconding, sir. I have to warn you ...' He completed the sentence, adding: 'You will please to come with me, sir, as soon as it's convenient.' The last part he had added because he was a considerate man, with a wife and children at home.

Henry was finally taken away, once more clad. The emeralds were taken as well. Athene had cried out that they belonged to her, but was told, respectfully, that she would have to prove ownership in the event. The money had gone. Her clothes were in the sea. She had been seen naked by a policeman. She was left alone, with the Maryland quilt at last clawed round her, howling like an animal with outrage, deprivation, cold, and grief. For the first time in her whole self-sufficient life she simply did not know what to do. This could not possibly have happened.

It was, of course, Nicholas Crowbetter who had caused it to do so. He had paid the man with the cigar to follow her and, if necessary, to go to the police.

The landlord, whose name was Joe, was in a quandary. He had, as was natural, gone up to the room as soon as the policeman had departed with his erstwhile customer, to make sure everything was all right; and it was not. The lady – she was undoubtedly a lady, or at any rate had been one once – stood with the Maryland quilt, for which Joe had some affection, wrapped around her naked form, no clothes in sight, evidently no money, and crying with a dreary wailing noise coming from her open mouth, which dribbled saliva out of one corner. Joe was sorry for her, but had a clear remembrance, having served before the mast for a portion of his youth, of orders from the bridge that a sailing ship in fog on the starboard tack must make one blast every two minutes, on the port tack two, and three in succession when the wind is abaft the beam. This wail or, rather, hooting note was on the other hand continuous and constant: he had never heard anything quite like it. The combination was too much for him one way and another, so he turned without more words and went downstairs to find his wife, who was peeling potatoes in the inn kitchen.

'Gawd, Maria, go upstairs to that poor bitch in first front right,' he said. 'Her man's been taken away by the peelers and she ain't got a penny nor no clothes, and can't hear a word for hollerin' and cryin' her bleedin' eyes out. Can't seem to say nothin' for herself either. Maybe she'll be better with you. I'll finish them spuds if you was to go up.' And he had begun to roll up his sleeves to do so, but Maria, without a word, had already dried her hands on her apron and gone. No clothes, indeed!

'I am sorry, madam, but you cannot stay here. This is a respectable house. You must leave at once.' The landlord's wife resisted an urge to snatch the valued quilt away from its present mishandling, but the last state would, in that event, be worse than the first. At the latter, emphatic word Athene realised her own predicament with renewed and fearful clarity. She could neither leave here as she was – she would certainly be arrested at once, like poor dear Henry, and the prospect of joining him in a cell at Harwich police station was hardly consoling, as matters stood – nor stay, because she could not pay the bill. She began to babble some explanation, but even to her own ears it sounded extremely lame. As for her eyes, from which the tears had begun to stop flowing, she could see the expression on the woman's face quite clearly, in fact much too clearly. Persons of a certain profession – the word prostitute would never be allowed to find a resting-place in Athene's conscious mind, let alone pass her lips – must be, no doubt, accustomed to being looked at in this way. She had never expected to have to endure such an experience; never in her life.

Still contriving to remain within the protection of the quilt, Athene drew herself up; a measure of spirit had returned after the late reflection. She looked Maria in the eye. 'You will kindly telegraph,' she said clearly, 'to my sister, Lady Witham, at Atherton Castle, to say that I am in great distress here – make the direction certain, if you please – and to come to my assistance immediately. My name, for your purposes, is Athene. Do this at once.'

'Who's to pay for all of it?' demanded Maria, with a trifle of increased deference nevertheless. Atherton Castle she had at least heard of; she didn't know about any Lady Witham, but if this person said a lady was her sister, something might come of it, only one had to be careful. She said she would ask Joe.

'Please do not delay; my sister will pay for all of it, and for anything else that is required,' said Athene desperately. Notwithstanding Sarah's last letter, she felt renewed confidence return, by some miracle, being as she was, and Henry – ah, where was he now? Athene began to howl again suddenly, and the tears flowed once more. 'I must, of course, stay here for the present, until help comes,' she said with difficulty, and wiped her face with the back of her hand; there was not even a handkerchief. A kind of prudence made her keep on the quilt, even after Maria, with a dark glance at it, had gone; it was as well, because just beyond the harbour lay the ship on which Henry should have sailed, still at anchor, her sails unfurled. Possibly, lascivious sailors could look through the window into this room. Athene decided to go and lie down again on the bed, finding herself trembling with cold and shock. Before that, the remnants of sense made her shut the casement dear Henry had so incontinently flung

open, as the wind still howled continuously through it. She
caught sight of a pink object floating out on the tide; her
corsets! It was as if all protection had gone with them. Uncle
Nicholas must never, never know.

Meantime, Henry's ship sailed away to the Hook of Holland
at last, her sails unfurled on a changing wind. Henry himself
sat in a police cell drinking a mug of hot tea, which was most
welcome.

The telegram, which had only been sent off at all after much
cautious consultation between Maria and Joe, finally arrived
at Atherton Castle while the family were at luncheon. It was
brought in by a footman with a tray, and he went straight to
the Earl, who was eating saddle of mutton, with some
difficulty owing to the endemic looseness of his false teeth.
     'My lord, as this was urgent, I took the liberty of bringing it
in.'
     'Good fellow, good fellow,' mumbled my lord, and tore the
envelope open. He held it away from him a little, passed it to
his wife by way of Witham, who sat at one side of the
unfashionable oak refectory table, and said through his
mastications that he didn't know what it was all about, but
Honoria had best deal with it and, if necessary, send a reply.
     The Countess perused it, raised her head, glared at Sarah,
and said: 'There need be no reply. Your sister is in some
difficulty, apparently, in an inn at Harwich. I suppose that we
must all three set out to go straight there after luncheon, as
the matter is –' She remembered the presence of the
footman, and turned to where he stood, carefully expres-
sionless as footmen are, and said: 'Pray order the carriage,
Holden; and you had best prepare yourself to accompany us.'
The man acted also as driver and, occasionally when the old
stableman was drunk, as coachman and groom. He was young
and strong, and would be useful in an emergency.
     As soon as he had gone out of the room Sarah said: 'I will
not go to Athene. I shall stay here,' and went on eating her
mutton. Honoria's dead glance, which had come to life in any
case on reading the telegram, fixed itself upon her
incredulously.
     'That is most uncharitable of you. I think that you should
accompany us. She is, after all, your relative, not ours. I do

not know exactly what is the matter; you would be in a position to elicit it from her. She sounds as though she were in some distress.'

Sarah muttered that she did not care how much distress Athene was in, it served her right; and Witham suddenly announced that he could not come either, as he was sickening for a cold. At this, the Countess forgot about the telegram and its contents and rounded on her son.

'You ought to have told me sooner. You should be in bed, with some hot lemon and a very little whisky. Go there at once; I will have the remainder of your meal sent in to you.' He had, she was convinced, a weak chest, and in any case the rest of them might well catch his cold, particularly in a closed carriage. She felt agitation rise, two courses of action at once being somehow forced upon her; she ought to stay and nurse Witham, yet she could hardly ignore the plight of Athene Crowbetter if Sarah's own half-sister – a further venemous glance was shot at her daughter-in-law, and Honoria reflected that with one thing and another, Sarah would long ago have received a sound whipping had she not been a married woman – were in such nameless difficulties as had somehow been hinted at in the telegram.

Witham lumbered off to bed, and Honoria thought of a solution. She said to Sarah: 'As you refuse to come' – it was useless, she had by now found, to force the girl to act if she did not choose to, except in a certain matter which was still insisted upon, though so far without results – 'as you will not, and it is most unkind of you, I will take your maid in any case; she seems sensible, and may help the poor creature.' She had in fact been creditably surprised by the way Betty had transformed herself, in a relatively short period of time, into a passable lady's maid.

Sarah shrugged, they all finished their mutton, ate the pudding, and Honoria rose to prepare herself for the journey, having first put her head round the door of Witham's bedroom to make sure he was comfortably in bed, to tell him on no account to leave it till he was fully recovered, and to promise to be back as fast as their somewhat antiquated carriage wheels could carry her. She then hurried off to put on her outdoor things, having looked briefly into the dining-room to make sure that Sarah had gone to instruct Betty; evidently she had, as she was no longer seated at the table. The Earl had his dental plate in his hand and was still picking shreds of recalcitrant mutton from between the porcelain teeth; he did not look up, nor did husband and wife say more than a curt farewell. They dealt together very little nowadays.

Sarah had gone meantime to Betty, who was overcome with awe. 'Lor', miss – m'lady, I should say – I won't be able to think of a word to say to her.'

'Nonsense, you know Miss Athene quite well from Hyde Park Gardens. Put on your warm coat; it is cold.' Sarah might not have much affection for most people, but she had a good deal by now for Betty; they were less like maid and mistress than two young friends, always allowing for those social differences whose absence would have embarrassed Betty far more than Sarah had they been dropped.

'I didn't mean Miss Athene, m'lady. I meant her ladyship. All that way, and in a carriage and nobody else with us. I wish you was coming.'

'Well, I am not. You will not need to say a word in any case; she will do all the talking needed. Look out of the window and enjoy the journey; it is quite long, I forget how many miles, but I shall not expect you back till late. Go straight to bed; I can do my own undressing.' She would go, she thought, for a walk.

The journey to Harwich proved entirely uneventful, and Betty did as she was bid and sat quietly looking out of the window at the flat rolling land; the country was dull after London, but she wouldn't go back and leave Miss Sarah – her young ladyship, that was – for anything. It was terrible what she had to put up with, and him coming in with the old woman and – well, you knew what happened quite well, although next door if not quite yet upstairs yourself. Her mistress had got used to it, Betty supposed. Otherwise she would probably have run away by now, he was so awful, and the old woman too.

Honoria said nothing; one did not talk to servants. She had brought enough money with her to deal with whatever emergency might have arisen; presumably it would be needed. Honoria passed the time in reflecting, almost amiably, on the recent returns from the investment of the Atherton coalfields in Crowbetter's Bank; they almost compensated for the existence of Sarah, who had proved herself to be a much inferior speculation. If nothing happened soon she, Honoria Atherton, would insist that the young woman be submitted to some form of medical examination. There must be something wrong with her.

Meantime, they came in sight of the sea, then the port, then the inn; today there was no wind and the sign hung dolefully. Honoria marched in, with Betty behind her, and demanded of Joe, who was at the counter, where the suffering Miss Crowbetter was to be found, as she had come to remove her and pay the bill. The man's face expressed relief.

'Gawd, I'm not 'arf glad to see yer, madam, and so will my wife be,' he said. A Miss Crowbetter, was it? He might have known she wasn't a Mrs, with the goings on there had been; they often wore wedding rings. This one who had come was an old trout, but obviously a lady; she was wearing a fur pelisse with a rope of pearls under it which Joe, who in his sailing days had reached the South Seas, instantly recognised as being quite something. He came out from behind the counter. 'What name shall I say, madam?' he asked, having lacked time, in the course of daily and evening custom, to reflect that a lady in pearls from Atherton Castle would probably boast some sort of title. Honoria left him in no doubt; beneath the pearls, her bosom swelled.

'I am the Countess of Atherton,' she said. 'Take me to this afflicted person at once.'

The encounter with Athene provided nothing unexpected from the reader's point of view. Betty concealed her giggles at the never-to-be-forgotten sight of old Miss Athene in her birthday suit, more or less, except for a quilt which by now was beginning to show signs of wear and tear. Honoria asked a few questions, paid the bill including that for Henry Laverton's previously imbibed brandies, and came to the conclusion that, in spite of everything, there was no hope of getting back to Atherton that night. They would have, in common mercy, to buy Athene some clothes; and by the time the shops shut, if indeed they were not shut already – one must hurry, the woman's weepings and wailings had taken up a great deal of valuable time – and one had had a meal, of which one was beginning to be in some need, and other things, they would have to stay the night. She had not brought night attire, and objected to the thought of Betty on a pallet at the foot of the bed aware that she, Honoria

Atherton, was sleeping in it in her chemise, so she arranged
that Betty should sleep with Athene, who would then be
suitably covered, as one hoped, and after breakfast tomorrow
they would all three return to the castle with all debts cleared
– one would of course recoup the expenditure from Nicholas
Crowbetter and he could investigate the whole business
further if he wished to do so – and the unfortunate woman,
who was after all a relation by marriage, could be nursed
there for a few days before being returned, like a sack of
damp straw, to London.

All this would take place, as most things intended to
happen by Honoria Atherton did, and in the meantime she
was able, by inconveniencing herself a little with haste, to find
a very inferior set of garments in a shop in a back street which
had not yet closed its shutters and whose owner, foreseeing a
good sale, refrained from putting them up until the lady, who
was evidently well heeled, had chosen what she wanted. Poor
Athene would have shuddered at the rough and poor quality
of the purchased garments at any other time, but she put
them on, with Betty's help, humbly and thankfully. It seemed
a very long time indeed since she had worn clothes at all. A
quilt –

Meantime, events had been moving at Atherton.

Sarah had gone for a long walk, inasmuch as it could be done
at all; she walked three times round the estate, looked at the
boggy land beyond the fence, reflected that something ought
to be done about it as it was not only dangerous but dull, and
returned to the house. The evening was coming down, and by
rights she ought to dress for dinner; but with her
mother-in-law away, no Betty to dress her hair, and Witham
in bed with his cold, she would be left in the sole company of
the Earl. It was not that Sarah disliked Lord Atherton; on the
contrary, she found him in some inconclusive way the sole
sympathetic member of the household. But he maintained
long silences, out of which he would at times come with
remarks conditioned by his Regency past such as 'When are
you goin' to get that filly in foal?' to his son, the filly being of
course herself. Afterwards he would relapse into the silence
from whence he had come. Sarah decided that she would
send a message to the cook to send her up a tray to her room,
saying that she felt unwell and would not come down to

dinner, and sent her polite excuses to Lord Atherton. Probably they would think she had caught Witham's cold.

She settled down with a book beside the lamp till it was time to go to bed, then undressed herself and brushed out her own hair. The book had been borrowed from the library, which was also the Earl's study, and when he was not in it, or else asleep, Sarah would go in there and muse without any great interest round the leather-smelling shelves. She was not by nature bookish, and had there been any other diversion reading would have bored her; but one had to pass the time in some way.

She yawned, used her chamber-pot briefly, and was about to get into bed, when the door opened and Witham came in, shutting it behind him. He wore an air of determination foreign to him, and his dressing-gown.

'What do you want?' asked Sarah unnecessarily. She loathed him by now; the state to which she had been brought by Honoria humiliated her, and she associated Witham in her mind with his mother, who had never once been absent in their prescribed weekly encounters till now. Now, because the Countess was away –

'Go back to your room,' she said firmly. 'You have a cold. I don't want to catch it. I don't want you here at all. Go away.'

But he did not go away, and suddenly the indignity of the whole business, her dreary life, the unspeakable people here, the loss of Hugo, everything, was too much for Sarah, ninth Viscountess Witham of Atherton. She bent, seized the chamber-pot, and hurled it straight at her spouse's head. Witham ducked, to her surprise – she had not supposed he could think or move so fast – and the pot hit the panelled door with a loud crash, shattering in pieces and leaving ungenteel dribbles down the doubtful Grinling Gibbons woodwork.

'I haven't got a cold,' said Witham. 'I thought –'

'You don't know how to begin to think. I loathe you. Go away. Go *away*.'

Sarah began to scream. She fought him off with her fists, or tried to, as he approached more closely; but his chest was like oak, and took no harm from the blows. She would have bitten him, but he was sweaty and the thought revolted her. At that moment the door opened and the Earl stood there, ready to go to bed, with his teeth out.

'What the hellfire's goin' on?' he demanded. 'Heard a

crash; thought the ceilin' was fallin' down. Might well happen by now.' He grinned, showing bare gums, then added: 'What're the pair of you about? Needn't ask, I dare say; get into bed, and get on with it. Thought you had a cold, Witham; don't give it to her; should've taken snuff first, shoved it up y' nose both sides. What're you hollerin' about, girl? Used to it by now, aren't yer? Ought to be; I hear everythin' through the walls, they ain't thick. Nor am I deaf, I can tell yer; gettin' on in other ways, maybe. I'd be glad of an heir; get on with it, I say. Go on, Witham; get her in calf while there's the chance. I know what goes on.'

He turned down the sheet, stood glaring at Sarah, who stopped screaming and climbed almost meekly into bed; there was, after all, nothing else she could do. The Earl gave a mild conciliatory growl and went out, shutting the door after him.

What followed should have given them both pleasure, but Sarah, long consumed by loathing and aversion, turned her head aside and endured passively what she had endured so often before, no longer caring whether her mother-in-law were present or absent. She even passed a few moments of the time in wondering idly how they were faring at Harwich; surely they would soon be back? When the Countess found Witham missing from his bed, she would come up here and take him away. That would be a good thing. Pretending he had a cold! In anyone else, it would have been a sign of intelligence. But Witham was an animal. One had only to listen to him now.

The animal proceeded to carry out his functions, however, as animals will, given freedom. Witham had never before experienced such strange joy and power; these, fulfilment at last, the entire pleasure of doing as he liked, for as long as he liked, with his own woman, were his, for the first and only time in his life. When, by the end, all having been accomplished, he started all over again, Sarah would, if she could, have closed her womb. As things were it was forced, by the processes with which Nature had endowed it, to receive, in the end, the long-garnered seed of the Withams, who had after all fought at Bosworth. When he had gone, she felt herself battered and outraged, but in some way different.

Witham went back to his room down the passage almost jauntily. If this was sin, he wouldn't mind committing it rather more often. Soon, however, his mother would be home, and the less said the better. He never said very much in any case.

The Countess, followed by Betty and assisted by the young footman, conveyed Athene at last out of the carriage into Atherton Castle. In common courtesy Sarah put in an appearance to greet the arrival, and was somewhat chastened to observe the difference in her half-sister's appearance. It was not so much the poor creature's clothes, which had always been dreadful, as her face and manner. The first was swollen with crying, the second had grown humble. The days of Hyde Park Gardens and Hugo's purloined letter were long, long ago. After a perfunctory kiss on the cheek Athene was led upstairs to bed, where she remained for a fortnight. At first Sarah visited her daily; after four days, she slept with her.

The reason was Athene's audible habit of nightmares. She had never had them before, having snored her way comfortably through undisturbed young womanhood. They no doubt stemmed from her recent experiences, which sounded unusually dire; and from the constant waking anguish at the thought of Henry in prison, Henry hauled up before the magistrates with a fuller trial pending and an unspecified sentence to endure; Henry badly fed, cold, deserted, abandoned by all his erstwhile friends except herself, his wife. Being dreams, however, grotesque variations and appearances occurred which were, on the face of it, nothing to do with Henry at all. Athene would cry out loudly in the small hours, waking the household but not, of course, herself. When she was awake she would cry quietly or else eat her food, which was a good sign; the plates, as Honoria remarked at once, were brought down again quite empty. Now and then there were attacks by day of sobbing and howling such as had disturbed Joe at the inn, but that affected a strong-minded community not at all. The nightmares did. Something would have to be done to prevent them, and although the Countess had no intention of letting Mrs Henry Laverton remain as a permanent inmate of Atherton, Athene was not yet in a state for common humanity – and even Honoria possessed a little – to return her to Hyde Park Gardens. Nevertheless the Countess, and the Earl, strongly objected to being wakened up in the small hours of the morning.

Sarah solved the problem in her laconic fashion. 'I shall sleep with her,' she said, 'then I can wake her up when she starts to yell.'

'That would not be at all convenient,' replied Honoria coldly. 'One of the maids may do so, if it is beneficial.' She had, as it happened, small experience in such matters; Witham's complexes had grown too deep for dreams.

'Let the gal do as she wants,' said the Earl unexpectedly. 'None of your business, Honoria.' He returned calmly to his breakfast porridge, well aware of the shattering effect his speech had had on his spouse; he could quell her on the rare occasions when he chose to do so. Besides, the gal was lookin' washed out; it was hopeful.

So Sarah moved at nights into Athene's bed, and although they would never be close to one another in either body or soul, the arrangement seemed to work very well. Sarah would shake her sister awake when she started to scream, or else slap Athene's face; then go to sleep again herself with the ease of the young. The suggestion had in any case been timely, because she had avoided Witham's last weekly visit with his mother by saying her courses were come upon her, like Rachel in the Bible, which made her unclean in the eyes of the elect. It was a lie, as they had not come, although by now they should have. However even Honoria could hardly bring Witham to her in Athene's very room, and Sarah found herself with the prospect of some freedom as long as Athene stayed. It compensated for the latter's snoring; Sarah was relieved, and fell asleep again easily.

At last, after the fortnight had elapsed, Athene was able to come shakily down to breakfast. As the days passed she grew more confident, and even ventured to make a little bright conversation, which both Earl and Countess resented so early in the day. Honoria began to examine more closely the prospect of her guest's early return to London. She mentioned it one morning, putting it as tactfully as her nature allowed; but it had the unforeseen effect of sending Athene into strong hysterics.

'Not back to Uncle Nicholas! Never! Never!'

Sarah, in silence, walked over and slapped her face, which had the usual effect in such instances. Then she went back to her own place, sat down, picked at the plateful of kedgeree which was generally a favourite of hers, turned suddenly, and was sick down the back of the Hepplewhite chair. They did not take breakfast in the dining-room.

Lord Atherton was jubilant; Honoria was satisfied in her conscience. She sternly forbade Witham to go near his wife now, later, or probably at all; she had her suspicions about what had happened while she was away. She reminded her son of the sin of concupiscence, which like many mistaken persons she imagined to have been the original sin of our first parents, thereafter denying them Eden: and impressed Witham so heavily with the grave nature of his propensities that he sat in gloom for a very long time indeed and hardly looked at Sarah when she happened to be present in the same room. This suited her very well, and as time passed, and she was no longer visited, she ceased to connect this train of events with the other which was taking place smoothly and predictably, inside her body, as she knew nothing whatever about pregnancy or childbirth. When she began to thicken, and later still to bulge, she summoned up courage to ask Honoria what could be the matter with her. 'You are in a certain condition,' was the only reply. Sarah went away bewildered, thinking she must be the victim of some fell disease, such as dropsy; but when the child began to kick inside her she arrived at some glimpse of the truth, and regarded it with a measure of vague benevolence; after all people did have babies.

By then, Athene had been sent with firm courtesy back to Hyde Park Gardens, and once there frantically ordered – it was at least a slight diversion – new clothes, new corsets, and a large quantity of writing-paper. She then wrote to lawyers, to influential persons of all kinds, but chiefly to Henry, who was by now in a cell by himself in Millbank Penitentiary. He did not reply, and Athene was uncertain whether or not she was permitted to visit him; she was too timid to ask Uncle Nicholas, who had preserved his usual silence about the whole matter, had asked no questions, and went out a great deal to his club.

4

Felix von Reichmansthal was back in Vienna. He had enjoyed Italy, and had imbibed infinitely more than Nick had done of the great art, beauty, and pervasive history to be found there. He had in fact lingered behind by himself when Nick went back to England. The legitimate son of Nicholas Crowbetter would have made a passable country squire, like his Uncle George; but travel had not increased his knowledge and he had stared, as his mother Jane would have done, with prominent pale-blue eyes at everything while saying nothing, and thinking less. He was evidently deaf to music, blind to beauty and ignorant of history. Felix was receptive to all three.

As regarded knowledge, Felix had no recollection of his mother till their initial Viennese visit, though all through his boyhood he had written to her dutifully once a week, sometimes receiving elegantly scrawled replies on pale-grey paper. Duty itself had been inculcated by Harriet Milsom at first, then by his masters at school; Felix was not by nature dutiful. When he had seen his mother at last, he had been amazed at her beauty; had drunk in every word she said, and had followed her advice about being careful in Italy about pretty girls; in round language, astonishing from so fairylike a creature, she had warned him about the dangers of the pox. This was in fact less prevalent in Italy than in Court circles in Vienna, but the warning was heeded. As Nicholas Crowbetter, who had never caught it, had admonished him about the same thing before he left England, Felix returned to Vienna still a virgin.

He was an extremely handsome young man. The honey-coloured hair of his childhood had darkened a trifle with the use of pomade; he could boast, which he never did, of a figure like a young god; and his golden eyes were striking

146

and reflective, though what he was reflecting upon was not always evident. He had interesting dreams. He was nineteen years old, and had never been short of money or, as yet, failed to achieve a single one of his desires.

Meeting his mother again, he continued to be amazed; she was not only beautiful, but wise and delicious in every possible way. Mélanie had not withered over the years, perhaps having put on a thought more flesh; Viennese food is rich. Felix could not imagine why she had married the Baron, who though kindly was boring and bald. No doubt Mama had succumbed to a sense of family duty and, also, had kept the name of von Reichmansthal for the sake of Wenzel and himself. Felix did not see much of Wenzel, who was occupied in some unspecified duty at the Hofburg and would shortly go to Bohemia, where a marriage had been arranged for him. Meantime, the Baron had been kind to Nick and Felix the first time, and had taken them to visit Schönbrunn and the riding-school, also to the Hof ball in the Rittersaal, with bored archdukes presiding at separate tables, and where the harassed and dutiful Emperor had danced with a stout noblewoman while the beautiful and eccentric Empress was, as usual, absent. This time, Wenzel was no longer present; and the Baron demonstrated a great affection for Felix. 'You are the son I have never had,' he stated, and embraced the young man. Felix felt sorry for him. To see the golden, spired and alluring city again was a pleasure in itself; to find kind hearts there better still. His German had improved, and he could make himself at home with the Viennese most happily. They found him attractive, as befitted the son of his mother. As for the late Count, he was forgotten; and nobody in Vienna had set eyes on Nicholas Crowbetter.

Mélanie took her son about. One day they were strolling arm in arm down the Führengasse. It was a bright autumn day, and Mélanie wore her customary green in a lighter shade than usual, with a brimmed matching hat and its curled ostrich feather. She was proud to be seen on such a son's arm, her elegantly gloved hand laid lightly upon it. Felix was as attractive as she had dared to hope – in fact she had expended very little thought on him over the years in England – and, given his father and his mother, as much so as he ought to be. She had never, least of all since her dull and prudent remarriage to the Baron, forgotten Nicholas

Crowbetter in his early state of impassioned lovemaking in London long ago. In course of a series of notable, though discreet, affairs Mélanie had found few since to equal him.

Lovers, nonetheless, were growing thin on the ground, like the dry brown leaves, already fallen, which lay here and there about the pavements. Perhaps it was because she herself was growing older, and though she did not feel or, hopefully, look it, all the world knew it. Moreover the Baron, although appearing totally unaware of such situations, kept a close enough guard to ensure that they did not happen often. In fact they could only happen at all when he was away at his estate near Graz. Mélanie was weary of him, wanted a new lover, and gazed reflectively at the tall golden creature who escorted her. If Felix, with his looks and charm, had been any other young man, she would promptly have seduced him. As it was, his education was still deficient in such matters, though she herself, not having known him previously, could think of him as an interesting stranger. In any case it was her duty, as his mother, to see about it; she did not care to have a son of hers spoken of as either ignorant or uninstructed. She smiled to herself beneath the green hat's brim; she knew very well where she would send him.

The crowds had thickened, and to Felix's reflective eye appeared to be streaming towards the Hofburg. He turned beneath the shade of his tall buff-coloured hat, of which he was proud, and courteously asked his mother, with whom he was enchanted to be seen, what could be the cause. They would hardly stream to see the Emperor; that punctual monarch could frequently be stared at reviewing his guards, and his lighted window viewed daily from four in the morning, when Franz Josef was unerringly to be found at work.

'It may be the Empress,' said Mélanie. 'You will be fortunate to see her.' They made their way between the sober coats and stiff hats of Viennese businessmen and the frivolities worn by their wives, bowing now and then to acquaintances, until they came on a carriage with gilded spikes, waiting in the street. 'It is the Empress,' said Mélanie. 'The gilded spikes are royal. It may be some moments before she appears. Her maids take three hours to dress her hair each morning, and she has no sense of time.'

It was more than moments, but the crowd waited patiently, chatting and laughing in the carefree Viennese way, while a little autumn breeze arose; then there was a sudden hush. A most beautiful slender dark-haired woman had come out alone, followed by ladies-in-waiting at whom nobody glanced. Felix himself was aware of nothing but the amazed silence of the crowd and of the Empress's magical loveliness. The most beautiful woman in Europe, perhaps anywhere since Helen, wore her hair, which reached her feet when loose, wound in plaits numberless times round her tiny head, like a coronet. Her cheekbones were high, her eyes very slightly slanted, like Mélanie's. Their glance came to rest briefly on Felix, then passed on. Elisabeth looked at no one, and entered her carriage still unsmiling, followed by her women. As it drove off, the watching people let out a long, held breath. 'It happens every time they see her,' remarked Mélanie. 'They can never quite believe that it is true. It is not often that she is seen, as today. She dislikes Vienna, and particularly the Hofburg. Now that her children are old enough she will leave them, and travel. It is hard on the Emperor, who loves her to distraction.'

'Why does she dislike the most beautiful city in the world when she is the most beautiful woman in it?' Felix demanded, still rapt like the rest. Mélanie smiled with closed lips, took his arm, and led him away. It was gratifying to have heard him give rise to so poetic an utterance; but she went on to inform him, for his own good, that the Empress was not popular despite the expected daze of admiration. 'I saw her look at you,' she said. 'She is not without an interest in young men. One of my countrymen, a young Hungarian officer, is said to have been with her on her yacht in the Mediterranean, but nothing came of it; the Emperor had him arrested that same evening before dinner. They say he sees, knows, and hears everything. Do not give way to illusion too readily, my son. The Empress has very bad teeth, which is why she seldom smiles. A great many of her close relations in Bavaria are mad. Perhaps so is she.'

She revealed her own still perfect teeth in a smile of open triumph. Felix gazed at her rather sadly. He wished that she had not told him about the Empress's teeth; he had wanted to preserve an illusion. He had seen beautiful statues, beautiful paintings, even, at a distance, other beautiful women; but Elisabeth of Austria surpassed them all. It was like a ballad or a song, and now Mama had spoilt it, no doubt with the best of motives. He was cheered a little when Mélanie let him escort

her to an outdoor café, its little tables not too full at this time
of day, and they sat down together and ate ices flavoured with
whipped cream, walnuts and chocolate until it grew too cold
to sit out of doors. Felix was still a boy at heart.

Mélanie von Reichmansthal had once had a French maid
named Leopoldine Guyon, who had given excellent service.
One day she had come to her mistress and had said that she
regretted, but she must leave. 'It is *les varices*, Madame la
Baronne,' she explained. 'I would endure them, but it is the
standing.'

Mélanie had not considered, and did not now, the
inconvenience a servant might well suffer in process of
arranging her hair for her while she herself sat at her mirror
changing her mind, but swiftly thought that Guyon, who was
shrewd, like most of her nation, might after all be better off in
a sitting position: she was not decorative enough for a lying
one. Mélanie let the woman work out her notice, and
meantime became almost familiar with her; after all, maids
know a great deal about their employers by the time they
leave. Mélanie became increasingly aware of the Frenchwoman's abilities, particularly as concerned money matters. Her
family were beet farmers in Calvados, but she herself had
saved a little, and preferred Vienna.

Mélanie had already decided that there were no ways to
employ Guyon any longer in the house. The Baron, with
benevolent firmness, preferred to make his own arrangements; almost the only way in which he reminded his wife of
Nicholas Crowbetter. Mélanie then turned her thoughts to
the capital itself, with its vast potential for shrewd women.
Taking Guyon and her *varices* in the carriage, she began to
look at properties in and about Vienna. Having come on the
right one, the Frenchwoman made no comment except '*Ça va
bien*,' firming her lips in a satisfactory manner under her mild
moustache.

Accordingly, the select brothel flourished, with the Baron's
money unknowingly behind it and Madame Guyon, in a black
silk gown and widow's cap, seated downstairs at the desk.
Nobody connected her with the scandal of black magic and
witchcraft in the time of Louis XIV, from one of the
perpetrators of which she was collaterally descended. Once
each quarter, and now and again on other occasions as well,
Madame la Baronne would call in her carriage to go over the

accounts and share out the takings. It was possible to keep the Baron in a happy state of mind about his finances, with a little over. Mélanie would come at night, when the polite world was mostly at the opera, and with a veil over her face: but it was hardly necessary to trouble with that last, the house looked so innocuous, with piecrust decorations on its pink exterior and immaculately draped muslin curtains at its shining windows. There was a formidable *Portier* to open the white-painted door and discourage respectable persons from leaving their cards, or, of course, to deal with the police if they should come. They never did, so discreetly conducted was the establishment and so carefully chosen the girls. Mélanie took the principal hand in this herself, sending as a rule for little Viennese shopgirls or maids, preferably virgins, looking for situations, and after inspection telling them that they would be better paid, more comfortable, and much better dressed, if they applied for a place with kind Madame Guyon, who would tell them much more. Guyon did this in her own way, on the whole with success, though one or two of the girls proved a little unwilling at first, till they accustomed themselves. Champagne was a useful means of persuasion, and there were of course others.

There was a particularly pretty and obliging little inmate named Sophie, demand for whom was so steady that Madame would not permit that it be wholly supplied. She had been perfectly innocent when she came, and the appearance of innocence remained deliciously, without and within. She was a charming girl, and her customers as a rule brought flowers and chocolates which Madame would not permit Sophie to eat, as they spoiled one's teeth – hers, of course, were like little pearls – and figure. Sophie had rosy cheeks, a small plump body like a cherub except that cherubs do not have little provocative pink-tipped breasts on a smoothly whipped-cream base; she could listen, which is important for all girls as customers sometimes grow garrulous; and she had a large quantity of glorious curly blonde hair. In short, she would be more than suitable to educate the young son of Madame la Baronne, home from England.

Felix was sent round to the house by his mother on foot. He carried a bouquet of flowers and a letter. Mélanie had said that it was an introduction to a little friend of hers, and the flowers were for her too. Felix, feeling slightly foolish, as he could think of no reason why he had to pay a polite call at

such an hour, made his way to the house as directed, and
thought that it looked pretty, with all its lamps shining behind
the muslin curtains.

He thought that Sophie looked pretty also, but blushed.
She was lying on a bed which was upholstered with pink silk
curtains and a matching quilt, and was quite naked. He had of
course seen the carved angels in German churches and
thought at once that, with certain differences, she looked like
them: but one did not as a rule meet young ladies under such
circumstances. He stood there, unable to think of anything to
say. He would have presented his flowers, but Madame had
taken them away when he entered, after feeling his muscles
approvingly.

Sophie laughed, her large blue eyes dancing between their
lashes. 'You are silent,' she said. 'This is your first time, *bitte?*'

'I – I –' Felix's wits were not dull, and he had already
realised what he had been sent here to find out. Sophie
seemed to read his thoughts and to sense his slight unease;
she was very sympathetic; it was after all one of her assets.
Also, the young Count was handsome. It would be a pleasure
to instruct him, as his mother had requested. In such matters,
Madame took one into her full confidence.

'Do not let anything trouble you,' she told him. 'It is quite
easy. We will be happy together, *vielleicht?*'

'*Vielleicht,*' echoed Felix. He then gave way to pleasant
sensations of all kinds.

Nicholas Crowbetter was beginning to feel his years.
Although the full vigour of his manhood had not abated and
seemed unlikely to do so – he continued to visit Harriet every
evening, and even took her advice, which seemed sensible,
about what to do about Athene, Henry Laverton, who was still
in prison but would unfortunately soon emerge, young Nick,
and Jane, who was not at all well he was most chiefly
concerned about young Nick. As heir to the Crowbetter Bank
and fortune, which was by now phenomenal, Nick should
have been ready to take his place with dignity, and some show
of interest, at directors' meetings, even though it would not
yet be necessary, or indeed proper, for him to say a word.
However today, having drunk more brandy at the meeting
than he was used to, the Crowbetter heir was discovered to be
asleep, gently snoring, in the midst of an instructive and, one

might say, conclusive discussion on the advisability of buying shares in Van Diemen's Land while they were still cheap. The faces of the various magnates round the table expressed pity, not for Nick but for his father; and if there was one thing Nicholas the elder could not endure, it was pity; after all, it was foreign to himself.

He summoned Nick to his study when they returned home, and castigated the young man so strongly that the latter's pale-blue eyes filled with tears. He tried to explain that he did not like working in the bank; that his arithmetic was uncertain and had always been so at school; that he did not understand money except to pay the grocer, and that he would much rather do something else. He was unable, however, to express himself clearly in face of his terrible father, whose Pan-like gaze was filled with the cold anger Nick dreaded more than anything in the world and always had, though he had tried to behave with courage. If only he could tell Papa that what he really liked was the country, and hunting, and perhaps farming in a gentlemanly way! Possibly some of the last sentiment was expressed in some way Nicholas could perceive, because he suddenly said, in a voice which grated a little,

'All you are fit for is to maintain cows and pigs, with others to do your work for you. I believe –' But Nick's face had expressed such joy that it was the nearest to liveliness it had ever achieved, and his father, most unusually, stopped in mid-sentence with surprise. Crowbetter's mind immediately swooped on the possibilities; one could purchase a seemly estate in the Home Counties, whose value would rise with time – elsewhere was of no great interest in such ways – and Nick could go there, live in his own house, entertain his neighbours, and marry, suitably of course, to perpetuate the Crowbetter line. Very often a grandchild resembled its grandfather.

He put the proposition clearly, his words falling separately like icy drops of water.

'I will buy you a country estate, a house, with fields and a home farm, where you may please yourself and live as you choose, with one stipulation; you must marry.'

Nick had not been sure what a stipulation was, but he knew about marriage, not, it is true, directly, but from hearsay. He nodded eagerly, thinking not of the bride but of the cows. He liked cows, with their gentle liquid eyes, long lashes and slow, reassuring ways; one knew in advance what a cow would do. A smile of pleasure was still on his face when he went upstairs to change his coat, gratifying the housekeeper, who was not without heart, and who commented later on to the upper parlourmaid, with whom she was almost on equal terms, that poor Mr Nick had had a bit of luck at last, whatever it was.

Nicholas, left alone, was cogitating. The bride must be of good stock, probably plain, that would not matter. No beauty; would marry Nick, even with the money. Neither would any woman of wit, though it was necessary that she possess intelligence. He had no knowledge of his son's kind heart, only of his lack of quick thinking, his absolute indifference to such matters as absorbed Crowbetter himself, such as the stock market, the secret international workings of the bank, the personages from England and abroad who came, the prestige built up over the years by himself and his father. No, the bride would have to be, in short, somebody whom no one else would marry.

Athene was less unhappy than she had been, although she had spent two years in bitter deprivation and, when she had tried to visit Henry in prison, two unexpected difficulties had arisen. Jane, quite out of character, had said that Athene must on no account be allowed to go, as she would bring home fleas. It had been at luncheon, and Nicholas was not present, or he could have told her that Millbank, as everyone knew who read the papers – but of course only gentlemen did – was a model penitentiary in advance of its time and that the occupants had single cells, proper food and enlightened supervision, and were kept clean. As Athene had pictured – how often on her bed, in the lonely hours! – Henry chained to the wall, on filthy straw, among noisome inmates like a herd of verminous cattle, she was relieved. At least he would have his privacy, which, as even Athene realised, he cherished, though of course solitary confinement must be a burden to gregarious people. Things were changing: in a few months she would be thirty, would pay Henry's debt, and would set him free, to return to her arms.

However a letter came from Henry, the first, despite all Athene had written, that she had had; he must somehow have procured writing materials. At first it chilled her a trifle; he made it clear, while remaining courteous, that he had no wish for a visit from her, or anyone else, though he would be enchanted to see her when they could meet openly again; that he was not uncomfortable, in fact very well, and that a warder had come to offer to instruct him in a trade, but he had declined. Athene was very much relieved; it would be incredible to think of Henry at some kind of vulgar workbench, with a saw in his hand; he, an officer and a gentleman. He added that a Quaker lady had come and offered to instruct him in religion, but he had told her that he knew about it already.

Athene yearned to encounter someone who had actually seen Henry, had perhaps even touched him – well, not quite, perhaps, as things were; would one, or would one not, shake hands? – and with a rare gleam of intelligence she wrote to the prison authorities to ask for the direction of the lady who had visited Major Laverton, her husband, very lately. A reply came in due course giving the name and address; apparently the lady was named Tabitha Nunn and lived not far off, which surprised Athene, as it was in some way difficult to think of a prison visitor in the vicinity of Hyde Park Gardens. However, Uncle Nicholas assured her – he was, of course, informed of the purpose of her journey – that some Quakers had more money than he had. He sounded quite petulant.

The house was near enough for Athene to walk, and as it was a first call to someone who was not already an acquaintance she had dressed herself rather carefully, in cheerful colours. She could seldom resist them, although for a long time she had felt that she ought to be wearing, as it were, widow's weeds till Henry reappeared from durance. However, the sight of the emeralds, which had been returned to her after Henry's trial by the efforts of Nicholas on her behalf, cheered her a little, and although she did not actually wear them on this occasion she began to look at them rather oftener than she had formerly done, with the intention of putting them on when Henry was free. The prospect exalted her; not long now, not long!

The door, which was plain, was opened by a sober young woman in a grey gown and frilled linen cap. Athene naturally took her to be a servant, and addressed her as one; was Mrs Nunn at home? One assumed that the Quaker lady visitor was married; the governor had given no indication in his letter; a strange omission, but surely an unmarried woman would not have been permitted to visit Henry alone, not that –

'Tabitha is preparing for the meeting,' replied the young woman, with her eyes cast down. Although apparently suppressed, she spoke in an independent fashion, and that and her use of Mrs Nunn's Christian name made Athene assume that she must be one of the family; perhaps a niece. In that case they dressed her very plainly. 'A meeting of what, my dear?' Athene asked kindly. She had once been to a meet of hounds, with dear Papa; but this could hardly have any connection. No doubt other visitors were expected. 'I hope that it is not inconvenient for me to call,' she said clearly, as the girl had said nothing. Perhaps she was deaf, or a little lacking. She looked up for the first time out of impersonal grey eyes, and replied quietly that she would fetch Tabitha, if it was needed.

The same variety of being came presently down the stairs; a little older, dressed in the same dreary way, and wearing an identical cap. This must however be the person who had visited dear Henry, and Athene's heart thrilled with anticipation. She pulled off her expensive glove and held out her hand, introducing herself fully, but trying not to sound condescending: it was difficult to decide on these people's class. Perhaps they had made their money quickly, and were not yet accustomed to one's own level of living and manners.

She explained her errand, and to her disappointment Tabitha Nunn replied that she could not enter into details at present; would Athene Laverton – Athene blenched at the immediate use of her Christian name, so very familiar, when one had only just met! – care to return, or else – for the first time the worthy woman hesitated – come as a witness to the monthly meeting? She spoke in as few words as possible, as they all seemed to do, polite comment, even agreement, evoking no response. They were certainly most strange.

The meeting was taking place, or was about to do so, in an upstairs room where about twenty persons sat in rows. They were all dressed in subdued fashion. They were mostly women, but there were one or two men, who kept their hats on. Two children seated beside their mother had been taught to look at the floor. Athene decided that, after all, they must be servants. She prided herself on being broad-minded, and having sat down – nobody had shown her to a seat, it was really most unmannerly – she bridled slightly, and looking rather, in that grey assembly, like an Amazonian parrot, waited. Nothing happened, and nobody spoke. Perhaps they were silent out of respect. Athene decided that it was, after all, her duty to make a little polite conversation to start the ball rolling, as young people said nowadays. Servants were often afflicted with shyness if one happened to meet with them apart from the exercise of their duties.

'What a very fine day it has been,' she said clearly. 'The weather is quite remarkable for the time of year.'

Nobody answered, and Athene began to feel a trifle mortified. After all, Mrs Nunn – she would *not* call her Tabitha – could quite easily have taken the time to tell her something about Henry instead of, as she had after all done, coming up here immediately to sit in complete silence for what was beginning to seem a very long time indeed. She did not even, as would at least have been civil, look up. Nobody did. These people had no manners at all. Their employer, who must be eccentric, should speak to them. Athene waited for a little while longer, then rose.

'Thank you very much for your hospitality,' she said politely to her hostess, if that was what one called Mrs Nunn. 'I find that I cannot wait after all; I have a pressing engagement. If you should visit my dear husband again, give him my love.' That, at least, was genuine.

Athene turned and showed herself out, downstairs, and into the street. Those had been the most extraordinary people she had ever met. She must tell it all to Jane, who was still not well. There was at least – she tittered slightly, in a kind of release – no danger of fleas from the prison; they had looked clean enough, even the men. She would write to the prison governor explaining how very peculiar they had seemed; Henry would hardly appreciate being visited by such persons. She herself had never been through such an experience in her life, which after all had had its varied side, when one thought of it. Ah, Henry!

Nicholas had been delayed by a conference with an important client, took him round to his club for dinner, and was late in reaching home. By the light of the gas-flares in the street, which had been disliked when they were first introduced as they made everyone look ill, he perceived the doctor's brougham standing outside his door. He frowned a little, and stirrings of some unidentifiable feeling rose in him; it meant that Jane was worse again. He was aware that he had married Jane for her money, that the money had hugely prospered the fortunes of the bank, and that he might have been a better husband to her. Perhaps had she been more intelligent he might have been; but he had never had much opinion of her wits. It looked as if young Nick had inherited them. There had been a slight ray of hope this evening; the client had been a Scotsman, and he knew another of that nation who had an unmarried niece, about Nick's age as it turned out, or a little older, intelligent, and with money.

'Why is she unmarried?' Nicholas had enquired; a pig in a poke – he had been down to see several estates in Wiltshire, and there had been a selection of livestock, in which he was not interested, in all of them – was not the kind of purchase he would make. In fact, if the girl proved suitable, there was no need to purchase anything at all; her parents would provide the dowry. Without dwelling on the reason for her single state, the client murmured something; Jamesina was the youngest daughter of a large family, and he supposed they took it in turns; he didn't know about such matters, but there the girl was, and he was fairly sure they would listen to reason if the matter was broached. Nicholas was still suspicious; a reason had not been given, and Jamesina, with her i pronounced as eye, was not as young as all that. 'They'll need to make a kirk or a mill out of it, else,' said the Scot, but Crowbetter did not know what he meant.

All this occupied his mind while he was admitted to his house, and he almost forgot about Jane till Harriet came down the upper stairs. He gestured briefly to her to go into her room, for he assumed that the usual arrangement would proceed; but Harriet stayed where she was, and he saw that she had been crying.

'Jane is dead, poor soul,' she said. 'She died at ten o'clock, quite peacefully. The doctor will be down presently, with the certificate.'

The doctor came, presented his condolences and the evidence that Jane's death had been due to natural causes, no mention being made of neglect, and Nicholas went up, as in duty bound, to view his dead wife. She lay heavy-faced and calm, and he realised that he could not remember when he had last spoken to her. A feeling of unaccustomed desolation began for some reason to reach him; he disliked change. Jane had always been there; the house had had a hostess. Now, what was he to do? Athene was impossible, and the thought of living here without Jane to supervise her was abhorrent; as soon as she was free of his guardianship, he would leave her to her own devices with Laverton and they could live elsewhere. That left Harriet. Gazing down, still, at Jane's dead face, he decided that it would be proper to ask Harriet Milsom to marry him. People would gossip otherwise, and she had, as he put it to himself, served him faithfully for many years. He drew the sheet back over Jane's face, went out of the room and downstairs; the servants were already draping the windows with black and closing the shutters, and the bank would have to be closed as well on the day of the funeral. Once that was over, things could go on as they had done before.

He had decided that it would not be proper for him to visit Harriet again until after the funeral, and once that was over – a large number of influential persons who knew Jane only as a silent hostess, but had at least dined at the house, came, and there were many tributes afterwards, Nicholas went to his study and left Athene and Harriet to dine alone, as he wanted to make up the urgent work not yet attended to owing to the day's ceremony, which had left him unmoved. He had a collation sent in to him, and ate and drank absently while still thinking of the contents of the closely covered sheets of thick, embossed paper lying on his desk.

Having done the work, he went, though it was late, to Harriet, feeling particularly in need of her. He thought almost affectionately of the calm continuing nature of his imminent marriage. There must, of course, be an announcement in the newspapers, as repectability was part of the order of things and, perhaps now poor Jane was dead, one of the *raisons d'être* of his intended proposal. He found that he was too impatient to undress, and went straight to her room. As usual Harriet was dressed and, Nicholas thought complacently, waiting for him as was customary. Her head was bowed and she did not greet him; the expression on her face conveyed nothing, and the black silk gown she nowadays wore made her look like one of the mourners; it was time, in all ways, to take it off.

Nicholas made the proposal in his own fashion. 'I have decided, as matters stand,' he said, 'to ask you to become my wife. As Mrs Nicholas Crowbetter you will, naturally, occupy a position in the world which you have not previously enjoyed. I know that you will behave with circumspection; you have always done so. The wedding must, of course, be very quiet, without guests. The news can be announced later.'

She stood up. She looked at him, and he realised again how fine her dark eyes were; she was altogether a fine woman, grown a little plump by now, but that did not displease him.

'I will not marry you,' said Harriet.

He was taken aback, but decided that she had answered out of prudence. This pleased him; he disliked fools, and Harriet had often sustained him with her wisdom, as he now recalled, not having had the leisure to think about it for some time. He smiled, revealing his by now darkened teeth.

'Come, come, my dear, there is no need to be hesitant. We are both growing old, and if –'

'I am not in the least hesitant, Mr Crowbetter. For years you have used me nightly as your whore and your adulteress. I endured it partly because I had not a penny of my own, and partly because of Jane. You hardly spoke to your wife, or thought of her, but she was capable of speech. We often used to enjoy one another's company quietly, without pretension, most of all without bitterness towards one another. Once I thought of going away, as a reasonably lucrative post was offered me; but your wife was so deeply distressed at the idea of my leaving her that I declined it. When she was dying she told me that I had been her only comfort for many years. Now that she is dead, on the very day they have lately buried her, you ask me to continue in the position of servitude I have been forced to occupy, without change except that the adultery will cease. I am chiefly concerned as regards that; it is the only thing that prevents me from being received into the Catholic Church, in whose faith and teachings I have been instructing myself for a very long time. I have managed to save a little over the years out of the pittance you pay me, and now that Jane is gone, I shall leave at once. I am going to the Ladies of Hammersmith, who will shelter me until I may become a full communicant. After that, I intend to enter a convent.'

'You –' He could not credit his own hearing; Harriet to leave, Harriet to become a Papist, Harriet to refuse his offer to make her Mrs Nicholas Crowbetter, Harriet –

He began to realise that he was as fond of Harriet Milsom as he could be of anyone. He relied on her. She must not be permitted to go. He began to try to persuade her, using the compelling charm he could use, and would always be able to do well into old age, for hopeful clients. But Harriet looked at him as though he were a stone.

'That is all I have to say,' she told him. 'Kindly leave my room. I am aware that you can turn me out into the street tonight if you so wish, but I should prefer to leave tomorrow morning.'

He had fallen silent; in fact, there was nothing to say. He stared at her for a moment, his mouth somewhat foolishly fallen open to reveal his missing teeth. Then he turned and went out of the room, as she had requested. A convent!!

Crowbetter did not go to bed, but went out of the house again and walked about the streets, losing count of time. The prosperous houses were left behind, and the Park; he walked he hardly knew where, although eventually, after a long time had passed, he recognised Westminster Abbey by the light of a quarter moon. The district beyond it was unsavoury, even dangerous, and Crowbetter knew it with half his mind, but still walked on. He had become aware of a savage need for a woman. Perhaps the exercise he was taking would help him overcome the need, as formerly; he continued to walk, but the bodily urge would not subside: in fact, it grew more urgent. He was driven at last to think of a prostitute, and found one eventually, standing beneath a lamp for custom with the resignation of her kind. It was the first time in his life that Crowbetter had been driven to one. He fumbled in his pocket and gave her a coin, not looking at her except to note that she was a scraggy creature. They exchanged no words while he satisfied his full hunger, for hunger it proved to be. After Harriet's plentiful flesh this skeleton was unsatisfactory, although better than nothing. So occupied was he that he did not notice, during the proceedings, that like himself she had remained silent. At the end, she spoke.

'You have not lost your former vigour, Mr Crowbetter.'
It was Maud, much changed.

Henry Laverton was released from prison three months
earlier than he had expected, because Athene could not
endure, or rather would not, to stay in the house with the
person her uncle had brought home the previous night and
who was present at breakfast. The episode of the Quaker
meeting was salubrious by comparison. Plucking up courage,
she told Nicholas in her loud clear voice that she refused to
endure the situation one minute longer, and stalked out of
the room, requesting the housekeeper to ask the cook to send
her a cup of tea and a lightly boiled egg upstairs.

Whilst eating the egg, it was borne in upon Athene that she
did not know quite where to go. She had no friends with
whom to take refuge, as she had never troubled to make any.
Henry, the thought and beloved memory of him, the
prospect, growing ever nearer, of his release (if Athene had
known, within two years absconding debtors would no longer
be arrested in the first place) filled her life and her mind.
Quite, quite soon she would see Henry again; and sat
reflecting on the fact for most of the day. Maud was not
present at luncheon, as she had been given Harriet's room, a
hot hip-bath, a comb, and was asleep between clean linen
sheets. The housekeeper, as Nicholas had foreseen, gave
notice.

When her uncle returned from the bank he sent for
Athene, who had not, after all, gone away. He was seated as
usual at his desk, sipping a well-earned brandy after the day's
work. The sudden realisation came to Athene that he was like
a great satisfied tomcat. Such a comparison was not, no doubt,
respectful, but one knew a little about certain matters by now,
and a tomcat was like – no, perhaps not. Henry was quite,
quite different, nobler, less chained to material things. He
would certainly never, never have brought such a creature
home.

To her sudden joy, Nicholas surveyed her with his golden
gaze and said: 'If you want your husband now instead of in a
quarter's time, I will make over to you all your money, shares,
investments, holdings, deeds, and specie. You may pay his
debt as soon as you choose, as well as the interest on it, which
is considerable. He may spend every penny of it on gambling,

and probably will. That is not my concern, and will soon be yours no longer. The moment he is free, by present law, the money is no longer yours but his. That is all I have to say on the matter, except that I will not continue to be responsible for either of you in the event of further debt. Spend the night here if you choose, or else go to an hotel. Tomorrow at eleven, come to the bank and I will arrange matters there for you to sign. It will take a little time to negotiate Laverton's release, and you will have expenses to pay a lawyer; keep enough to do that, or Laverton will be in prison again. Now get out of my sight. Mrs Humble, who in future will be my housekeeper and hostess here, is coming down to dinner. If you care to join us, you will use her with civility. Otherwise I wish you a good evening.'

Athene stood there with tears pouring down her face, but they were tears of joy. Henry at last, at last again, after so long! But she was not fluent in gratitude, and only said politely and tremulously, 'Thank you, Uncle Nicholas. I am *most* grateful,' and, still quietly and joyfully weeping into a lace-edged handkerchief, ascended to her room.

Athene did not come down to dinner, but Maud did, in a black silk dress that had belonged to Harriet and hung on her loosely, but could be taken in. She had combed her hair, looked clean and, by now, fairly respectable; after all, life had forced a great many things upon her against her inclinations. She sat down in Harriet's place, and the soup was served. They ate in companionable silence.

During dinner, which Maud ate like a wolf, Crowbetter observed her. After the day's rest she had somewhat begun to resemble her former self, although her face was bruised in one or two places, and she had lost a good deal of weight. He thought that with proper feeding and treatment she might, given a little while, become acceptable again in other senses than one, but there was the question of Humble. Afterwards, as they sat over coffee, he asked her outright.

'He's the same as ever, and always will be,' said Maud dully. 'He'll probably wonder where I am. He might come here: that's the trouble, as he's got his rights. Otherwise I'm pleased enough to stay; one customer's better than a few, and the food's good.' She grinned suddenly, and he saw that she had lost a tooth. 'Humble knocked that one out,' she said, noticing the direction of his glance. 'He used to black my eyes, or beat me black and blue if I didn't bring home money. He'd fuck me as much as he liked for himself, then turn me out on the street. At the beginning he'd stand watching in a doorway, to see I did as he'd told me, I expect. We was in a lodging-house at first then, a measly place with pallets on the floor. There was others in the room and he used to do it to me there, among them all. At first I minded, then I got used to it. You can get used to anything, come to think. I'd sleep during the day, that was something. Joe Humble couldn't get a job again, not with horses; that might've been his trouble, or a part of it.'

He noticed the deterioration in her speech and words, the accustomed twang of the soliciting London whore. He asked her outright, as it worried him somewhat, if she had caught the pox.

'Naow,' said Maud. 'I was lucky, I s'pose. I got in the family way twice, I think it was Joe, but you use a crochet hook. I learnt most things. After a while I'd made enough money at it for Humble to set up a fruit stall. I could've squashed the fruit in his face by then, but I didn't. It was worse for me because it meant he could afford to get drunk every night, and he'd wallop me whether I brought home money or not. All this'll interest you, I don't think, you being a gent. I ran away once to my stepfather, but he said he'd get the police to me if I came back. There was nothing I could do but carry on.'

'I will take care of you,' Nicholas said. 'We will buy you new clothes; you will eat proper food. If the servants object to your presence here they will be dismissed, and they know it. You have nothing to fear if you stay inside the house or go straight into the carriage. Humble cannot harm you here. You have endured enough, and I feel that it is my own fault; that is an admission I rarely make, but I make it now. I will atone if I can, and if you will permit me to do so.'

Maud grinned her lopsided grin. 'I remember the carriage,' she said. 'I ought to, wouldn't you say? When I think how it worried me at the time, it'd make a cat laugh. Nothing worries me any more. I'm not a lady now, that's it; nothing to keep up with, when all's said and done. It's a comfort, in a way.'

He smiled. 'You will become a lady again,' he assured her.

'Not 'arf I won't,' said Maud, 'living here with you. I s'pose the rest is all dead, or else gone away.' She looked round the empty dinner-table: Athene, Sarah, Jane, Nick and Felix, all gone. Harriet she did not remember.

Crowbetter found her talk more entertaining than it had been, by a long way. In fact, he was enjoying her company. Next day he had additional cause for pleasure. He had spread out *The Times* to read at breakfast, and scanned the columns while Maud consumed kidneys and bacon, scrambled eggs, hot buttered toast and coffee. Nicholas looked up suddenly, his expression gratified.

'You will be delighted to learn,' he told her, 'that Sarah, Viscountess Witham, my niece, has given birth to a healthy son.'

'Good for 'er,' said Maud, removing a shred of bacon from between her remaining teeth. Outside, the carriage door slammed as Athene, followed by the maid who had replaced Temple, was driven off to her hotel.

The labour had started at night while Sarah lay in a pleasant natural sleep, as Witham was no longer allowed to come near her. She awoke to a nagging pain in the small of her back, thought it was cramp, and changed her position, but presently the pain came again. It came and came, getting fiercer, increasing in frequency; presently it grew unbearable, and she would have screamed, except that she did not want Honoria to come in, as would certainly happen. She got up instead and woke Betty, who was within call because the Countess had expressly ordered that she herself be sent for at once if anything happened. Betty ignored it, and said – she had a large family of brothers and sisters at home, and had seen at least some of them arrive – 'Walk up and down, love, it's the best thing, for a bit at any rate,' and then remembered that one didn't call her young ladyship love; but Sarah was past minding. She walked, biting her lips, up and down the bedroom floor; then suddenly something inside her burst, and a quantity of warm fluid gushed down to the floor, making marks on the carpet. Sarah began to cry. 'It's the waters,' said Betty equably. 'Never mind the mess; it means the baby's coming soon.'

The baby! Swelled up to the size of an elephant, the shape of a frog, Sarah could take no comfort in the thought of it. It was thrusting down her in the way Witham had thrust up her, and directly connected, as she now realised, with that event.

She began to howl softly, hands clutched to her body, then clenched hard together; at last Betty led her back to bed, saying gently that she would fetch the Countess, if it was really wanted.

'No,' breathed Sarah, sweat beading her brow; and managed not to scream through abominable pain, for some hours until the baby's head at last showed: a black head, like Witham's. Betty showed her how to lie, and said: 'There, now, dearie, it won't be so bad after the head comes. I got to press on it 'cos that's what they do. It'll come, anyway.'

She pressed, and Sarah stuffed her pillow against her mouth with the agony of the birth; then whatever it was came out, and it was a boy, to all appearance normal if not beautiful. Betty wiped its nose and mouth with her apron, laid it aside and went back to her exhausted young ladyship. 'He's all right, he is,' she said. 'He'll do. We'll tell the old – we'll tell her other ladyship he was born sudden, like. She'll never know. Couldn't have done anything I didn't do, if that much.' She was kneading Sarah's stomach. 'You go to sleep now, m'lady, and it'll be all right, you'll see.'

It was all right. When Honoria came next morning to view her grandson she congratulated Sarah and also Betty, saying everything had been very well managed and she quite understood that in the haste of the event there had been no time to call her. Then she addressed Sarah from the foot of the bed.

'Now that Witham has an heir, he will no longer visit you regularly. The sin of our first parents was concupiscence, it must be indulged in solely for the procreation of children, and women must suffer pain in childbirth, as no doubt you have found for yourself. It is right and proper that this should be so.' Honoria bridled a trifle at thought of the new and degenerate habit of using chloroform to relieve labouring mothers of their appointed torment. She remained also singularly uninformed, as a great many people still are, of the nature of original sin.

The baby, who was to be named Lawrence, slept like the dead in his cradle. He was very ugly, but the Earl was pleased.

Laverton had been fairly happy in prison. He enjoyed solitude and his own company never grew wearisome to him. He duly exercised in the yard with the other inmates, but did

not particularly look forward to it except for the outer air,
slightly polluted as it nevertheless was by the nearby
industrial discharges into the Thames. Visits from well-
meaning persons left him unmoved, and the prospect of not
having any at all from Athene was attractive in itself. He read
her letters briefly, did not reply, and was glad to be free, as it
were, until he was released, when there was the money to look
forward to. Meantime, what he chiefly missed was a good
game of cards.

Nevertheless Henry was beginning to chafe at circumstances, and the news of his early release gave him a certain
amount of satisfaction. He had his own clothes returned to
him, shaved – the moustache had been grown again in prison,
but it had not regained its military glory; it drooped and was a
trifle drab, which doubtless prosperity would cure – and was
put in a hackney, sent by his wife, to the hotel where Athene
was now staying since leaving Hyde Park Gate.

Athene was waiting for him, tremulous and tearful, in the
suite of rooms she had hired for the occasion; they contained
Biedermeier furniture, a well-fed aspidistra and a large
double bed. Henry glanced at the bed and shuddered slightly.
Athene had put on weight, and two years of unwearying
damp devotion in solitude had left its marks on her
countenance. She was, in short, not wearing well. Laverton
decided that he could not face it. After all, the money was in
the bank.

'And how is my dear, dear love after all these years? I have
waited so long to feel your arms about me again; so very long.'
She clasped him to her large, corseted bosom, and Henry let
himself be submerged for a matter of some moments; after
all, he must keep the old girl sweet as long as it could be done,
if only for the sake of peace, to which he had grown
accustomed in the cell. It was rather like having brought a
small, blinking owl out of its twilit privacy in the hollow of a
tree into strong daylight, though the simile stopped there as
Athene released him, held him away from her and looked
fondly into his eyes, which had grown somewhat bleary.

'We will have dinner early, dearest, and then, perhaps –'
Henry had already decided that there would be no
perhaps. After dinner, of which he already felt in need, he
would tell her that he did not feel at all well. They went,
accordingly, down to the dining-room, and as they ate and

drank their way through several courses Athene's face, from where she sat opposite him at their small intimate table, grew coy and almost dimpling. The experience was so horrible that Henry almost forgot to enjoy his sweetbreads, of which he was fond and which Millbank Penitentiary, reformed as the inmates' diet had lately become, did not include.

He absently ordered more wine, and Athene sighed with happiness. It was so delightful to be able to abandon oneself, one's very all, to the man one loved; to a man at all, in fact; that was to say, gentlemen knew about wine.

They had returned upstairs when Henry broke it to her that prison life had sapped him and that, for the present, he did not feel that he could make her happy in certain ways. 'I'm tired,' he said, and sighed fairly convincingly, turning away as from a sight of Eden. Athene was convinced, and of course repentant and sympathetic; would dear Henry perhaps like to see a doctor tomorrow? As this was the last thing Henry wanted, he gave a non-committal grunt, started to undress, and got himself into the soft and extremely comfortable bed, as near the far edge as possible. After the prison pallet it was luxury untold, and Laverton reflected briefly that life from now on would be a good deal less hard on a chap, then fell asleep.

'I understand, dearest,' said Athene softly, brooding over him like a giant mother eagle. Henry did not see or hear her until later, when her habitual snoring woke him. He decided that in future they would sleep in separate rooms.

Next day, he went to Crowbetter's Bank and transferred Athene's entire fortune from there to Coutts's. The chaps went to Coutts's. He had once had an account there himself. If needed, they would give him an overdraft.

Sarah was going for a walk. The baby was asleep, she had fed the little brute and he would soon be weaned, and there was a letter from Hugo. She had managed to purloin it from under her mother-in-law's nose and intended to read it in privacy.

She walked to the furthest point of the estate, where there was a small spinney. Sitting down on a fallen trunk from the large oaks which had once flourished there, she laid the envelope briefly against her cheek. She had not, it was true, thought of Hugo for a very long time, as she had been submerged in her own bitter happenings, but they had loved one another; one does not altogether forget an only love. She remembered him now, and how they had waltzed together at Hyde Park Gate, joyous and happy and young; and she could remember that always, whatever they made her do here, because sooner or later that old bitch would want Witham to have more children and would bring him back to her bedroom and the whole business would start again.

She opened the letter. It was not long, and was written in Hamburg.

2nd April, 1865

Dear Lady Witham

I heard of your marriage, and must congratulate you on the birth of your son. I hope that you are happy. I myself was not so for a long time, particularly as you did not answer my letter. Nevertheless I hoped that you would wait for the two years I asked, but you did not.

I myself am about to be married. Her name is Agnes Kloster. She is the niece of my chief at the bank here, where I have received promotion and they are pleased with me. Agnes is a good young woman and will make an excellent housewife. I am fortunate. They are giving us a small house in Altona. My mother is dead and I shall not return to London.

Ah, Sal, why did you not wait? We were so happy!

My love, my love. I will never forget you. I wish you all happiness. I will not write again, and you must not answer.

Your devoted servant,

Hugo Loriot

The tears were in Sarah's eyes, and presently one spilled over and ran down her cheek. She sat very still for a long time. At last she realised that it had grown cold and that she must either walk some more, or else go back. She thrust the letter inside her bodice and climbed over the fence; she could endure the confines of the estate no longer, round and round and round them as she walked every day. There was a bog on the far side, as she had been told, and she would be careful; life was ugly, but she had no wish to die. She prodded her way with a stick she found, and presently traced out a dry path, walked a short distance, and looked about her. The world had widened a little; there were more trees. Trees didn't grow in bogs. One day – she would come here again – she would go and explore further on; it made a little brightness. Perhaps she would come tomorrow.

Felix continued to be happy in Vienna. According to
Continental custom, he not only shared with Wenzel the late
Count von Reichmansthal's title, but also his fortune. Wenzel
did not grudge him his share, being himself now comfortably
married to his Bohemian heiress, with estates near Budapest.
As for the indulgent Baron, who had no children of his own
(Mélanie had been unhelpful), he doted on Felix sufficiently
to have adopted him as his heir. The young man therefore
had money, birth, good looks, address, and an education. He
was to be seen everywhere; driving round the Rings, riding in
the Prater, waltzing among the brilliant uniforms in the
Rittersaal with jewelled heiresses possessing sixteen quarter-
ings as well as other attributes. He had been presented to the
Emperor, who had made dutiful conversation with him and
had invited him to shoot at Ischl and at Mayerling; but never
to the Empress, who by now had acquired a villa on a Greek
island and spent a great deal of time there. Young Count
Felix – the happiness of his name was regarded as a portent –
was the despair of hopeful mamas of young marriageable
daughters; despite every effort, he was not to be ensnared. As
he was evidently not a cold-hearted young man and loved
dancing, they wondered why. If they had asked his mother,
Mélanie could have told them: Felix continued to be faithful
to pretty Sophie in the house with rococo decorations.
    One day he had come to Mélanie and had announced that
he wanted to marry Sophie. He made the announcement
blushing, like a great boy. She reflected that he should hardly
have been one by now after the care she had bestowed on his
enlightenment. 'That is impossible,' she replied coldly. 'When
you marry, it must be to a person of the nobility.' In fact,
looking afresh at Felix, she did not welcome the prospect of
his marriage to anyone at all.
    He was slim, tall, handsome, broad by now of shoulder with
riding and fencing, and reminded her in some indefinable
way of Nicholas, without the prudence, the coldness, the
selfishness. It was like looking at Baldur the Beloved, of
whom Mélanie had not heard, attired faultlessy in well-cut
clothes. She had, however, heard vaguely of Apollo; perhaps
that would serve. At any rate, she neither wanted Felix to
elope with Sophie nor to lose his quite evident joy in living,

which itself made him attractive to her. She congratulated herself, not for the first time, on having produced such a son. At the moment, however, Felix was looking woebegone.

'If you will give me your solemn promise not to marry this *Weibchen* while you are away together, you may take her on a little expedition,' she told him. 'The Salzkammergüt is very beautiful, with astonishing mountains.' Mélanie cast down her eyelashes, which for her age were still moderately thick and which she had always continued to darken, and remembered a hectic four days spent some years ago while the Baron was away on some business or other, in the company of an engaging dragoon near Salzburg. 'Go soon,' she said to Felix. 'I have no wish to be hard on you, my son. Arrange it with Madame Guyon, and set off together.'

Felix wondered how his mother knew Madame Guyon, but did not ask; he was in too agreeable a state of expectation to think of mundane things. He rushed to the rococo house, went straight to Sophie, who was dressed in a pink satin négligée so early in the day and had not yet done her hair, and kissed her repeatedly. She was pleased to see him, as he would divert her thoughts from something which made her sad; the necessity of providing for one's old age enough to have to marry a rich widower who had proposed to her, and who had sufficient money to keep her in cream cakes for life and, accordingly, losing delicious Count Felix, whom Sophie loved and much preferred to all her other customers.

Felix peeled off the pink négligée and they made love on the bed, and while they were there he told her that his mother had arranged a little holiday for them both. 'If Madame permits,' said Sophie cautiously, for Guyon had not forgotten her own old age, which was a great deal more imminent than Sophie's, and she liked to increase her savings as steadily as possible.

However Madame proved surprisingly amenable, and they duly travelled by the broad dark smooth-flowing river past trees and a great golden monastery, and laughed and drank beer and on arrival made love wherever they could, among the trees when they got there, in the little private stone sitting-rooms of the pretty Salzburg cemetery, and in inns; especially a certain charming inn in the mountains, which last could be perceived through its bedroom window, that is if one had time to look. No lovers had ever loved more frequently or with such abandon, and Sophie gave up being at all prudent as one could always blame the widower.

However, too soon it was time to go home.

The Baron had, as formerly stated, a country estate near Graz, where he kept stallions. Their pedigrees engrossed him constantly and he made a great deal of money from their performance. He was, accordingly, absent from Vienna for months at a time. This suited Mélanie, who seldom accompanied him there; so when she said that she was going to join her husband for some weeks, Felix was slightly surprised, as he knew the Baron bored her and she loathed the country. However he dutifully saw her off, and hastened to renew his lovemaking with Sophie.

But Sophie was not there. She was not, as Madame put it, available. Felix stared at her, aghast. What had they done with Sophie? Where had she gone? She was reserved, as he thought, for his use alone, but it might possibly be that there was now another customer influential enough to have obtained her. The thought displeased him quite remarkably. In fact, it made him ill.

The cold eyes of the Frenchwoman regarded him impersonally above her moustache. 'Sophie will not return,' she said. 'She is married. We have other girls; there is Amie, Germaine, Theresia, Pépi –'

Felix, his face white, wept. 'How could it happen? She did not tell me. She did not –' But he fell silent, and slumped in a satin-upholstered chair; what was the good of asking this calculating old woman why his love had betrayed him? Sophie must have known, while they were in the cemetery, while they were in the inn –

He declined the other girls; they did not interest him. 'Wait,' said Madame, who disliked losing custom, and was not devoid of feeling so long as it did not interfere with business. 'We have a particular room you cannot yet imagine. In it is a lady who is unlike anyone you have ever known. She is particular, and will not take every man who comes. Nor will you see her face; she wears a mask. She will survey you, and if you do not please her she will send you away. If you are chosen, you will experience far more than Sophie ever taught you. You will learn what most men never dream of. You will forget everything but that you are with her, and I promise you that you will return.'

'What is her name?' asked Felix sullenly. It would be better than going home to the empty house, to think of Sophie in a husband's arms; already her betrayal had made her begin to fade from his mind and, in spite of himself, his curiosity was stirred. It would be, he supposed, the same as going out and getting drunk. He might as well try this woman.

'Her name is Lilith.' Poldine Guyon spat out the last consonants carefully; they were unfamiliar in French, but she had been instructed in everything.

Felix was led to the room, which had an antechamber in which he was told to take off his clothes. Madame had led him up herself, but quickly went back to the desk. He stripped, and saw himself naked in a mirror which covered the whole of one wall. There were candles lit, though lamps glowed in the rest of the house. They showed him his body, perfect as a Greek athlete's, perfect as the Discobolos. His heart had begun to beat with a feeling he recognised as mild fear, but could not imagine why; he had never been afraid. The thought steadied him and he went in, to a further room which was large and draped in black. On the bed lay a woman, appearing headless because the black velvet pillow, the black velvet mask, the lace about her neck, as for a ridotto, revealed only her body in the light of two tall candles. Felix had an erection at once. It was the most beautiful body he had ever seen. The small perfect feet were crossed; the ivory arms beckoned gracefully. She did not speak. She did not have to. He knew that he was accepted. There were no words between them.

He went to her. He knew what to do. He thanked – whom did he thank? It was in some way not right to mention God here – someone, whose name he could no longer remember, that he was no initiate; that he knew enough, had experienced enough, to wring a delicious moan of satisfaction from her at last, after a long caressing of the ivory body as though it were that of a goddess, and he a god; no fleeting youth, but Apollo. Her hands traversed his flesh; the very touch of her fingers enthralled him. He lost count of time, of whether it was night or day. He had her many times; she received his seed. The candles burned low. In the end he fell asleep, and woke to find himself alone on the empty bed; Lilith had gone.

'Madame is not available. Perhaps Tuesday.'

Felix was aware of sharp disappointment. He had come back

eagerly to the rococo house, full of strength and certainty, consumed with intense desire; and now, this Frenchwoman at the high desk told him, in the same cold voice she had used concerning Sophie, that Madame would not see him. Felix turned on his heel and went out, spending the evening in a restaurant, and later walking aimlessly about the streets; he had already been walking all day, waiting till the hour when he might go to Lilith; staring at shop windows without seeing them, passing by acquaintances who, in anywhere other than Vienna, would have been offended, but being Viennese they smiled at one another and said: 'He is in love at last, the young Count; it was time.'

Perhaps Tuesday. Madame Lilith must be a person of some importance, as she was evidently not to be dictated to, like the girls. Felix grew determined to break the spell of silence, to ask her who she was, knowing nothing, as he did, at all of her besides her name. Lilith! Lilith! It was strange, in some way dark, even archaic; he had heard it before, but had forgotten where.

He had a core of common sense and next day and the next, read a book; but he would go back on Tuesday. He would go back as often as she would receive him. The strangeness of the experience titillated and intrigued him; she was different from other women in some way Felix could not describe, and yet beautiful, so beautiful, a silent Aphrodite. Who was she? Who was he himself? He had felt close to her beyond the common closeness of lovers, and would have lain with her night after night, all night, again and again, till the candles burned out; then yet again, in the dark.

That was really the trouble. Lilith was unavailable because she needed a rest. Felix had been given a very good education.

She kept him waiting several times as the weeks passed, partly to increase his desire for her and partly to savour, on her own part, the amusement of the whole thing in privacy. When he came, it was as it had been before, and the next time, and the next. She had taught him a good deal by then that he did not know, and would certainly never have learned from Sophie, by now contentedly eating her cream cakes in a prosperous middle-class parlour and already losing her figure a little. All her life she would think of Felix with a certain wistful recollection, and his son was to prove very like him in feature,

though short and plump, with blue eyes like her own. He had
been conceived in a cemetery, but it did not seem to make him
melancholy, and the former widower thought that he was his
own, so everyone was contented.

On their ninth night together, Felix was determined to find
out who Lilith was. He had tried on previous occasions and
she had not spoken, only raising her white palm in a
forbidding gesture, and in silence. Tonight, he had made up
his mind to see her face: even if it were deformed, if it
showed traces of smallpox, perhaps – even a birthmark.
There must be some reason for so determinedly hiding it
from sight. He would be merciful; he would continue to love
her. At the end, when they had fulfilled themselves yet again,
he stood up from the bed. The golden eyes of Nicholas
Crowbetter looked down.

'I must know who you are,' he said. 'If you will not take off
that mask I shall do so myself.'

She gave a low pleased laugh, and pulled the string. The
mask and black *merletto* fell away, leaving her naked except
for a little tricorne hat. It was his mother.

He remembered screaming aloud with horror, with the
sudden awareness of an old, old sin for which a king had
blinded himself, a sin forbidden even in a society where there
was no God; leaving her, hearing her low satisfied laughter as
he seized his clothes, huddled them on in some way, and
rushed out into the night.

Mélanie watched him go. It had been diverting; a new
experience, and she was beginning to find them difficult to
obtain. But he had, to be frank, exhausted her even before
the obligatory nine nights together, which made the total
piquancy of the whole business, were completed; besides
which she would genuinely have to go down to Graz to
persuade the Baron that the expectations of becoming a
father were not beyond him; not now.

The old post-coach trundling into Germany was no longer
used except for the occasional passenger who was too
eccentric, or too poor, to pay for newer methods of transport.
It took a long time, a wheel had been known to come off in
the mountain passes between Vienna and Prague, and the
roof leaked. The driver, who was likewise old, flicked his

whip occasionally at the tired horse and felt relief that the single passenger, who at first he had decided was either drunk or crazy, had been able to pay his fare, merely saying that he wanted to travel as far as the coach went. This meant Prague, Leipzig, with a turn off for Zwickau, then back again on the road to Halle, Goslar and Hanover. The young man could not quite afford Hanover. At all these places one relieved oneself and, if necessary, had a meal at an inn.

The young man, alone in the swaying coach, stared ahead at him without seeing anything but darkness, without and within. Felix knew nothing but that he must get away from Vienna; as far as possible, to the ends of the earth, to the uttermost parts of the sea. *If I fly to the uttermost parts of the sea, Thou art there.* That no longer meant God, but his mother. He had tried, after lurching blindly again about the streets of Vienna in the cold dawn, to find a church, had come at last to the cathedral, battering on the doors with his fists, but they remained shut; it was too early. In any case, baroque angels and little chapels like caverns containing the bones of saints would hardly console him. He had, by now, no religion. He was nothing and no one. Such money as he had in his pocket had covered the fare as far as Goslar. What would happen afterwards to him he did not know. No doubt, if he wrote to Crowbetter's Bank, they would fetch him back to England; but Uncle Nicholas with his golden eyes like Felix's own had been his father. Felix was sure of it now. He had no wish to see his own eyes looking at him, knowing what they had seen and what had been done.

He closed his eyes and tried to sleep, letting the sight of forest and hill and town pass by. There were always houses, always streets, always towns; one town, one street was like another. He did not want to remember Vienna; but a voice within him told him he would never forget. He was changed from what he had once been, no longer like other men. He had been singled out for a particular evil. He was nothing, an instrument: no more.

'Goslar,' said the driver curtly. He held the door open for Felix to get out, disgruntled because he would receive no *Trinkgeld* as the boy had no more money. Also, he was anxious to get back to his wife in Hanover that night; she owned a sausage-stall in the market beside the Leine.

Felix stumbled out. He began to walk without any sense of direction or of place, hearing as if in a dream the coach rumble off, left alone in the gathering dusk which showed him only half-timbered houses, old and inhabited by no one he knew, and irregular streets, down which he walked uncertainly. There were churches, at which he gazed without seeing them; the thought of beauty was alien now. Also, one could not eat candles; and he realised that he was hungry. The hunger began to gnaw at him in a way he had never been permitted in all his life to know or imagine before. He had nothing left with which to pay for a meal; perhaps if he looked for an inn, they would take his watch as payment.

He had some memory of finding one and being refused food; they told him to take himself off, thinking the watch might be stolen; wild-eyed, white-faced and dishevelled young men were not the debonair Count Felix of Vienna, and customers in such situations were not welcome. He was turned away; and the smells of cooking made him long for food, then emit, at last, thin vomit. He had not eaten for days; he had not had a drink of water. After vomiting, he longed for water more than anything.

He knocked at a door, and a maid opened; when he asked for a drink of water and even a crust, she slammed the door. 'You are worse than the friars,' she told him. 'Go and look for them; they have already been.' Her German was less guttural than Viennese, with hissed s's; the back of his mind was aware of it. But he was desperate, and could think of nothing but water, water; was there a river or not? He tried to remember one, with bridges; had that been here, or in Leipzig, seen briefly as they passed through? He could not remember; he was tired, very tired; and hungry, and the night was coming down.

He saw what he took at first to be a woman with a flapping skirt, then realised that it was the friar the girl had ridiculed, wearing his long brown habit. He carried his bowl, full of scraps from the day's begging. St Francis had eaten disgusting food as an act of humility. Where had he himself heard that, in all the world? He would offer his watch to the friar, in exchange for scraps.

The little man – he was small and plump, and his name was Brother Heinrich – came nearer, said 'Grüss' and held out the bowl, as of custom. Felix heard himself speak; his voice was still his own; in some way the fact surprised him.

'I will give you my watch in exchange for that food,' he said. 'I have not eaten for very many days.' He had in fact lost count of the days; they had travelled, stopped, waited, then started again. The friar shook his head, smiling; he would not take the watch. Felix stared hungrily at the bowl. There was some bacon among the rest, but it would be salt, and would make him thirstier than ever. His stomach revolted; he could not eat it. 'If I could have some water,' he said, 'only some water –' and lurched unsteadily. The friar had little shrewd black eyes, and a pleasant smile. He nodded a couple of times; he had not at first seen, in the dusk, that this young man was not as able to give as he was in need to receive. He needed help; he needed shelter, perhaps in the infirmary.

'We have a well,' he said quietly. 'Follow me, little brother.'

He took the boy's elbow to guide him on the way; Felix was almost unable to walk any more. He must be nursed back to health, in body and in spirit. Franciscan brothers had faced leprosy unafraid; they did not entirely content themselves with begging for scraps.

Young Nicholas – he was no longer known as Nick, having become a respected member of the squirearchy, whose father, of the same name, was seldom nowadays seen by anyone as he was pursuing his usual avocations with increasing contentment, though he still looked in occasionally at Crowbetter's Bank – had been married, in unspectacular fashion, some time ago at Hyde Park Gardens to his Scottish bride Jamesina, who had come down, with her uncle, from Edinburgh. At first sight there seemed to be nothing wrong with Jamesina, although she was no beauty; but that could hardly have been expected, given all the circumstances. She was of medium height, thin, strait-laced and melancholy, with dark hair, a long nose and a sallow complexion. She seldom said anything, which suited Nicholas as he seldom said anything himself. He found no difficulty in performing his expected duties, and Jamesina evinced no particular surprise. There was not, however, much pleasure in it, and he was pleased when his wife announced, in a slightly rasping Edinburgh accent, that she was in a certain condition and she thought that it would happen in May.

Jamesina had one eccentricity; she liked her tea laced with

whisky. At first this startled Nicholas, but he assumed that it was an accepted habit in polite circles in Scotland. What he failed to note was that, as time went on, Jamesina was taking less tea in her whisky and, by the end of a few malodorous months, no tea at all. In the end, she was found lying on the floor, even further beyond speech than usual. Nicholas helped to carry her up to bed and her maid unlaced her; but the incident perturbed him. Nor was the sight of her flaccid body slumped on the bed an attraction.

He went out to where the cows grazed in the near field, and stood watching them. As always, he loved cows; loved the pigs which rooted in his woods, because it made better bacon, but they knew him and he liked to scratch their backs. He even loved the bull. It was decidedly pleasanter outside than in, and when he saw a little milkmaid come out to the cows, with her stool and pail, he was happy; she was new, but seemed to like working in the dairy. She had a birthmark on one cheek, which made her shy. It was difficult to imagine her the worse for whisky. Her name was, for whatever reason, Geraldine.

Geraldine bobbed when she caught sight of him, but the cows needed milking, and she went duly from one to the next, presently carrying the first filled pail back to the churn. He had been watching, knew that it was heavy, and took it from her, which perturbed her. 'Oh, sir, you shouldn't be doin' that.' She had brown eyes, he thought, less like a cow than a deer, with long lashes. The rest of her was plump. He was happy in her company.

'It is too heavy for you,' he said gallantly. 'I am stronger than you; why should I not carry it?'

'Because you are the squire, sir.'

She spoke gently, and they walked along together to the dairy with Nicholas carrying the pail, in silence; it was a companionable silence, not like the ones with Jamesina. He began to be present at the milking every day, and hardly a word was ever said between them, but they understood one another. Once she told him that she had brothers and sisters at home, older than she was, but they were all married; nobody would marry her because of the birthmark; they said it was where the devil sucked at her.

'But he doesn't,' said Nicholas. His dim brain was stirring with a certain determination. It was a great deal more comfortable being with Geraldine than being with Jamesina.

Whatever his father said – and Nicholas was no longer so greatly afraid of his father now that the latter was seldom to be seen and growing old – whatever anyone said, he loved Geraldine and he did not love Jamesina. Jamesina could have her whisky – he would not stint her – and he would have Geraldine. It was a simple solution and contented everyone.

They moved into comfortable quarters above the stables, continued to go down together to milk the cows, and Nicholas discovered for the first time in his life the real and thorough pleasures of the bed. In course of time Geraldine was to bear him eight children, and none of them had birthmarks. When Jamesina died of drink some years after giving birth to a son who looked the same as everyone else, with his mother's melancholy features but not her propensities – in fact, the third Nicholas Crowbetter was to grow up into a shrewd financier, no doubt helped by his Scots blood – his father married Geraldine. They came back to live in the house, which ceased to smell of whisky, and were happy for many years together until Nicholas, who had been out hunting on a wet day, came home soaked, forgot to change his clothes, caught a chill and died of pneumonia like his Uncle George. Geraldine died shortly afterwards of grief; she should have made him change his coat, and she reproached herself. She had loved him greatly, and life held nothing more.

Meantime, the sharp-eyed boy who would inherit Crowbetter's Bank began to look about him. The county, who had ceased to call, began to make fresh overtures, but the third Nicholas Crowbetter did not heed them. He had decided to sell the estate – the bastards of different ages could all go to the devil, his father had left them provided for – and to live in town.

5

It took Laverton five years to run through most of Athene's money, but long before that she was begining to suffer bitter disillusion. Henry seemed to delight in giving her pain; he was often spiteful, most unkind, as she told herself, and had only acted as her husband at all on two or three occasions, once when he wanted some change, and twice when he wanted the emeralds.

It had been perfunctory. He rose from her bed – his own door he kept locked when he was inside, so that she could never go to him, which had hurt her more than he perhaps intended, dear Henry – and asked her where her emeralds were. Athene, lying on the pillows, stared at him in surprise.

'What are you going to do with them?' she asked. Henry was buttoning his trousers. He was, if one thought of it, like a little strutting cockerel, with a red nose for a beak. Why did she love him so? It was the first time she had asked herself such a question, and his next words left her without an answer.

'I shall lodge them with Coutts's,' he said curtly. He would do nothing of the kind; he would take them to a certain eminent jeweller and get the best price he could. 'They are not safe here, and they are no doubt very valuable,' he added, not unkindly.

'Perhaps I might wear them more often,' she suggested timidly. The glance he gave her she would never forget. It was contemptuous, sour, and brief. There might never have been anything between them, such a short time before. He was nice to her so seldom; and his next words when they came were the worst of all.

'They don't suit you; they were put together for a woman with looks.' He turned away, and Athene suddenly sat up in the bed and began to wail.

'Why are you so unkind to me, Henry? Why? I don't believe you love me at all. I don't believe – I don't – after all the years I waited – and now –'

The tears had come, and the inevitable hiccups. He turned briefly and regarded her, still with dislike. Her mouth was a black cavern, wailing open like the usual great pink mask of Greek tragedy with a hook nose. The tears rolled down her plump cheeks and stained the coverlet. She was yammering words as she always did and it did not matter what they were. Laverton jerked his head.

'Get me those jewels,' he said. 'I pay the bills here, don't I? Get off that bed and bring them here; get on with it, you miserable old cow. I have an appointment.'

She continued to howl and wail, having hardly heard him, which was no doubt fortunate. Laverton strode to the chest and pulled open every drawer in it till he found her jewel-case, and took the lot. Athene was by now gasping protests from the bed, and Laverton wanted to get out of the room. He left her still hiccupping and went past her into the corridor, his mind pleasantly filled with the thought of the appointment, a series of which had already cost him a good deal of Athene's money. It concerned a gambling den which had a select separate brothel, known only to the few, where there were Indian boys. Henry had relieved his irritations there on several occasions.

Athene sobbed herself to sleep, and when Laverton returned, full of brandy, in the small hours, he made love to her again a little; after all, life was more tolerable if there was peace, and it was dark, so she could not be seen. He told her, as she gasped and sighed with bliss, that he was going to employ a young Indian valet to look after him; the valet would sleep in his room. Athene's heart sank; an Indian! And they would no longer be private, only the two of them, and what had just taken place was so delightful; perhaps she had misjudged dear Henry; after all she seldom wore the jewels, and doubtless they would be safer at Coutts'.

Henry stole away thankfully, and locked his door out of a certain acquired prudence. He had at least contrived to break it to Athene that the boy was Indian. She could get used to the rest. The prospect cheered Laverton's morose nature, and he became almost civil to his wife at breakfast, which was always sent up. Afterwards, he went to his club, as she noticed he so often did. She sighed a little; it would have been pleasant for them to walk arm in arm down Regent Street together, as had happened so long ago; but gentlemen had their own avocations. She herself thought that she would go for a little walk there, perhaps even doing some shopping, for remembrance's sake. She thought, on the way at last, about Henry's club; he had not been admitted to Boodle's or Brooks's, and had of course not troubled to apply to White's or the Carlton. Athene was therefore uncertain which club it was, but Henry went there a great deal, so if it made him happy she must let it do the same for herself. Otherwise –

It was at this point that she came upon the famous jeweller's, which Henry had promptly visited. There were the emeralds, displayed in the centre of the window, their green fire blazing, the surrounding diamonds outshining all the rest. Athene gave a strangled cry, and fainted in the street.

The manager of the famous and very expensive hotel where the Lavertons had stayed now for some years, Athene's dream of some cosy little house for Henry and herself never having been permitted to materialise, was perturbed. Granted, the Lavertons were long-standing customers, and Major Laverton had for some time settled the bills regularly and tipped everybody with a lavish hand. But of late he had been increasingly erratic, had once been allowed to run up a bill for three months, then paid up grudgingly; he had always come in at all hours, hardly ever sober; but his wife, with whom the manager had some sympathy, had seemed respectable – one understood the money, was, or had been, hers – and when she was brought home limply seated in a cab, with a policeman sitting beside her to escort her into the hotel, her hat over one eye and her appearance dishevelled, to say the least, it gave the hotel a bad name. The manager, a courteous man, decided to speak privately to her husband. Perhaps Mrs Laverton drank in secret, which was her own affair and no doubt consoled her. He himself would merely make it clear that, with regret, Major Laverton must look for other accommodation for himself and his wife as soon as was convenient.

Meantime, Athene was put to bed, not by her personal maid, who had left long ago, but by the hotel linen-maid, who

unlaced her corsets. Left alone, for once Athene did not burst
into dreary weeping. She was gradually becoming filled with a
cold determination of late quite alien to her. Before her
marriage she had been narrow and aggressive; since then, she
had experienced almost every kind of misery; now, she was
like a sheathed sword, which at the proper moment would be
fully, and effectually, drawn. After all, she was a Crowbetter.
The pale-blue eyes brooding under the heavy lids were like
ice; Athene's mouth had firmed at last instead of drooling.
She would say nothing when Henry came in; nothing at all.
She would endure whatever came, for the meantime at least.
It was not so difficult now. She no longer loved him.

Henry came in presently with an Indian boy. They went
into his bedroom together, past Athene; the boy gave a
respectful little bow. Later she found out that his name was
Satki. He was extremely beautiful, brown as polished wood,
with a slight, erotic swagger. He might have been seventeen.
His manners were faultless. When he smiled, his teeth were
like pearls. Athene took leisure to reflect that dark-skinned
persons usually had beautiful teeth, and wondered why.

Over the days, her life continued as usual, except that
Henry, who otherwise ignored her, came once and stood over
her in a state of rage. He spat out at her that they had been
asked to leave the hotel and that it was her fault for making a
fool of herself. 'By God, I believe I shall go alone,' he said.

Athene looked at him steadily. 'When all my money is
spent, I have no doubt that you will,' she replied calmly. That
silenced him and he went back into the bedroom with Satki.

The sounds that frequently came from the bedroom had at
first puzzled Athene, as they were the same, roughly speaking
– and it gave her no pain to remember it now – as Henry had
made on that unforgettable occasion at the inn at Harwich.
The possibility took some time to register in her mind that, in
fact, they might be. She listened as the days passed, again
without pain. She was steel and flint now. Nothing could hurt
her any more.

Next time it happened, she was ready. Henry had ceased to
visit his club. When the Indian boy was not with him in the
bedroom Satki would move, soft-footed and gracefully, about
her room doing whatever Henry requested of him, except for
the one activity which always took place next door. He ate his

meals, presumably, with the hotel staff. When he would go in with Henry, the door would be locked behind them as usual. One day, Athene could tell from listening that Henry had forgotten to lock it. The moment had come. She moved as swiftly as a panther – and Athene had never felt like a panther before – towards the sounds, turned the handle and flung the door open.

Satki was lying face down on the bed, his buttocks exposed. Henry was busily conducting certain proceedings. When he heard the door open he turned his head and, when he saw his wife, his spiteful little face contorted in fury.

'Get out of here, you damned ugly interferin' bitch. Go to hell.' Athene stayed where she was. Satki wriggled free, and vanished discreetly in some fashion. Henry was left in his opened underwear, spitting with deprived rage, his pointed nose red as rubies. Athene regarded the ugly sight he made with detachment. She spoke calmly.

'Fasten your underwear when you can. I have certain things to say to you before I leave you, which I should have done long ago. I used to love you. I no longer do so. You married me for my money and now that is spent, you have no further use for me. You have treated me with spite, unkindness, betrayal, meanness, and falsity. You have never given me a word of kindness or done a tender act. You have never even given me a gift, or taken me with you about town, or out to a theatre or a restaurant. You were ashamed of me. What becomes of you now, after you have run out of money again, I do not know, nor do I care. Take yourself out of my sight; I am going to pack what I have left, and go. Fortunately I have the cab fare left out of such allowance as you grudgingly made me. It was not very large, but in future I shall have to live as a woman who is no longer rich. It is perhaps as well that I have learnt to contrive.'

She turned and went out. He had heard her in astonished silence, and even with some stirrings of compunction. When Athene's eyes flashed like that, she was a damned fine woman. He supposed that he had used her badly. 'I suppose –' he began, but from where she was putting a few garments into a Gladstone bag – after all the rest could be sent for later – Athene replied almost absently.

'I have nothing more to say; go where you choose and do as

you choose. I have no wish to see your face again. It is even uglier than mine.'

Nicholas Crowbetter was not surprised to be told that Athene had returned to Hyde Park Gardens: he had expected her long ago, and he knew exactly what to do. Rumours had reached him of Laverton's behaviour, as he heard most things sooner or later and, in any case, Coutts' manager was a member of his club. Although bank managers preserve confidentiality regarding their clients, there are certain ways of making facts known without betraying this; and one way and another Nicholas was enabled to make an annuity payable to Athene out of the ruin of her fortune, although she would never be rich again.

He did not, in the least, however, want her back as a permanent inmate of his household. He was extremely comfortable with Maud, and even the obnoxious Humble had been dealt with; he had appeared one day at the bank, blustering his way in, and although the clerk would have fetched the police if necessary rather than trouble Mr Crowbetter, Mr Crowbetter had happened to come out. He was met by a stream of abuse, but dealt with it in his cold fashion: and the upshot of the whole thing was that he told Humble to his face that he would receive a small allowance, paid once a month, provided he left Maud in peace and did not molest her or try to see her again. Since then Maud's fears had faded and she was, in fact, putting on so much flesh with good food and contentment that she would soon begin to rival Harriet Milsom. Nicholas, therefore, found Athene somewhere else to live. It was a small, respectable private hotel, and she stayed in it for the rest of her life, at last playing acrimonious three-handed cribbage with two other old ladies in the shadow of yet another aspidistra in the corner near the window. Nicholas continued to keep an eye on her welfare, but did not let her trouble him.

All that, of course, occurred long after the events about to be related. Ironically, if the Married Women's Property Act had become law four years sooner, or if Henry had been kept in prison for a little longer, Athene's fortune could have been at least partly saved and things might have turned out very differently.

*

The third Earl of Atherton was found contentedly dead in the leather armchair in his study when his grandson was three years old. This was a mercy, as he had not lived long enough to realise that the boy resembled his father with a similarity mostly achieved by tadpoles. Honoria, henceforth the Dowager Countess, but undeterred by that fact, proceeded to mould the child into shape in precisely the same manner as she had moulded his father. She whipped young Witham herself whenever he did wrong, or when she thought he did; took him to meetings of the sect almost before he could speak; and generally reduced him to the almost vegetable obedience which was still manifest in the behaviour of the new Earl. As for Sarah – Honoria never quite managed to think of her as the Countess and deferred to her wishes in no way at all, continuing precisely as she had begun – Sarah had become a silent, thin-faced, sullen creature who endured the fourth Earl's renewed weekly supervised visits passively and without interest, with closed eyes and averted head. Honoria, who had decided that it was time there was another, perceived that Atherton, as he was now, was in danger of falling into sin again. She lectured him again so heavily on the subject that he became increasingly fearful, unfailingly obedient and, accordingly, not effective. Whether for that or for some other strange reason, perhaps her loathing, Sarah, Countess of Atherton, did not conceive. This time, Honoria was adamant; there must be some cause relating to the earlier birth still remaining; perhaps a blockage. One did not discuss such things. Sarah must submit to a medical examination.

Sarah endured this added humiliation in silence and apathy: she no longer cared what happened to her. Fortunately the doctor was new, young, progressive, and tactful. He made the investigation gently, having requested the Dowager to remain outside. This made Honoria bridle; she had expected to be present, like the owner of a brood mare or a valuable greyhound bitch. However Dr Andrews looked her straight between her dead eyes and said that the Countess had a right to privacy like everyone else, and should see her doctor alone.

Presently, he asked Sarah certain questions. He had found nothing wrong with her, and told her so. He could tell – he knew human nature and had the enlightened views about women's rights which were already spreading in knowledgeable circles – that this most unhappy girl was in a state of despair, that she cared for nothing at all in life, least of all her husband or her child. Sarah suddenly opened her turquoise eyes and told him a great deal. Long before the end, he was shocked and appalled, and he had seen poverty, suffering and crime.

'I will speak to Lady Atherton,' he offered, but Sarah shrugged from where she lay.

'Please don't. Let them go on as they are. At least she pulls him off me. If she wasn't there, he'd stay. He did once, and that's how they got their heir. I don't want more children of his, except that I might die this time. I wouldn't mind that. I don't mind anything any more.'

She closed her eyes, and he saw the long brown lashes that were almost all that remained of Sarah Crowbetter's beauty. He took her hand: his grasp was warm and dry.

'I will try to make things easier for you,' he said, 'but there are few ways in which I can do so, after having heard you speak. I can at least tell your mother-in-law that there is nothing wrong with you, which in conscience I must do. When you are most unhappy, remember that you are young, in a position to do a great deal of good, and that there are women whose husbands beat them and even knock an eye out, and the law as it stands cannot touch them. We must hope that matters will improve for women. I am glad that I have met you. If you need me at any time, I will come.'

Sarah thanked him, but did not watch him go. The fact that there was nothing wrong with her meant that it would happen again, perhaps tonight. She would endure it; she had done so before, and must continue. The doctor's coming had made no difference.

Meantime, the doctor himself was informing Honoria that he prescribed cod liver oil and gentle exercise. Her toad's face bore no expression other than a slight firming of the lips. Sarah went for walks; that ought to be sufficient. She would bring Atherton to her tonight. He had been lethargic lately, and – her mind gave a twist of dry unaccustomed humour – perhaps he needed exercise as well.

The end of it was that Sarah was permitted to take longer and longer walks. Often she walked over to visit Betty, who had been married in the previous year to a large devoted tenant farmer named George Plunkett. Sarah had not troubled to find another personal maid. It didn't matter what she looked like now, and she could put a comb through her own hair.

Betty and George were enjoying farmhouse tea, the young wife having adapted herself to cooking and baking in the same way as she had changed herself, with shrewdness and efficiency, into a lady's maid and had assisted Sarah at the birth. Her husband adored her, and his tiny apple-cheeked old mother did so too, sitting as usual in a rocking chair beside the fire, smiling to herself and knitting a shawl. Sarah, midway through a buttered drop-scone and honey, noticed the shawl. Betty saw her looking, and blushed.

'I'm expecting,' she said proudly. 'I waited till next time you came, m'lady, to tell you.' The young farmer and she glanced at one another, with a deep look of contented love. Presently he went out, to milk the cows, and Betty said, with a long clear glance at Sarah,

'That's the way it ought to be, the way it is between Plunkett and me. It's lovely. I know it isn't for the likes of me to mention it to the likes of you, but I know what you've put up with, and I thought I'd tell you, well, that there are other ways, kinder than you've had. Granny 'ud tell you so too, but she's deaf. That's why I'm able to speak out so; forgive me, m'lady, if I've spoken as I shouldn't. But I'm so happy I'd like you to be happy too, only I know you ain't.'

'Let me know when it's born,' said Sarah. 'I should like to come and see it.'

She went away a trifle cheered, for some reason; and walked back to Atherton against the wind.

Far away in Goslar, Felix had lain for some weeks in the infirmary of the Franciscan monastery, too ill to know where he was. At times he was in delirium, at others crying out with fearful dreams; mostly, he lay in a kind of lassitude, not caring whether he lived or died. They fed him; they washed and cared for him. He grew used to the sight of their brown habits moving across the tiled floor, of their worn patient hands touching him. By degrees he learned the names of the different brothers; Brother Heinrich, who had brought him in; Brother Robert, Brother Franz, Brother Schwartz. The last was a dark-complexioned man from Thuringia with a black beard and black hair, always cheerful; there was a common sensation among them of cheer and calm thankfulness, and at last, when Felix was stronger, he asked Brother Heinrich, whom he knew best, the cause of this general contentment. The little friar's black twinkling eyes looked at him.

'We have humility, and the love of God,' he said. 'We have nothing of our own, and that is restful. If you remember, I would not take your watch. You still have it; it has not been stolen from you here.'

Felix looked at the watch, then about him at the other inmates of the infirmary floor, lying on their pallets; there were men with sores, a man with a hernia, a madman who raved, a man with a fever, a man whose head shook constantly. They were all nursed and cared for, as he himself had been. Yet how had it been done without any money? He asked Brother Heinrich, who replied calmly.

'Our founder, the blessed Francis, would not permit money to be used, at the first; he was angry with a friar who had accepted some, and made him bite it in his mouth and throw it on the midden. Now, it is true, we accept a little: one must be practical. But God provides; whatever we need, we pray for, and it is sent.' He smiled, and bustled off into Goslar with his begging bowl. Felix lay and listened to the bells ringing for prime, terce, sext, matins, lauds, vespers, nones. He had never been to the chapel. It was still difficult to get up and walk. He would make the effort tomorrow, perhaps; he was still weak.

Next day, he asked Brother Franz if he might come to the chapel. This brother was more silent than the rest, and only smiled. Felix took this to mean that it was not forbidden, and as soon as he could walk again with steadiness, went in.

It was simple and plain, less ornate than the churches in Vienna. There was a silver crucifix above the altar which shone in the faint light. Some few people were in there already, towards the front; Felix slumped at the back, feeling dizzy; then, as the rest were kneeling, made himself kneel also. They were waiting for something; the sense of expectancy was strong in the narrow place. Presently a strange brother Felix did not know came in, ready vested, and began to say Mass.

The rest went up to receive Communion, but Felix did not dare. He had been instructed and confirmed, in his youth,

under orders from the Baron, but he felt, by now,
irredeemably soiled; his guilt would not leave him, and he
dared not go to confession with that particular sin. He was an
outcast; he knew it, and had known it since the beginning; but
he wanted to stay here. The thought of going out into the
world filled him with terror and disgust. The world was filled
with evil, and had in any case rejected him. He must stay on
here, among the gentle brothers. He must stay, if they would
permit him. Surely they of all people would not cast him out.

He spoke to Brother Heinrich, and the little friar's eyes
showed sympathy. 'Why do you not go to confession for this
sin, whatever it is?' he said. 'Then you would be free to join
us, if you chose, and otherwise to go on your way.'
'I have no way on which to go. It is a sin so terrible that it
would never be forgiven.' Felix hid his face in his hands. 'I
cannot speak of it,' he said. 'It is with me day and night, but I
cannot speak.'
'God is infinitely loving,' said the friar gently. Felix raised
his head; since his illness the handsome features had grown
thin and drawn.
'He cannot forgive this. If I might stay here – I will do
anything that is asked of me, sweep floors, prepare food if I
am taught –' He thought of the elegant meals served up to
him in Vienna, the varied sausages, the liver soup with tiny
dumplings, the fluffy cream cakes Sophie had so loved. But
he must not think of Sophie; the Salzkammergüt was long
ago, in another life. He must not remember anything, or
anyone; he must live from day to day.
'We must see if you can be accepted as a lay brother
meantime,' said Brother Heinrich. 'Such a position is not
binding in any way. It involves menial work, it is true, but the
others will show you what to do, and you are apt to learn.
Later, when you are at peace within yourself, we can consider
further what is best to be done. Meantime, you may wear a lay
habit, and –' he smiled – 'sweep floors.'
It occurred to Felix that Brother Heinrich must be of
greater importance than had at first been evident. Everyone
seemed equal here. He could be content among them, if only
he could forget the past. He would try.

He swept floors daily, with a long-handled broom made of

securely tied birch twigs from the mountains. He swept the
dorter, the cells, the corridor, the chapel, the infirmary. He
scrubbed the flagstones of the passages and outer court daily
with ashes. He carried in wood for the fire which cooked such
food as was given or sent, and washed the bowls and plates.
His hands grew red with the tasks, his face set. If anyone from
Vienna had come upon the once handsome and sought-after
Count Felix, they would have passed by without knowing
him. He would do any menial task, anything that was asked of
him, but one thing he would not do; go out into the world
with Brother Heinrich and the rest, carrying a begging bowl.

It was not that he minded begging; he minded very little by
now; but his mind was still sick. He could not face the outside
world. The mere thought of walking down a street in Goslar,
a street anywhere, sickened him. He would prefer to stay in
the monastery for the whole of his life; once he told Brother
Heinrich so. The friar looked at him keenly.

'God made the world, and man, and the creatures in it. If
you will not come into the town, why not go into the
mountains? The Lord Himself went there very often, to find
peace.'

For a long time Felix would not go, but one day he
persuaded himself, and went, sidling out of the little postern
at the back of the monastery. It abutted on to green fields,
and beyond them reared hills; in particular one round distant
peak, at which Felix stared for a long time. Later, on return,
he found that the peak had fixed itself in his memory, but he
was not sure why; it was not as high as the mountains above
Salzburg, the very thought of which gave him pain.

He asked Brother Heinrich about the peak, and the friar
gave him a strange look. 'That is the Brocken,' he said. 'It is
best not to go there.'

'Why, good brother? It is not so very high.'

'It is best not to go,' repeated Brother Heinrich, and cast
down his eyes. Felix, who would not otherwise have thought
of going, began to want to do so. He thought increasingly of
the peak, whether sweeping, eating, or lying at night on his
pallet bed. He would hear the bell ring for nones and terce
absently, as if they belonged to another world; which, in fact,
they did.

About that time – he had been there for nine months –
Mélanie von Reichmansthal opened her mouth and yelled in

torment as his child gradually forced its way out of her. It was a son, and Mélanie died afterwards; when all was said, she was not in first youth. The Baron, who had a kind heart, shed tears, but was glad that at any rate he had an heir. He decided to call the child Felix, after that other, golden creature whom he had adopted and who had disappeared almost a year ago. One had searched, but there was no trace. This little boy would atone.

Christmas came and went, and after it Felix asked if he might become a Franciscan novice. The joy of the Midnight Mass for Christ's birth, the sight of the filled chapel which he had helped to decorate with holly and fir, the sound of the bells, and the feast afterwards – well-wishers had sent wine and plucked geese, and a great cake with raisins in it, for the friars did much good in Goslar – cheered him, and bore him up on a feeling of exaltation which replaced, for the moment, the pervading image of the Brocken peak. Afterwards, this returned to him, but as though it had faded further away; at times, however, when he was slack in prayer, the image returned, and loomed again in his mind. He took advice in the confessional, was told it was a visitation of the devil, and to watch and pray; Felix tried to do so. He also worked very hard, although another lay brother had come to replace him at the sweeping and the scrubbing, the carrying in of wood and water, and the cleaning out of the fire. Felix had to spend a great deal more time at his prayers; the office, the litany, the prayers of St Francis, must be learnt by heart, along with many others. He had grown used to rising early in the morning; matins, prime, terce, nones divided the day, and the Angelus at midday and at six. He also resolutely took his turn, first with Brother Heinrich and then by himself, with the begging bowl about Goslar, though as a novice he was not allowed to speak.

This was the trouble. He was still very personable, and the maids who answered the door often tried to inveigle him into the kitchen. They pretended it was for a good hot meal, but Felix knew, after the first attempt, that it was for something else as well. He confided his doubts to his confessor and was absolved, but the ghost of the young man who had been so prodigious a lover in Vienna and the Salzkammergüt would not be laid. This troubled Felix constantly.

He grew restless, and as the snow melted in the streets of Goslar and winter turned to spring, freeing the timbered houses from their frozen thraldom, Felix became afraid of going into the town at all. In less than a year, he knew, he would have to take his final vows; and to betray the brothers then would be worse than what had happened in Vienna. The confessor had told him to pray, and he prayed without ceasing; but the sight of comely girls hurrying past could not leave him unmoved. Moreover, the image of the mountain had returned. It troubled him night and day. Felix never deliberately looked towards it, keeping the sight of it over his shoulder; when he had to turn in that direction he purposely kept his eyes on the ground, mutely holding out the bowl for food or money. But he was not comfortable, either in his mind or in his body. He became determined to climb the Brocken and face whatever it was that so perturbed him, haunting his very sleep.

He spoke of it to Brother Heinrich, who was still his mentor and who had told him, at the beginning, on no account to go near the Brocken, without explaining why. On hearing of Felix's determination to do so, he repeated the same thing. 'Do not go there,' he said. 'It is evil.'

'The only thing to do with evil is face up to it. Christ did not run away from devils; He made them run away from Him. I have decided that I must do the same, or I will never be free.'

'You are not Christ,' said Brother Heinrich. 'It is true that He will help you. But to ask Him to do so on top of the Brocken is to put even Him under strain. It is very evil. There are several months to go before you take your final vows.' The novitiate lasted for a year.

'I cannot take my vows till I have climbed it, and I would rather go now, without more delay, and be done with the matter,' replied Felix hotly. 'Afterwards, I shall be a calmer man and a better novice. At the moment, everything is confusion. I can no longer concentrate on my prayers. I intend to go tomorrow.'

'Tomorrow is the worst day of all,' said Brother Heinrich. He cast his eyes to the ground.

'Why? Why?'

'I may not tell you. As you yourself say, you must face this evil for yourself. It may be that you will not come back here. In that event, Christ's peace be with you at the last. Go tomorrow, if you will. It will be by then the first of May.'

Felix spent the night in fervent prayer. He felt almost uplifted by it, in body as well as soul, like the great saints had been. Early in the morning, he went to Mass, then drank some water, broke a loaf of bread and ate some, then presently set out. Brother Heinrich, who was watching, saw him go with sadness and deep affection. He knew that he would never see the young man again.

Climbing a mountain is never an arduous business at first, and Felix anticipated no difficulty. Franciscan sandals, in fact, made the going easy, being light and flexible, like walking freely in bare feet but with the protection of leather soles. However, at the beginning there was no protection needed; only cropped or longer grass, an occasional pheasant running out of the latter, and a thin scattering of young trees. The ground sloped up gradually, until he came to the foothills. These were young mountains, formed when the continent of Africa moved, enclosing the ancient Sea of Tethys in a narrower basin, forming the Alps, forming volcanoes; but there were no volcanoes here. As he went on and upwards, Felix decided that Brother Heinrich could not have known what he was saying; he must have looked at the mountain, decided that its humped shape was evil, and avoided further acquaintance.

It was then that the bells began to ring out all over Goslar. They did so every day, but Felix realised how far he had come from them already; the church bells, the many convent bells, the great bell of the monastery itself. They were ringing the Angelus. *The angel appeared to Mary, and she conceived of the Holy Ghost. Behold the handmaid of the Lord. And the Word became flesh, and dwelt among us.* But Felix climbed on, crossing himself: nothing would make him turn back now. The three times three chimes, then the nine, faded into silence; and he found himself at last on a forest slope.

The trees were thick, the slope grew steep, and he had to struggle to part the branches; perhaps he had wandered off the way. The effort of fighting through them delayed him, and he imagined that the early summer light had faded; before he came out, he even found himself in a green dark; but on the upper slopes the sun still shone, though there had been showers of rain.

It was then that he saw a strange thing; himself, seen

against a cloud, surrounded by rainbow colours. He wondered if he had gone mad; he crossed himself, and muttered a prayer. When he opened his eyes the cloud had gone, and the image with it. Had he known, it was what climbers called a Brocken spectre; but Felix did not know, and he climbed on with trembling limbs, convinced now that something evil awaited him, the accursed; that that sight had been a forewarning.

The Brocken was closer now. He could see its hump, bald as a man's head on top, thick with trees below. He was filled with obstinacy; he would not go back without having scaled the peak, not for all the warning images the devil could send. As he scrambled up the slope, he heard, as if for the last time, the far-away bell ring out for lauds. His strength was almost exhausted; he longed only for rest. He came to the top, which bore some kind of cairn or pillar; he surveyed the green panorama of the Harz range, the blue lake spread out below; then lay down, meaning only to refresh himself till he had gathered enough strength to descend, and return to Goslar.

When he awoke, it was night. He was conscious at once that he was not alone. There was someone there, someone, something evil; he could smell it, and was afraid. There was a strange whistling noise in the air, which might have wakened him. It floated round him, mingled with the evil, wreathing like a mist. Gradually it took the form of a woman, naked, her light hair floating. It was his mother. He gave a cry of horror, and struggled up, with intent to flee; it did not matter that he could not see for the mist and dark, it was better to break his neck on the mountain than to stay here, with her; but she was not all there was. He heard her laugh, and the whistling down the wind increased; on they came round him, nearer and nearer, the women, come from all over the world, prancing, breasts bobbing, with the click to the tongue, the suck to the cheek, the nip to the thigh. It was the coven; it was Walpurgis Night, and when they saw him by the risen moon they laughed aloud, joined hands, and danced in triumph round him.

'Why, here's a fine young devil!'

He ran frantically about the circle, trying to break out. Hands seized him, and ripped his habit off; now he was as naked as they. He could smell their acrid female sweat; it pervaded everything, roused sensations in him he had made himself forget – when? Why?

Time stood still, then whirled backwards, widdershins about. Somewhere far below, he heard the monastery bell ring for nones. It was like an echo from another life. The witches ran round him, one after the other presenting themselves; one after the other he served them as they came; some were the comely girls he had not dared follow in the streets of Goslar. Others were of no known country, no known time. He did not again see his mother. When they had done with him he fell, exhausted, to the ground in a deep sleep. He woke in the dawn to find everyone gone, and himself naked and chilled with dew. The brown habit lay not far off, torn to fragments. He would never wear it again.

Later, he wrapped a piece of it round his waist, fastened it with the girdle which lay nearby like a white snake, and crept down the side of the mountain. He was tormented by hunger and thirst, and spent some time slaking the latter in the clear waters of the lake, and pulling grass to eat. He did not know, by now, where he was or where he was going. It was like the time he had fled from Vienna. He could not now, he knew, return to the monastery. Brother Heinrich had known what would happen, and had bidden him farewell. Felix took such ways as came, staggering up and down hills, not knowing where the paths led. The night had passed; by now it was very early morning, and he no longer heard the sound of bells. A red glow in the sky seemed like sunrise. As Felix went towards it, however, he knew that it could not be; the sun rose on the other side of the Brocken. He continued to approach the glow, timidly. He was worse off than before; by now, he had neither money nor clothes. He had ceased to marvel at anything that had happened to him.

He found that the glow came from several great furnaces, and that men almost as naked as himself were working them, even so early. Felix stumbled towards them, taking comfort from the sight of their naked backs, shining with sweat in the light of the fires, and from the heat itself, which warmed him. Men were stoking, shovelling, raking some matter which gave off an abominable stink like the pit of hell, making the air dark with choking fumes. Weak and almost delirious as he was, Felix knew it must be the sulphur mine at the foot of the Rimmelsburg, a lesser mountain towards which he had no

doubt wandered while deliberately skirting the town. Brother
Franz had told him of it out of one of his silences: the mines
had been worked for a thousand years, and there was in
addition silver, lead, copper, gold, and zinc. The information
cropped up in Felix's mind, like a lesson learned long ago by a
schoolboy, not of importance now; the main thing was that he
was hungry.

He went up to the nearest man, laying a hand on his
shoulder when he had done shovelling. The man swung about;
his face was black with corroded sulphur. He saw a ragged,
exhausted young figure with wild eyes, golden like the eyes of
Pan; but Willi Kreuz had never heard of Pan. He only knew
that here was something strange, clad only in a loincloth.

'Who are you?' he said suspiciously. 'What do you want? We
get on with our work here.'

'I too can work,' said Felix. He spread out his ruined hands,
still rough and red from scrubbing. 'I cannot work unless I
have food; I am hungry. Will you give me work? I will work
for a week for food only. I have eaten nothing since I came to
these mountains.' He did not name the Brocken. Kreuz's eyes
narrowed, burnt red at the rims as they were with sulphuric
vapour.

'They need workers,' he said, 'But it is not my task. Lothar!
Lothar! A fellow here wants work. He says he will work for
food only. It is possible that he is mad.'

He grunted, and turned back to his shovelling. Felix reeled
with hunger, exhaustion and the pervading stench. But he
would stay; he would work; he would eat, and later receive
money. With the money he would buy clothes; and then he
knew what to do. He knew already, even now. But it would
take a long time.

He worked in the sulphur mines for a year. At first, he would
not have lived, let alone done the shovelling and used a pick,
without food and lodging. That he found both, and at once,
was due to the woman named Hannerl who sat over her
outdoor fire with a cauldron, stirring soup. Most of the men
had wives who fed them – there was a small community, living
in huts up the slope – but Hannerl was there for those who
had none, and in any case all the men, when they needed a
hot drink on a cold day, would go to her when they had a
moment's leisure, pay her, and receive a mugful to keep them

warm. This was a summer day, however, and custom was
slack. The man named Lothar, who had taken Felix on to
work, jerked his head and shouted at Hannerl to give this fool
soup, and he himself would pay her later. Then he went off.
Felix stood before Hannerl. She was stout, perhaps fifty,
clad in layers of clothes like an onion, even in summer. She
stank a little. Her hair was contained in a knitted cap. When
she raised her eyes from where she sat, they were small and
blue, fringed with stubby dark lashes; it was possible that she
had Irish blood. Felix thought that she might have been up
the Brocken, but did not remember or ask. The smell of the
soup itself was pleasant; it had been made with a beef bone,
and as she ladled it out Hannerl put a sausage in. 'There,' she
said, and handed it to him with a grimy fist. 'When you have
drunk it, you will feel better. Do not gulp it; it is hot.'

He had already done so, and burnt his mouth; but soon felt
steadier. He drank down the soup eagerly, and when it came
to the sausage seized it in his fingers, and wolfed it. Hannerl
said nothing, but refilled the mug.

'I know what it is for a young man to be hungry,' she said. 'I
have a son. He is in prison in Hanover. He once stole money.
When I can, I go to visit him. He looks like you, except for the
colour of the eyes. They do not feed him enough, and I take
him bread and *würst*. Where will you sleep tonight?'

His heart sank, for the thought of making love with her was
abominable; he wanted no more women. But the blue eyes
gazed at him steadily, and Felix replied with truth that he did
not know; it would be warm enough to sleep outside, near the
furnaces.

'Not when winter comes,' said Hannerl. 'I have a hut which
you can share, if you will. There is a separate pallet. It will be
useful, you understand, to have someone to be there when I
am away, visiting my son. It takes me two days, and often
when I come back something has been stolen, though I
haven't much left to steal. I must not lose my cauldron ladle,
for instance. If you can guard that for me instead of my
having to take it along, I will be grateful.'

She spoke in the ordinary peasant German of the region,
but like a great lady. He wondered what her history was apart
from the son, but never found it out. Meantime, he accepted
gratefully. The hut in question was made of wood, crazed and
leaning sideways, and its roof leaked in the rain like that of

the post-coach from Vienna. But the pallet was no worse than any other, although Felix caught fleas; and Hannerl fed him by arrangement with Lothar for the first week, after which Felix was able to pay her himself. Also, it gave him a place to bury his weekly money; he kept it in a tied piece of rag in a dug hole in the corner near where he slept, and covered it over. When he was away at work he dragged the pallet over it. Every now and again he would feel the earth to see that it had not been disturbed. He grew silent and acquisitive, and the men mocked him and called him Hannerl's *Geliebte*, but there was nothing of that between them. They got through their working day, hers with the cauldron, his with the shovel and pick; his muscles grew strong, his mind determined. Hannerl would cook his breakfast, and a meal at night to strengthen him, as she was able to get into Goslar for stores, bones and sausages; but Felix never went there, though he heard the bells ring out still.

'If you will buy me a coat, a pair of trousers, two shirts, two pairs of hose, and a pair of shoes, there is no need for a hat.'

The year had passed, and Felix handed over half his money to Hannerl, who was going as usual into Goslar to buy food. Nobody had pilfered it, and Hannerl herself was trustworthy. She nodded, and looked at Felix sadly; she had grown very fond of him. It had been like having her son with her again.

Felix saw her off; he would not come himself into Goslar. He was ashamed of meeting any of the friars; they might be about the streets. They would only say, he knew well, 'God go with you' gently, and offer him no reproach; but he still reproached himself. He would wait till Hannerl returned with clothes, then make his way to Hanover.

All that day he worked with concentrated fury, the sweat pouring from him. He shovelled sulphur, the smell of which would haunt him for the rest of his life. It was difficult to breathe because of the fumes; the men frequently died of lung troubles in the end. But the mine had maintained him, and so had Hannerl; he prayed, the first prayer in a year, that no accident would befall her on the way, that she would not be robbed; in that case, it was all to do again.

But she returned. She had brought him a pair of thick trousers, of good woollen cloth; a coat of the same, and it was again summer; shoes such as a peasant might wear, and heavy

Strumpfelhosen. The shirts were of flannel. Felix did not complain; went to tell Lothar, as it was courteous, that he would be leaving; and somewhat to his surprise received the man's good wishes. 'You have worked well,' said Lothar. 'Good workers are hard to come by. If you will stay, I will put you on to silver smelting; not everyone can be trusted.' But Felix declined, although it was pleasant to be assured that, if all else failed, he could come back.

Then he went to say goodbye to Hannerl. He took both her hands, which were never clean, and kissed her blackened cheek. 'I cannot begin to thank you for all you have done for me,' he said. 'If it had not been for you, I should have died.'

'Well, you did not do so,' said Hannerl cheerfully. She smiled till Felix was out of sight, then allowed herself a tear or two, which fell into the soup. She would miss him badly, and her son, whose name was Ludwig, would not be out of prison for a long time.

Felix obtained a lift in a turnip-cart, making its way slowly to the Leine market. He offered to pay, and the sullen individual who drove it pocketed a coin; there was no talk between them as they lurched on, which was restful. Already Felix felt the improvement in the clean air after the Rimmelsburg mine. The turnip load was heavy, and the driver skirted Goslar and Salzgitte, even Hildesheim; there were better prices to be had in Hanover. He did not explain any of this to Felix, who was in any case not interested; but it was pleasant to feel the tired horse take on a new lease of life as the slopes ironed out into a flat green plain, and the town of kings came in sight.

He was set down at the market, and did not wait to wander about its stalls, which sold everything from sausages to lace. He asked the direction of the nearest bank, walked there, and demanded to see the manager. A pop-eyed clerk looked at him doubtfully. This rough fellow was a peasant, and dirty. One had been instructed to keep undesirable customers from troubling the Herr Geschaftführer.

'I regret,' he began politely, but Felix the aristocrat of Vienna raised his head; behind red-rimmed eyes, hair filthy with soot, a grimy face and coarse hands like a workman's, the Crowbetter blood in some manner revealed itself. 'Show me in,' he demanded, and the clerk, in fear and trembling – he would be reprimanded afterwards, perhaps refused advancement, one could never predict – showed him in as he had requested to the manager, who was not, in fact, engaged, but reading a newspaper.

Felix bowed. 'I will not take up very much of your time,' he said in his excellent German. 'I am the son of Nicholas Crowbetter and I desire to return to my father in London. If you will assist me, he will of course refund you with the appropriate interest. I can give you no guarantee, but if you are doubtful, and will write to him at once – I will give you his address – I can live frugally in Hanover for a very few days. But as I am short of ready money, I would be grateful if you would speed negotiations as much as is possible.'

The manager had been coming slowly out of irritation into astonishment, then, at last, attained great eagerness to please. In fact, he had met Nicholas Crowbetter in London at a directors' meeting some years ago and had never forgotten it; everyone had heard of Crowbetter's Bank; and, memorably, he had noted Nicholas's compelling golden eyes. The same eyes looked out at him now, challenging, demanding, implacably and, at the same time, pleasing; and the manager's Teutonic soul longed in any case to reunite a child with its father. Whatever had happened was none of his affair; this was Nicholas Crowbetter's son. It would also be good for business.

'*Mein lieber Herr*,' he said, 'facilities will be made available without delay.'

Felix was glad that he had decided to tell what he had always known, within himself, to be the truth.

Nicholas Crowbetter spent more time at home these days, though he still went to the bank. In the evenings, he and Maud played chess. She knew the rudiments of it already, and it gave Nicholas pleasure to teach her the more subtle gambits, in the intervals of which he could, as he had used to do, watch the steady progress of her bosom, which under appropriate treatment was swelling again agreeably. For the same reason he would permit her to sit with him across the table after dinner for a share of the port; he seldom entertained guests nowadays. Accordingly, he was present when the butler came to announce that there was a young man outside, asking to see Mr Crowbetter; he had put him in the hall, but he did not think that, perhaps, he should have done. This admitted confusion on the part of an English butler said a good deal for Felix's persuasiveness: as had been made manifest also to the Hanoverian bank clerk, he looked like a peasant and spoke like an aristocrat. It was all very difficult.

Nicholas went out. The young man was Felix, in a state totally different from that in which he had left London. Nicholas asked if he had eaten, and he had not; food was made ready, hot water carried upstairs, and Felix was scrubbed down in a hip-bath and had his hair washed thoroughly by Maud, who could turn her hand by now to anything. After drying in front of the fire he was put to bed, between clean sheets. He fell asleep at once, and was not present at breakfast. Nicholas left word that he would see him on return from the bank, but on no account to present himself there.

On return, he sent for the young man to his study. There was a degree of information to be got out of Felix, but not all. It was evident that certain happenings in his life had changed him from a rich, carefree youth to a chastened and sober man. This did not displease Nicholas, who had given up an unusual portion of time during the day to pondering Felix's future.

'You have,' he said into the determined silence, 'forfeited the settlement the Baron so generously made upon you, because he did not know what had happened to you. You sent no word to him. Now –' He realised that Felix might be ignorant of Mélanie's death, and continued gently, ' – I am in close touch with Vienna, as you know; and I have sad news for you. Your mother died in child-bed about a year ago. The Baron is, naturally, proud of his son, and has disinherited you in his favour. One cannot blame him.'

Felix had turned so white that Crowbetter thought he was going to faint, and having little patience with such attitudes continued coldly, 'You should have been prudent, but all is not lost,' he said. 'My own heir is, of course, my grandson, the third Nicholas Crowbetter. I believe he also shows an early interest in finance. That is very encouraging for me, and I have made him the co-heir of Crowbetter's Bank, together with my dear Maud. Parliament acted too late to save Athene's fortune, but it will protect Maud from her rapacious husband provided she continues his allowance.'

Felix had heard the last words not at all. His mother dead in childbirth, of his child; the child to inherit everything; and if he

spoke the truth, everyone would be disinherited, including
himself. There was no way of putting the wrong right, of
making anything better. He stared at Nicholas, whose golden
eyes, with increased age, were beginning to make him
resemble a lemur. The birth must have taken place about the
time he, Felix, entered the Franciscan monastery, long, long
ago.

'You have not yet heard all I have to say,' said Nicholas
quietly. 'I am prepared to offer you a place in Crowbetter's
Bank if you will work hard, remain sober, and manage to live
on a much smaller income than the one to which you are
accustomed, without getting into debt. It is my duty to
provide as much as I can for my heirs. You cannot start at
once; you must have clothes measured by a tailor, and your
hands are not yet those of a gentleman. Wear gloves at night,
after using rosewater. I will meet your tailor's bill. Is there
anything you have to say? I can think of no other future for
you, unless you marry well.'

Felix shuddered. 'Sir – I am grateful – there is one thing –'

He did not explain it all; he was beginning to have much
recourse to silence. Last night, as he lay asleep, he had had a
clear dream of Sal. They had grown up together, had romped
together, and he realised that it had been in this same bed
that she had spent her marriage night. He remembered her
set, unhappy face as she went out next day to the Atherton
carriage. If he might see her once more –

He framed his request. Nicholas Crowbetter dropped his
gaze. He had heard that the Atherton marriage was not
happy – it could hardly have been expected to be so – but,
after all, there was an heir. If Sarah was cheered by a sight of
her young relative, so much the better. He himself, content in
his body, would not interfere if two young creatures came
together; in fact, he had always secretly blamed himself for
grasping at the noble marriage before he had seen the
bridegroom.

'Go, by all means, but not in those clothes,' he said evenly.
'You had best see my tailor today.'

Sarah had been sitting in bitter reflection in her private wood,
where she went now almost every day, either threading her
way across the boggy land or else returning there after she
had visited Betty, a mile along the road. The ground here was

covered with moss and ferns, damp because it had lately rained, but Sarah did not care if she caught a chill, or, in fact, if she died. In the past, she had known some vague desire to hold on to life, but that was gone; what, after all, had she to live for? To breed little apes, at her mother-in-law's command. Last night, it had happened again; Witham – she could never remember to call him Atherton – had been brought to her bed, the Dowager had stayed nearby, and had pulled him away before he had had enough, and she herself more than enough. Atherton disgusted her. She loathed her marriage. Her life was nothing. Apart from Betty, she had no friends. The county had called at first, but Honoria's peculiarities had set her apart from the beginning, and as Sarah had hardly been permitted to say a word during the visits they had formed no opinion of her either. It was day after day the same, and night after night; as for her son in his nursery, the sight of him revolted her. She began to give way to the dreary crying which sometimes engulfed her when alone; and heard a horseman approaching on the road.

This was unusual, as few passed by on the way to Atherton. Presently he came back. The sound of hooves stopped, and instead there came footsteps, light, determined, young. It was Felix. Sarah stared in amazement. It was like seeing a god descend from the sky. He flung the horse's reins over a branch, and came to her.

'Sal!'

He held out both his hands, and she saw at closer view that he had changed from what he had once been; the hands were red and calloused, his face lined, with deep furrows running between nose and mouth. What had happened to him? He was young, her own age. 'What –' she began, but the ruined hands had seized her own, and held them.

'They told me you were here,' he said. So she had been watched; they knew. 'Who told you?' she heard herself whisper. It was intolerable to think that the Dowager had sent him. But she saw him smile.

'I saw nobody but the groom, and would have left my horse there, but I wanted to get to you quickly. Why have you been crying? Why?' She was thin, he thought; thin, harder, older, with a set mouth.

His finger traced, very gently, the course of her tears. She suddenly began sobbing and told him all about it. It ended with her lying against his breast, against the expensive riding-habit made by Crowbetter's tailor. Nicholas Crowbetter had been good to Felix; had offered him a horse from his own stable, as it was more direct to ride to Atherton than to take the post-chaise, and there were no trains.

Felix comforted her. He did so in the only way he knew, for there was nothing else he could offer her but love. He had no money to maintain her, and the Countess of Atherton could not in any case reasonably elope with a clerk from Crowbetter's; and Crowbetter's was, for him, meantime at least, the only refuge. So they made love. Felix showed Sarah what love ought to be; the mutual kissing, the time allowed for the cycle to rise, the ecstasy when it does; the aftermath, the lying in surcease together, the contentment, the fulfilment. Sarah's eyes were closed; he kissed the long tear-beaded lashes. They murmured together of many things, and of nothing, still murmuring. Sarah was fully happy for the first and only time in her life; she kissed him gratefully again and again, on his mouth, about his lips, on the furrows that should not have come there, that her fingers tried in vain to smooth away. She nibbled his ear. They made love again. The time passed. It began to be evening. Beyond the trees, a further light rain had begun. Sarah started to shiver, and he was awakened to chivalry for her.

'You must not be cold,' he said tenderly. He had never been as tender, even with Sophie, long ago.

'Your arms warm me. Don't go. I don't want to go back.'

'I will return tomorrow, at this time, in this place. I promise. You should go now, before the rain grows too heavy.'

They kissed, lingering at it, and then at last she went; a slender shadow in the growing twilight, soon gone along her secret path. Felix was filled with ecstasy and triumph; he would see her again; he would take employment as a country yokel, anything. Meantime, he loosed his horse, and to exercise it, and give vent to the power and glory in himself, galloped up towards the moor, round in a wide circle, joyous and free, the Brocken forgotten, everything forgotten except love, which he knew at last.

Unfortunately, Sarah, in the same state of mind, had omitted to warn him about the patches of bog, and it had been raining. The worst patch of all was one that had claimed several men's lives, mostly farmworkers lurching home drunk on Friday nights. This was a Tuesday, and Felix was not drunk; the horse knew, however, as all horses will, that the place to which it had been guided was dangerous, and stalled in mid-gallop. Felix was thrown over its head into the bog with such force that he sank almost at once, his cries for help unheard, the only trace of his going a few dimples in the sour black mud. As for the horse, it veered about and, riderless, galloped away; losing the direction of the inn where they had been staying, so that the innkeeper there never knew what had happened and assumed that the young gentleman had absconded without paying his bill; on and on, for several miles, till it was caught at last by a prudent ostler who, seeing that it was too valuable for hire, sold it reasonably well even further away from Atherton than it had started.

Nobody, therefore, knew what had happened to Felix. Nobody would know until twenty years afterwards, when the bog was drained and his perfectly preserved body, stained dark green, was rescued from the sucking embrace of the immemorial mud. Nicholas Crowbetter, having thought, like the innkeeper, that Felix had absconded, no doubt at the prospect of steady work in the bank, meantime gave up any search for him in disgust: after all, something of the kind had already happened with the Baron. Nicholas paid the tailor's bill, assumed the horse was taken also, and forgot the matter as not worth remembering.

As for Sarah, she went back to the wood next day; and waited and waited for many hours. At first she thought Felix must have been delayed; then she realised that he was not coming. She said nothing to anyone, but her bitterness began to corrode her again, like a cancer; he had betrayed her. It might have been expected; she was no longer beautiful. Felix – he had always been irresponsible, if one remembered – had taken his pleasure on her and had then departed. But she could at least remember that pleasure; and there was another one waiting. Within a few days, her menstrual period should have come; and it did not. Her whole life became a fierce hope that, despite his betrayal, it was Felix's child she bore and not her husband's. As the embryo grew in her, she willed this constantly; it would be a comfort to spite the Athertons. Honoria had not seen Felix come, only the servants; and everyone was used to Sarah's vagaries of staying out late. She thickened, and waited, and having declared, at the earliest possible date, to Honoria that she believed herself pregnant, the loathed nocturnal visits ceased. Sarah was, accordingly, left in peace to await the birth, and to remember ecstasy. At the least, Felix had given her that.

The Dowager Countess was a person of principle, as will have been surmised. At some inconvenience to herself – the housemaid was a good worker, and the groom had been a tolerable groom – when she found the pair in the bushes together, she dismissed them both at once, without references. The housemaid fled crying into oblivion, but the groom took his revenge. He used, unknown to himself, the method employed by Mélanie von Reichmansthal to rid herself of her first husband a generation earlier.

In fact, he went further than Mélanie had done, and considered the separate occupants of the carriage. The young Countess didn't go to the sectarian church; if she had, he would have waited till Monday, having some sympathy with her. The old bitch – none of the servants thought of the Dowager as anything else – would be there, and his Lordship, for what he was worth, and probably the boy. In a sane man's opinion, the sooner the world was rid of the lot, the better. The former groom – he had been given no notice – worked cautiously on one wheel, till it was loose; weakened the traces, as Mélanie had done; and furthermore inserted unobtrusive tin-tacks under the mouthpiece of the carriage-pony, so that sooner or later, under whatever hands, it would bolt. With luck, this would happen at the ford, where the wheel would come off at the same time, plunging everybody into the water. If nothing worse happened, they would at least be thoroughly soaked. The ex-groom then collected his belongings and went on his way.

Unfortunately, things went slightly askew in a manner he had not intended. The Dowager had her share of patronage, and she considered it her duty to stop off at the farm on the way to inspect George Plunkett's and Betty's recently arrived baby, a healthy boy. Atherton, who was driving – it had not been possible to find anther groom in time – and little Lawrence were supposed to wait outside in the carriage till Honoria emerged. Meantime, the pony grew restive; Atherton was no more capable of controlling it than anyone

else would have been, and it galloped off, with the present
Earl on the box and the next one bouncing about inside.
Young Lawrence set up a wail, which was to be his last sound
on earth; Honoria came out of the farmhouse door to witness
only a cloud of dust; and the carriage careered on, losing its
wheel, till at last the ford was reached with the lopsided
carriage overturning suddenly and dragged in that position
half across, when the traces broke, freeing the pony.
Atherton lay gasping in the current, his neck broken;
Lawrence, last Viscount Witham, drowned shortly in his own
vomit. The Dowager, brought along in Plunkett's farm cart,
for once did not continue on to chapel. Driven home again
afterwards, the dead eyes stared ahead. It was essential for
Sarah to give birth to a son. The news could hardly be kept
from her, but it must be broken as gently as possible. As for
oneself, that mattered very little; but the next heir, failing a
son from Sarah, was the celibate and extremely nervous
clergyman who had presided at Witham's and Sarah's
wedding, and could not be relied upon to continue the line, as
he was now in his middle fifties, and must perhaps be
persuaded to marry; but of course not yet.

As the young Countess had expressed a wish that the doctor
who had examined her should be present at her confinement,
Honoria was forced to accede. It was in fact politic to let Sarah
have whatever she wanted meantime, though a doctor was a
luxury not usually considered necessary at a birth. The
Dowager was further disturbed when Dr Andrews brought
chloroform with him. She expatiated once more on the sin of
our first parents and the according obligation on women to
suffer pain. The young doctor looked her straight between
the eyes.

'This is the Countess's wish, and she is my patient,' he
stated. 'I shall require you, Lady Atherton, to go out of the
room.'

Honoria, who had again expected to be present – there was
no Betty now – bridled, as formerly, but eventually, with
further persuasion, went. Sarah was in labour on her bed. She
let the pains come passively, exhibiting a languor which
alarmed the doctor; after examining her he took her hand.

'It will not be so bad this time,' he told her. 'It is a second
birth, and normal. The head will come first, then the worst

part is over.' He showed her the bottle of chloroform and the mask, which he would soak when the pains grew bad, and she herself could hold it over her face.

The pains grew worse, Sarah made no effort, and the doctor knew it might be a long business; most men would have left and returned, but Bob Andrews would not. The maids came and went, with hot water. Sarah began at last to strain and moan, biting her lips; she seized the mask, and a minute after placing it over her face, gave birth.

'It is a beautiful little girl,' said Andrews gently, holding the child up for her to see. Sarah's turquoise eyes opened for a second between their long lashes: she saw the baby, gave a little mysterious smile, then died. Andrews was uncertain why she had done so; she had been healthy, and the birth had presented no complications. Afterwards, he admitted to himself that it might have been because she had no more wish to live. Such things happened.

The Dowager was not too greatly disturbed; Sarah had outlived her usefulness. No doubt she had died as a result of the wrath of Heaven called down by the impious use of chloroform, in direct opposition to the clearly expressed instructions in the Book of Genesis. As for the baby, it would be called after herself; she would presumably, as her own health was excellent, live to bring it up in the way it ought to go; and in proper course there would be a suitable marriage to perpetuate the Atherton blood. The fact that the child had honey-coloured hair did not alarm her; her own, when a girl, had been something like that colour, although nobody would suspect it now. However, when the child's eyes opened, they were a clear green. She was, in fact, the image of her paternal grandmother, Mélanie von Reichmansthal. This, of course, was one thing the Dowager did not know, and could not altogether account for.

6

Young Honoria's upbringing was relatively simple; when she did wrong, her grandmother whipped her. If she sang or, worse, whistled, she was lectured, threatened, and reprimanded for that or any other sign of joy. Worst of all was the punishment for the slightest untoward movement, the least inattention, at sectarian meetings; for these she was not only whipped immediately on reaching home, but forced to stand in the corner facing the wall, with her hands behind her back, while the Dowager consumed Sunday luncheon, generally roast lamb, potatoes, a vegetable, and gravy. Accordingly, by the time she was fourteen, young Honoria found it politic to keep her eyes cast down and behave, outwardly at least, like the other sectarian young women.

Her one relief was the farm where the Plunketts lived, George and Betty, with their ever-increasing brood of children. Honoria was permitted to stay for two hours, having been escorted there by the eldest Plunkett girl, who was in due course employed at the castle as between-maid. Freda was, like all the Plunketts, solid and dependable, and the Dowager felt that she could trust her with the custody of Honoria. If the old woman had known, the chief delight of all the children, including Honoria herself, was to repair to the wood where she had unwittingly been conceived, play hide-and-seek and tell earthy stories. Afterwards, and after a good farmhouse tea, Freda would escort the young lady back again to the castle.

One thing became increasingly disturbing as the years wore on. The Dowager, by now stouter than ever and with a determined waddle replacing her former stride, had developed the habit of inviting the present Earl, the clergyman, to dine and sleep. He had been persuaded to take the name of Atherton-Studeley-Crowe, but meantime refused to give up his living. He would sit with his eyes cast down, say grace at meals, but little else, and depart to the relief of everyone including himself. For a long time Honoria could not understand the reason for these dreary visits. When she was sixteen years old, her grandmother told her.

'You are now of an age to be married, and you will marry the Earl. The ceremony will take place quietly here, without guests, although naturally an announcement will be placed in the gazettes.' The Dowager could never bring herself to refer to newspapers. 'You may have a new dress made for the occasion, and you and your husband will stay here. Mr Atherton-Studeley-Crowe – I should say, Lord Atherton – will give up his living on his marriage; he will have other duties.'

Honoria heard her in outrage. Married to that old man? She knew, or rather had an idea, what marriage meant; it meant, or should mean, being like George and Betty, happy in each other's company and producing more and more children. But she could not imagine what any children of herself and the Earl would be like, or what – well, he –

'Grandmama, he is not very young,' she ventured timidly.

'Youth is a sinful time,' replied the Dowager. 'There are desires and errors from which I trust I have shielded you fully in the course of your life. I cannot live for ever, and it is best to place you in the hands of a responsible, older husband. You are impulsive and can be wilful. There is also the title.' The dead eyes glared, and Honoria almost ducked away, thinking of the birch-rods, reposing in their brine bucket to keep supple, in the cupboard. At least, when she was married, Grandmama would have to stop that. Aloud she said, 'When is the ceremony to take place? I – I should like time to have the dress made.'

The Dowager, pleased at her granddaughter's lack of resistance – it was a tribute, after all, to her own training of Honoria – agreed in a gracious manner that the dress might be made indeed, and Honoria escaped. That night, in bed, she lay and thought. Next day, without Freda, she went to the farm.

George Plunkett, Betty's eldest, was a decent and dependable young man who helped his father. Honoria came upon him when he had just completed a haystack. The smell of dried grass was all around them, and the sun shone on George's bare arms, which below his rolled-up shirt sleeves were lightly downed with golden hair. Honoria found the sight pleasing. They knew one another very well from the days in the wood, and she had no difficulty in broaching the subject to him.

'He's in his late sixties,' she said, 'and it's been decided. Can I marry you instead? I should prefer it. I don't care in the slightest that he is an Earl; his breath smells.'

George was in a quandary. He was, as it happened, walking out, young as they both were, with a girl named Lizzie, whose mother had a bakery in the village. Titles apart – and it wouldn't be suitable for him to marry the Lady Honoria in any case – he couldn't let Lizzie down; she had started sewing chemises for her bottom drawer already, and they had planned everything. But as he did not answer, Honoria's eyes filled with tears. They spilled over on to her cheeks, wordlessly.

'Show me,' she said after a moment. 'Please show me what it's like, George. With him, it'll be awful.'

Pity claimed him, and he laid her gently down among the scattered hay, and showed her. She also showed him; in fact, he was dazed and astonished by her response. The demure girl he had known, in constant fear of her terrible grandmother, vanished, and in her place there came below him a fairy creature, an arc of ivory and rainbow, with a passion he would never forget; in fact, he forgot himself. The latter development worried George for a long time, until he heard that nothing of that kind had happened to the Lady Honoria, either before or after the marriage. In fact, George Plunkett had done a favour to the bridegroom; the new Earl of Atherton could not have deflowered a daisy. He did his best, however, in such other ways as were left.

The wedding night of Honoria and the Earl proved worse for the groom than for the bride. On first coming in, bashful in his nightshirt, he had made her kneel beside him in prayer for a quarter of an hour, then turned his eyes aside as she climbed into bed. As Honoria by now knew what to expect, and found that it did not happen, she was presently able to go to sleep very comfortably on her own side of the bed, while the wretched man castigated himself on the other. He had never in his life permitted himself to look at, or think of, women, much less cohabit with them; but this disturbing creature, whom he had watched unfold from a delicate chrysalis into a butterfly – the new Earl was a devoted botanist and nature-lover – troubled him in a manner which he was only just beginning to understand. He trusted that, perhaps, tomorrow night, or the night after –

Honoria, questioned by her grandmother next day, was purposely vague. The Dowager had not, as with her son and his bride, interfered on the wedding night and all the others except one. She would not have considered it proper; after all, the Earl had been a clergyman. But Honoria was unsatisfactory. Asked directly if anything had happened, she replied, 'I believe so, Grandmama,' and one had to leave it at that. This state of affairs continued for several weeks, when certain sounds, coming from the bedroom, convinced the Dowager at last that all was well.

Thereafter, the Earl could not leave his bride alone. He would summon her furtively from whatever she was at, and even forgot to pray; the new power in him, feeble though it was, entranced him, and so did she. Honoria put up with it; to pass the time, she would recite to herself fragments of poetry which a passing governess, not entirely under the thumb of the Dowager like all the rest, had taught her; and stare without feeling at her labouring husband's false teeth, reposing in a bowl nearby. As time went on, he in his turn grew poetic, reciting verses aloud from the Song of Solomon. It was diverting to be informed that her breasts were like two young roes that fed amongst the lilies and that she was the only one of her mother, while his dry hands caressed her smooth young body under the nightgown. Long before he had finished, she would have grown sleepy; and generally slept at once, taking no more notice of Atherton. He had one advantage; he did not snore.

At last he inveigled her into the bedroom by day and requested her, in a devious fashion, to take off her clothes, also unpin her hair; he liked to run his dry fingers through it. He had locked the door coyly behind them; the maid had already been in to do the room. Startled – it was almost time for luncheon – Honoria obediently undid her dress, slipped out of it and her petticoat, and let the Earl's eager hands unlace her stays, which she hated wearing. When she was naked, he laid her on the bed, climbing upon her immediately, wetting his lips with his tongue in anticipation. Honoria did not know Chaucer except in a slim bowdlerised version made available by one of the governesses, so the context was lost on her; but the Earl's eventual gruntings, his pantings, his increasing efforts, began to sound increasingly laboured. Shortly, they ceased, and Atherton's head, with its few remaining white hairs, lolled on her breast with saliva dribbling out of its mouth. It became evident that the Earl was dead, whether of exhaustion or pleasure would never be known.

Honoria had never seen death before, and she ran screaming and naked out of the room, her hair flying, down the corridor, calling for help. The person to encounter her was, of course, her grandmother. The Dowager was scandalised at the ivory body, the very sight of Aphrodite.

'How dare you show yourself in that state? Cover yourself at once! Supposing the servants should see you? Where is the unfortunate man? What were you –' She took a deep breath, stopped asking unnecessary questions, hustled Honoria back to her clothes, surveyed the Earl's corpse briefly, and said in a hollow voice.

'This is the last blow of all. Unless you are to bear a child, the line of the Athertons is extinct. Put on your dress; we must order mourning immediately.' She went away, and Honoria dressed meekly, as she was bid. It was to be the last meek action of her life.

She was meantime put into stuffy mourning, and it was summer. The county called to condole, and while the Dowager as usual dominated the conversation, Honoria gazed at everyone out of her green eyes and said nothing. As a certain marchioness remarked afterwards to the Lord Lieutenant's wife, it was evident that the young woman was as odd as her mother; an access of grief for the husband could not perhaps have been expected, but one assumed civility, and had received very little. One would not call again, but, of course, there would be the funeral.

The Earl, his false teeth replaced in his head, lay in an oak coffin which was closed early for good reasons. After the funeral service, which was taken by a visiting clergyman, he was placed in a row in the ancient vault which, like a kind of Kaisergruft, contained the mortal remains of Athertons from the time of Charles the Second, everyone prior to that having been killed elsewhere or scattered during the Civil Wars. The old Earl lay there, and Witham and Lawrence, and poor Sarah, her silver handles darkened long ago. The last Atherton, or rather Atherton-Studeley-Crowe, slid into place uneventfully beside them, and the grille clanged shut. Afterwards, there was a collation for the mourners, then everybody went home.

Next day, kind Betty called. She had waited till everything was over. She was admitted to the young widow, although the Dowager's conditions were strict; mourning must be maintained for a year, with no visitors other than those commiserating about the death. Perhaps Betty could have come into this category; at any rate, she went straight to the girl and took her in her arms.

'I've got something to say, dearie, and I'll say it fast, in case *she* comes in,' she told her. 'Don't waste any more of your life; now you're a widow, you're free. You could even have a bit of fun if you was to go to London, on your own; even your poor mother was given a season, for a little while, that was. You've never had anything of the kind, and while you're young, go and enjoy yourself. There's plenty of money in Crowbetter's Bank. I know, because the late Countess, God bless her, told me so. The Athertons paid it in, to buy her, that was. You're as entitled to it as that old bitch. I'm speaking plain, because it's time someone did. Don't let her bully you; you take your rights.'

Honoria smiled. 'I have written to Great-Uncle Nicholas already,'she said. 'I had the same idea, without knowing much about it. I have never been out in the world.'

'You'll get on in the world all right: bound to,' said Betty wisely.

On Sunday, Honoria refused to go to the sectarian meeting. The Dowager was ruffled, but assumed that a proper regard for mourning was at last having its effect on her granddaughter. She inclined her head, went off by herself, and came back in the usual anticipation of roast lamb, vegetables and gravy. To her shocked astonishment, Honoria was by now wearing a low-cut dress of pale blue. Toads swell up, and so did the elder Honoria.

'What –' she began, but the young Countess seated herself,

and in front of the serving-man it was not proper to resume. They waited while the roast meat was carved and served, the dish of roast potatoes proffered, the gravy poured. The plates were large, deep, and Royal Worcester. The young Honoria began to eat placidly. The elder could not. She stared at her plateful of succulent food, then at her granddaughter's bosom, which was improperly revealed to a degree that reminded the Dowager of the lamentable occasion of the Earl's death, when Honoria had after all fled down the passages in a condition which was never again to be thought of. 'I assume,' the Dowager began dreadfully, 'that you have gone out of your mind. Fortunately only the servants have seen you. After luncheon, you will go upstairs immediately and change into your widow's weeds. I am astonished that you should have left them off for one moment.'

'I do not intend to wear them again, Grandmama,' replied Honoria, raising a forkful of cabbage to her mouth. 'I did not dislike my late husband, but I have no reason to mourn for him; he was forced upon me. Now that I am a widow, I may do as I choose; and I am leaving here and going to London.'

The Dowager turned grey as ashes. Her mouth opened; she gasped like a landed fish, then fell forward, her face in her untouched plate. As it happened, her nose and mouth were submerged in the gravy, and her snortings thereafter resembled those of a large pig in a trough. The serving-man had gone out when they commenced to eat, and Honoria did not call him back. She waited till the Dowager had finished her snorting, and was lying limp and flaccid, drowned in her own gravy. Then she rang the bell for the servant.

'My grandmother is dead, I believe,' she told him. 'She has had a seizure. There was nothing that I, or anyone else, could do. Please arrange to have her taken elsewhere.'

As the serving-man remarked later to the upper housemaid, with whom he was on terms, the young lady was fairly cold-blooded; but you couldn't blame her if she had let the old bitch drown in gravy. Most others would have done the same.

Nicholas Crowbetter had been a trifle bored when he received, at the bank, a letter from the widowed young Countess of Atherton, asking if she might stay with him until she found herself a domicile in London. His position as Sarah's trustee had expired with her death, and any connection he might have with her daughter was after all nebulous; moreover, he was extremely comfortable with Maud and did not want to be disturbed. However, he did not like to be discourteous, and wrote rather stiffly to give the Hyde Park Gardens address, and to say that Lady Atherton would be most welcome there until she found other accommodation. He did not commit himself further.

When, therefore, his butler announced that the Countess had arrived, and was waiting in the smaller drawing-room, Crowbetter expected to find a pudding-faced nonentity in dowdy mourning. The reality, rising gracefully from her chair, almost knocked him backwards. There, in an old-fashioned bonnet and a dress put together by a country seamstress – he had been right about the clothes – stood Mélanie von Reichmansthal.

Nicholas was, as has been amply demonstrated, a prudent man. He was also perceptive. He made himself remember that this girl was his great-niece, and that any unheralded leaping of the blood she promptly caused him was inconvenient, to say the least. He realised also, with the quick addition and subtraction that had made him a prominent international merchant banker, that Felix and Sarah must have met for at least five minutes before that graceless young man disappeared. (Within a year or two, they would dig up the body where it lay still and deep, but Nicholas would never know, as it could not be identified.) Also, he bore in mind what had happened to the last Earl, a fate described in circumlocutory fashion by the late Dowager when she was writing her last letter to him about shares.

He therefore approached Honoria, kissed her affectionately on the cheek, and held her away from him, saying fondly, 'I am glad to see you. By all means stay as long as you like. I have been receiving small company, but I will remedy that; the world must certainly see you, but first, my dear, we must have you properly dressed.'

Nicholas was a man of his word, and very little of the Atherton money had been spent on Honoria in the short course of her life. He called in Madame X, who designed and made clothes for the Princess of Wales, Lady Randolph

Churchill, and other leaders of society; Madame was
enchanted to have such a figure to work on, not to mention
carte blanche as regarded expense. By the time she had
finished, at least for the present, Honoria was able to be seen
in little swooping hats, resembling baskets of flowers,
elegantly gowned and carrying a tiny parasol to protect her
ivory skin from the August sun; driving in the Park, with
Nicholas beside her, proud as if she had been his own
daughter: few remembered any connection he might have
had with Mélanie, but if they had done so, or remembered
her at all, they would have considered the whole thing
touching and romantic. As for Honoria, she was enjoying
herself; various great ladies who were still in town, having not
yet departed for the shooting, bowed, and she and Nicholas
bowed back. It was all of it a prelude to ·her formal
introduction into the great world; who would present her at
Court was not yet clear, but someone would be found. In any
case, without waiting, Crowbetter intended in the early
autumn to give a little dance at Hyde Park Gardens. It was a
long time since he had done so; come to think of it, a very
long time indeed. It would be nothing elaborate, suitable to
Honoria's widowed state; an orchestra and ices, and she
herself should be his hostess. After all, there was nobody else
suitable; Maud would not do, and Athene was worse, by now a
confirmed cribbage player in her private hotel.

Maud herself put up with the whole thing placidly. She
knew that it was unlikely that Crowbetter would displace her
now; they had made each other comfortable for too long.
Besides, they had not finished their last game of chess, and
subtly, like Penelope's web, Maud used the gambits he himself
had taught her to confound him, dragging the game out to
last for weeks, then months. She would not, in fact, be entirely
unsuitable as a director of Crowbetter's Bank, but she was
certainly unsuitable to host Honoria, and knew it; on the
evening in question, she would retire prudently to her room.

One problem remained. When Crowbetter mentioned the
dance to Honoria, she was for once put out.

'It would be lovely, Uncle Nicholas, but I have never been
taught to dance. Grandmama would not permit it.'

So he hired a dancing-master, and the strains of the pianist
floated down again as they had done long ago. The master,
an anaemic individual, fell in love with Honoria at once, and

began to make a nuisance of himself, but before dismissing him she had learnt the polka, the Lancers, and, most importantly, the waltz. She began to look forward very much to the party; it was the first one of her life.

Meantime, Nicholas had received an interesting communication from the Baron in Vienna.

28 July, 1883

Lieber Herr Crowbetter!

Forgive my addressing you in my own tongue, but my heart fills itself with joy; I am so proud of my son.

Felix — I called him after the unfortunate young Count, of whom no more has been heard — has done well at everything. He is all I could wish. As a parting gift from my dear wife, whose portrait, draped in black, hangs before me as I write — he could not, if I could after all not keep her with me, be improved upon. He is very handsome, not unlike the poor young Count, in fact almost his double; there is no doubt some inheritance here through my lamented cousin Franz, my wife's first husband. It is the same blood, after all.

I intend Felix for a diplomatic career. It will be suitable to his rank; he is an apt linguist; and he has already rubbed shoulders with the world. I sent him first on a tour with his tutor, to Paris, Berlin, Copenhagen and The Hague, but not St Petersburg, which at present is too dangerous. In all these places he excited admiration by his presence and his manners. The ladies, of course, made much of him. He came home, and as I feel he has been suitably educated in all ways — he is twenty — I am sending him, alone except for his valet to London, to meet such personages as the Prince of Wales; Felix is a fine shot also. I cannot tell you the number of his accomplishments; he has never disappointed me. He has brought my old age great happiness, is affectionate, and has atoned for a great many things. Ach! I will not specify. It is pointless now.

What I would ask of you, my old friend — we have corresponded often over banking matters — is that you will be a father to Felix while he is in London. He will remain for three weeks, then goes on, at his own pace, to Dresden and Stuttgart. His address while with you will be (here followed an address in St James's Square) *and I have instructed him to call upon you at the earliest opportunity. I am sure that you will be pleased with him.*

Your very devoted servant, mein lieber Herr,
Eitel von Reichmansthal, Baron

The paragon did not call, and Nicholas Crowbetter knew an increasing desire to set eyes on him. He could not, in nature, be the double of the earlier Felix. The Baron's sentimental soul must have imagined it. As things were, and from the sound of him, however, he would be the ideal second husband for young Honoria. Nicholas had grown very fond of the girl, but at his age he preferred not to have to make as much effort as he had already done in the direction of social occasions. This small dance would be enough, certainly, for Honoria to be seen by the right people, if she had not been so already. The third Nicholas, and his newly married wife, an heiress, were to attend; Crowbetter himself had by now permitted more and more affairs at the bank to leave his own hands and be grasped by those of his extremely capable grandson. He was not troubled about the future of the firm; it would continue. As regarded Honoria, if the young man saw her he would love her, and if he did not, then some other young man would. Felix von Reichmansthal had received an invitation; one could do no more.

Honoria was dressed for the dance in white crêpe, closely fitted, its skirt draped and sewn here and there with silver roses. In her ears dangled the sparkling Atherton diamonds, which had reposed in the bank for so many generations that their setting was fashionable again. Her hair was piled in a tower of honey curls, with one silver rose pinned in it. Her bosom, magnificent for so young a girl – her mother had been the same, one recalled – was well if not fully displayed, and on her white-gloved arms gleamed the Atherton bracelets. It would have been vulgar to wear the necklace as well; enough was enough.

She stood with Nicholas to receive the guests, inclining her head as to the manner born; certainly she would make a diplomat's wife, he decided, if only the future diplomat would show up. No doubt he intended to look in for an hour, as young men did who had other engagements. Nicholas recalled, long, long ago, staying up all night at Crockford's and winning against Count d'Orsay, and afterwards flinging the money at Maud, in a certain place. Well, he was too old now for all that tomfoolery, and so was she, but there was always chess. Where the devil was that boy from Vienna?

After the last guest had arrived, Felix came. He was tall, slim, elegant, with honey hair and golden eyes. The eyes looked into those of Crowbetter, who received the kind of shock which is inflicted once in a lifetime. The boy could only have those eyes if –

Dumbfounded, he heard the orchestra strike up; and the new Felix saying to young Honoria, gazing at her intently, 'May I have the honour of the first waltz?'

They flowed into one another's arms; there was no other word to describe it. They waltzed; others were already waltzing to the lilt of the music. The third Nicholas Crowbetter was doing so with his pretty little dark-haired wife, who would shortly try to find other partners as her husband was a trifle too uxorious. Felix and Honoria danced as one, her white skirts whirling, her hand firm in his, his other arm hard about her waist. They were pressed close against one another, golden eyes looking into green. They were already an entity, soon to become one flesh.

Nicholas saw it, and gave up trying to reason out who Felix was. It was too late to change anything now. He was beginning to feel tired, and would shortly go up to Maud, but meantime turned courteously to his nearest neighbour.

'It is a peasant dance originating in Germany,' he said. 'So many of our customs now are German.'